O9-BHJ-204

HEARTWARMING

Her Unexpected Hero

—

Cheryl Harper

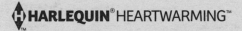

H HARLEQUIN® HEARTWARMING™

Recycling programs
for this product may
not exist in your area.

ISBN-13: 978-1-335-51063-1

Her Unexpected Hero

Printed in U.S.A.

www.Harlequin.com

"The only Kingfisher I'm concerned with is you."

Caleb bent his head closer. "And the only Callaway I want you to relate to is me." Something clicked as soon as he admitted that. It was true, so true, but his emotions didn't matter unless Winter felt the same.

"I don't suppose you'd like to support the arts in Sweetwater." Winter took a step closer and tugged on his jacket. "The gallery could use a wealthy benefactor like you to attend the grand opening next Saturday. Bring your checkbook, of course."

"I'll be there." He needed to go. She should walk back inside where it was warm, but she wasn't moving away. Not even after he gave her the answer she wanted.

"But don't buy the bunny painting. That one's mine." She smiled up at him and it was impossible to stop. Caleb bent his head slowly, carefully, and pressed his lips against hers.

Dear Reader,

When you think of home, does a certain place come to mind? For me, it's the house I grew up in, my mother on the couch with a book and a beagle at her side or my father's truck winding along mountain back roads. The places we love shape us.

For Winter Kingfisher, the mountains of eastern Tennessee are her first love and she'll fight to protect them, even if it means losing everything she's worked for. Caleb Callaway has orders to challenge Winter and her resistance to the Callaway family's plans. I hope you enjoy reading how well that works out for him!

To find out more about my books and what's coming next, visit me at cherylharperbooks.com.

Cheryl

Cheryl Harper discovered her love for books and words as a little girl, thanks to a mother who made countless library trips, and an introduction to Laura Ingalls Wilder's Little House stories. Whether stories she reads are set on the prairie, in the American West, Regency England or on Earth a hundred years in the future, Cheryl enjoys strong characters who make her laugh. Now Cheryl spends her days searching for the right words while she stares out the window and her dog, Jack, snoozes beside her. And she considers herself very lucky to do so. For more Information about Cheryl's books, visit her online at cherylharperbooks.com or follow her on Twitter, @cherylharperbks.

Books by Cheryl Harper

Harlequin Heartwarming

Otter Lake Ranger Station

Her Heart's Bargain
Saving the Single Dad
Smoky Mountain Sweethearts

Lucky Numbers

A Home Come True
Keeping Cole's Promise
Heart's Refuge
Winner Takes All

Visit the Author Profile page
at Harlequin.com for more titles.

This one's for my parents.
They're gone, and I miss them and home
every day, but I'm grateful for deep, deep roots.

CHAPTER ONE

"DOES ANYONE ELSE smell that…?"

Winter Kingfisher glanced up from her phone as Macy Gentry paused to take suspicious whiffs of the air over their corner booth at The Branch, the answer to nightlife in Sweetwater, Tennessee. It was Friday night, prime time for fun and rowdy crowds, but still so early that the first unofficial get-together of Sweetwater's single ladies was tame. Subdued. Almost boring.

The way first dates or professional networking opportunities can be.

Scanning blog posts and headlines, hunting for either the Kingfisher or Callaway name had distracted Winter from the awkward silence in the booth. Not to mention any untoward odor.

News of her part in ending an engagement with the man planning to be governor had had a longer life cycle than she'd imagined. For almost a decade, she'd worked with her fiancé, Whit Callaway, Jr., in Knoxville's political arena to make sure all his press was favorable. Going head-to-head against the Callaways, one of the wealthiest families in Tennessee, in order to save her brother's job as head ranger of the Smoky Valley Nature Reserve had meant she'd returned the ring and landed both Kingfishers on the front pages.

Unfortunately, the coverage varied wildly from favorable to "literally the worst," but it had taken a turn for the better for the Kingfishers. She was the scorned woman. The innocent one. Her brother, Ash, had rightfully become a hero again. Whit Callaway's campaign had faltered.

Was saving The Aerie worth the hassle of canceling a society wedding, losing her job and her plans for the future?

Winter shifted on the hard wooden seat and tried not to focus too closely on the answer to that question.

After two months, Winter could feel her chance to directly challenge Whit's political campaign evaporating. Getting even was not the Kingfisher way, but what about a little payback?

But instead of forcing her way onto his opponent's strategy team, what was she doing? Rusticating at home and not much else.

Well, other than reading about Governor Richard Duncan's terrible record on education and teacher pay while she waited for this first get-together to be over. Could she help this guy win reelection? Yes.

But *should* she?

It would serve Whit right for not listening to her. If he'd stopped his family's plan to develop a lodge at The Aerie and destroy one of the most important areas of the reserve she loved, they would still be together. He would still be winning, and Winter would be by his side in Knoxville.

Not here, where she definitely did not seem to be winning anything.

Governor Duncan needed better advice. The solution: a Kingfisher heading up his reelection campaign. Win-win. For her, at least.

"I'm not sure exactly what it is, but it's flowery. What is that?" Macy sniffed again. "Roses?"

Before Winter could change the subject, Christina Braswell stood. "Hamburgers all around. Don't waste your time with anything else on this menu. Trust your waitress friend to know." She marched over to the bar and returned with a tray of drinks and hamburgers in baskets.

Macy craned her neck, clearly searching for the fresh spring meadow tickling her nose. Since her brother's girlfriend and coworker at the Smoky Valley Nature Reserve had become a staple at Kingfisher family dinners, Winter knew there was no way Macy would let it go until she had the answer.

"Lavender." Winter tugged her denim jacket and patted the large Choose Duncan Again button she had pinned to the lapel. "The fragrance is lavender. My mother grows a lot of it. If she has a signature scent, it's lavender."

All the women at the table turned to face her.

Christina held up a frosty mug in a salute. "She does speak. So far, the only forms of communication I've seen have been glaring at your phone and sighing. Your brother is a better conversationalist and he mainly speaks in single syllables."

The criticism hurt, even if it was true. Neither she nor Ash were known for their easygoing personalities or sparkling conversation. Smarts—yes. Determination—yes. Easygoing charm? Not so much.

"I've got a lot going on right now," Winter snapped and then realized it was so untrue. "Or I should have, I guess. I don't have a job yet. No one on Governor Duncan's re-election campaign will answer my calls, so that shoots my whole 'make a difference in Tennessee politics' plan in the foot. My engagement to a perfect man from a wealthy family destined for the White House is… Yeah, if you can read a newspaper or blog, you already know all about that. The smell? It's lavender. My mother insists that I use the shampoo she makes herself from the organic ingredients she grows in her garden. Does it smell nice? Yes. Does it lather? No. Does it do anything other than strip every bit of gloss and shine from your expensive haircut?" Winter poked the frizzy fall of dark hair over her ear. "Hard to say. I'm still only a month into the experiment. It may totally remove every hair from my head. That's the way life is going right now."

You're griping about shampoo. Your whole life is wrecked, but what you complain about is the state of your hair.

Yes. I deserve to complain.

Oh, poor baby. Rich husband fell through, and all that schooling and job experience have left you at the mercy of... What, again?

Angel on one shoulder, self-doubt and pity on the other. That was why she was exhausted.

For half a second, Winter was relieved to let off some of the pressure of the worries boiling in her brain. Then regret washed over her. Letting people know she was struggling was an un-Kingfisher thing to do. Her family handled their own problems.

Christina's eyebrows shot up. "Okay, you do have a lot going on right now, up there in your brain, anyway." She pointed a french fry around the table. "But Winter Kingfisher can spin all that on a dime. You know it. We know it. Some of us have halfheartedly resented you for it for decades, ever since they stood in your 'most likely to succeed' shadow." Christina nudged her burger closer. "Take a bite. Take a *breath*. We can help. Some of us are professionals at picking up the pieces after everything falls apart."

Christina had nailed her problem right on the head. Winter should be above this... floundering. The fact that the bad girl of Sweetwater was giving her a pep talk took some consideration, but Winter appreciated it. She picked up her drink and took a sip because she couldn't decide whether to agree or disagree, and that ambivalence was irritating. She'd never hesitated in her life.

Now, having someone order her dinner for her was a relief.

"When Astrid and I first started planning this get-together, I had a much rowdier vision in mind. Young, single women. On the town. A bar with real choices other than beer and *light* beer. With all the excitement over the showdown with the Callaways about the proposed lodge at Otter Lake and the…" *Breakup.* That was the missing word. Macy shot a worried glance at Winter before straightening in her seat. "*Holiday.* Christmas slowed us down, but I'm glad everyone could get together tonight." She jammed her straw three times to loosen the ice in her drink and glanced toward the bar. "When we get on a regular schedule, we can move this out of town. The Branch is our starting point, not where we end."

The petite blonde seated across from Astrid, Leanne Hendrix, said, "I'm happy to have a chance to get out." She tugged on the shoulder of her T-shirt, the hot-pink uniform of Sweetwater Souvenir, the shop she'd been asked to run. "I'd rather sit here quietly with you guys than clean my apartment and binge-watch some television show."

More awkward silence stretched over the table, but Winter silently agreed. She'd had to come to terms with the fact that she needed new friends. More friends.

"That's it. We aren't going to let gossip keep us apart, not anymore." Christina slapped her hand on the table. "In fact, let's come up with a name. It'll be like our little club then. We could do jackets."

"Have you lost your mind?" Macy drawled. "Let's start small. Dinner. A *successful* dinner." She pointed at Winter. "This girl is half a second from bailing on us, and we haven't even eaten our burgers yet. Let's make it through one night."

Christina rolled her eyes. "Fine. You want to start small, we'll start *small*."

Something about her exasperation amused Winter. She wasn't alone. Finally, their booth's atmosphere was closer to being a party than an interview going badly. How long had it been since she had giggled like that?

When everyone turned to look at her again, Winter said, "You guys would be off to a better start without me. I'm not in the mood to party lately. I should get my burger to go."

Before she could stand, Macy grabbed her hand and held tight. "You are staying. You're eating. And if you want to talk about everything that has gone wrong or could go wrong or will go wrong or how you're going to conquer the world next, we are here to listen to it. You may have been too cool for all this *before*, but I am not. I want to be able to call *someone* when I need to talk about *things*. This is why we need girls' nights out." She shook her finger at Christina. "That is not the name of our group."

"Eat your burger. Burgers make everything better." Christina waved hers and took a big bite, staring around the table until everyone followed suit.

"You could smuggle your own shampoo into the bathroom." Macy pressed a hand to the center of Winter's back and ran it in small circles, her expression one of extreme concern. "Before I got to know you so well, I was pretty sure you were too cool to notice my existence. A lot of that had to do with how amazing your hair was. Sleek. Shiny. Every day. Like magic."

It took Winter a second to realize they'd

returned to her shampoo challenges, and the good hair was in the past tense. She understood the impulse. On the list of problems she had, it should be the easiest to solve.

Winter's whole life had fallen apart, and Macy was ready to cry over her hair. That was how well her mother's shampoo was working. Every time Winter stared in the mirror now, she was reminded that life had taken a fuzzy, out-of-control detour.

"I could, but it's pretty clear when I use my own stuff. The fact that I can run a brush through it gives me away. The lectures you get for bringing plastic bottles into my mother's house, and on the expense of salon shampoos, and the devastating research some companies perform on animals, although not mine, because I did my own research and paid twice what I needed so I could use it with a clear conscience but whatever, Mother… All that together?" Winter snatched the butterfly clip holding her bangs back out of her hair. "Nobody has time for that every day, not even the unemployed."

Clearly, her new friends were not quite certain how to react, but their small smiles and twitching lips were another reason to laugh.

And that felt good.

"I never appreciated the small things before," Winter said, "but the small things have gotten much, much larger lately." The tiny pinch of the butterfly clip she'd stolen from her mother's stuff was easy to focus on.

"Any idea how long you'll be staying with Mom and Dad?" Macy asked. "Ash has room in his cabin and there's a couch in my living room. The space isn't much, but you're welcome to it. And there's no way I'll lecture you about your shampoo." Macy lowered her voice, and added, "Unless you won't let me use it, too."

Christina elbowed her in the side affectionately.

"What? She has good stuff. Her hair was legendary." Macy held both arms out to the ladies as if to say no one in town would blame her. "Before all this, I could hardly talk to Winter because she was so…together."

Before. Macy didn't have to explain before what.

That was something else everyone at the table knew.

Before the governor had read the environmental-impact report of the new lodge being planned for the Smoky Valley Nature Reserve and decided to attack his political opponent, Whit Callaway, Jr., over the damage to Tennessee's resources and history.

Before the lodge, which the Callaways were pushing through on the land they owned but held in reserve for citizens and voters in Tennessee, stalled and they turned on the head ranger, her brother, Ash.

Before Whit had threatened her brother and led Winter to end their engagement and showed his true colors.

Before she'd begged Caleb Callaway, Whit's brother, to fix everything, except her job and her engagement.

Winter had had it all together before that.

Begging was not an option for Winter Kingfisher, but she'd done it for the reserve and her brother, and a chance to keep the life she'd set up.

She'd been the public outreach officer for the reserve. She'd been juggling Whit's campaign with one hand and a society wedding with the other.

Now her hair was a mess, although it had nothing on the rest of her life.

"This is temporary." Winter had repeated the same words to herself so many times she was beginning to wonder if they had lost all meaning. "First, I find a job. Since both the reserve and politics seem to be out of the question…" This was where she stalled time and again. "I'm open to suggestions."

"I have all the time in the world for you at the library. Unpaid volunteering doesn't help with the money, but the kids love your story times. You would not believe how many crayon drawings of Rabbit tricking Possum I've seen since you told that story two months ago. It's like you have some special connection to them." Astrid narrowed her eyes. "Have you ever considered teaching?"

Winter's immediate panicked reaction, complete with shaking her head so hard her frizzy hair whizzed in front of her face, had them all fighting back grins, until Astrid drawled, "Okay, crossing that off the list."

"I like to tell stories. Kids love stories." Winter balled up her napkin. "That doesn't make me a teacher. Teachers mold young minds and keep them in their seats. Storytellers waltz in, capture their attention and waltz back out. Me? In front of a classroom all day long? I'd either arrange them into military formation or take cover under my desk. Either way, it would end in tears for one of us."

"Not teaching. Not the reserve. How are

you with food orders?" Christina asked. "The campground is staffed, but this place could use some help." She wrinkled her nose. "Your tips would be better if you could fix your hair, though."

"I was a hostess at a restaurant in Knoxville all the way through college." Winter studied the beat-up interior of The Branch. Surely she could manage drink orders and the limited menu here. "How different could it be?"

As she glanced back at her companions, no one seemed convinced. Before she could argue that she'd discovered quickly how to suggest appetizers and the perfect pairing of wine, Leanne leaned forward. "The skills are different here, hon. Are you good with your hands?"

"Like, writing?" Winter mimed holding a pen and scribbling on a small notepad.

"That and often picking up broken things." Leanne motioned at the big, noisy crowd of fishermen that had come in.

Sweetwater depended on the tourists attracted to the area by the nature reserve's trails, campground and lake. During the busy summer season, the main street through town enjoyed a steady stream of families shopping for souvenirs and breakfast, lunch and dinner. Late February was slow on Otter Lake, but there were still groups of folks that visited the campground for a weekend away. Since this was the only place in town serving beer, The Branch was must-see Sweetwater for nightlife.

"Have you searched for jobs in Knoxville or Nashville?" Macy asked. "I know your parents want you here, but the options open up in the city."

She had, but Knoxville was too close to Whit, and Nashville wasn't close enough to Otter Lake. Moving there might open up a spot for her on Richard Duncan's campaign team, since she clearly had the insider info on Whit Callaway, but there was no safety net in Nashville. No Otter Lake, either.

On the other hand, in Nashville, she wouldn't have to worry about every person she passed on the sidewalk, neighbors who'd known her for her whole life, wondering how she'd messed up everything so spectacularly.

"I'd like to find something here. For now. Later…" Winter let the sentence trail off. If she managed to win a spot on the governor's team, Nashville would have to work. Until then, she'd stay home. She loved this place—

the reserve's beauty, the stories of the people who grew up there—and all she'd ever wanted to do was teach other people to love it, too. Working for the reserve and plotting Whit's race to win the state capital had been a solid plan. "I can wait tables. I've always been a good multitasker."

"You could pick it up, for sure. And the tips are decent. Unfortunately, the urge to drink them all away means no working here, not for me." Leanne turned her root beer in a slow circle. "I could talk to Janet. She mentioned finding a part-time salesperson for the art gallery she's opening next to the souvenir shop."

When everyone nodded and pointed in relief, as if they'd been certain she'd be a failure at waiting tables, Winter tried not to take it personally. She'd once taken success as a guarantee, but right now she was riding a wave of disappointment. All things considered, the art gallery was a better alternative for her than delivering burgers and beer.

"Better to have two chances than one. I'll ask Sharon on the way out if she needs any help waiting tables." Winter nodded at the fake smiles surrounding her. "And I'll call Janet on Monday to find out if she's hiring.

I need more than one option in this job market. I handled a lot before. I can do both of these things." They nodded, so she did, too.

And she immediately felt better. Having a plan had always soothed her concerns.

To do anything more, she had to smooth out her life. Winter tugged her fingers out of her tangled hair, resolved to get herself together.

When the Callaways were faced with opposition to their plans to build at the reserve, they had targeted her brother as the villain of the story. Because of them, Ash had faced public criticism and the potential loss of his job as head ranger.

Even though they'd had no real proof of his guilt.

And after she'd spent years at Whit Callaway, Jr.'s side. Their engagement hadn't stopped the drive to punish Ash.

Winter might have expected that from Senior, who valued the family's standing above almost anything. That was business. Her anonymous release of the environmental-impact plan to the governor had been the same. Just business.

But the fact that her fiancé had gone along

with his father's efforts to hurt Ash? That's where the pain came in.

Her best revenge would be to get so stinking happy that Whit Callaway gnashed his teeth when he remembered her. To do that, she had to get out of her parents' house. Obviously.

She had a life to rebuild.

CHAPTER TWO

CALEB CALLAWAY WAS certain no man his age should still be summoned to the dinner table like a rebellious teenager. Living in Nashville meant he could come and go as he pleased most of the time. Until a few months ago, he'd dropped in at the family manse whenever the mood hit. His mother celebrated every visit. His stepfather disapproved of his choices, and his brother turned everything into a competition. Going home was work. Holidays were a requirement. Every other day of the year, he lived well and visited the Knoxville Callaways when it was convenient.

Then Winter Kingfisher had barged into his office, tilted his world sideways with her passion for the Smoky Valley Nature Reserve and her own family, and convinced him to be some kind of hero. At that point, the Callaway family welcome mat had been rolled up and locked away.

Not even Christmas had brought about a

thaw in the standoff. He'd spent it in Hawaii. Alone. The less-crowded beaches had been nice. Realizing that he was traditional enough to want cold and snow and fireplaces and Christmas ham served at his mother's table had been surprising.

The discovery that all the acquaintances who liked to eat out on his reputation and credit dried up like snow in Waikiki the minute Callaway money disappeared had surprised him more than it should have.

Getting caught in the mess between the Kingfishers and the Callaways hadn't been his idea, and being drafted to run the lodge project had seemed a long shot.

His stepfather, Whitney Callaway, Sr. ran Callaway Construction. Always had, always would, and the two of them got along better with miles separating them.

The longer his family's silence had dragged, the more Caleb had been convinced Senior had realized the error of his decision to make building the lodge his stepson's penance for interference. Senior liked control. He wouldn't give that away.

But something had changed and his stepfather had made a personal call to tell him to come for dinner. Tell, not ask. Senior never had been much for asking. That was most of their problem: communication.

The fact that he was parked next to a fountain complete with a spitting fish, the centerpiece of his parents' ornate oval driveway, uncertain of his welcome for the first time in his life, was Winter's fault.

Well, hers and his own uncharacteristic generous streak that had made it impossible to tell her no when she'd asked for the favor that had gotten him in this mess.

Irritation that he'd been shoved into the middle of Callaway drama threatened to boil over until Caleb had thrown on the brakes. He'd made his own choices. Were they heavily influenced by a beautiful woman? Sure. And if he ever met Winter again, he'd make sure she understood how she'd upended his life.

For now, dinner.

"Come on, man. The sooner this begins, the quicker it's all over, and life goes on, right back on the road to Nashville," he muttered to himself. Caleb ran a hand down the silk tie he'd added at the last minute, then grabbed his suit coat off the hanger in the back seat. Showing up to his mother's house for dinner without a jacket would lead to Extreme Displeasure, Caleb's nickname for the tight-lipped frown Senior often gave him. His stepfather was committed to upholding the family's stature, and that required dressing for dinner like Victorian royalty.

Dinner was going to be rough, but the only way back to normal was through the fire. Senior would say he'd changed his mind and could trust no one else with the completion of The Aerie lodge. Caleb would nod in serious understanding while sighing inwardly in relief, and life would go on.

Before he slid out of the SUV, Caleb judged the distance between his parking spot and the gates at the street. "One minute or less. I could be free."

Caleb pulled the keys out of the ignition, stretched out the kinks and slipped on the jacket. Then he noticed the mud on his boots.

He'd stopped on the way out of Nashville to tour a land parcel with Mitch Yarborough, luxury home developer and father to Caleb's on-again, off-again girlfriend, Melissa. Caleb could still feel the hard thump of his heart when Mitch had offered him the chance to be the builder of every lot in the gated community. The key words were *state of the art*, *high end* and *best of the best*.

"Four months." He had that long to add to

his crews in order to be launched into Nashville's big-time home-construction firms. Was it too soon to tell his stepfather?

This was the challenge he'd been dreaming of for years. His right hand, Carlos Lopez, was ready to lead his own crew, but meeting payroll after doubling his team would be tough in the beginning. Summit Builders would struggle under the bills. A loan of Callaway cash would make it all easier.

Tonight wasn't the right time to ask for money, but it was tempting to spread his good news.

After a hurried dig through the back seat, Caleb found a brush and did his best to knock the mud off his boots. Would it escape their notice? No way, but at least he wouldn't leave any evidence behind.

"Good enough." Caleb tossed the brush back onto the floorboard and slammed the door. As he rounded the bumper, the front door to the Georgian-style family mansion swung open. Instead of a maid, his mother was framed beautifully by the glowing fanlight and transom windows.

"I wondered if you were going to come inside or make a break for it." His mother kissed his cheek as he paused in front of her.

The familiar scent of her perfume would always carry him home.

"Me, too. It was touch and go." Caleb shoved his hands in his pockets, aware all over again of how he didn't belong here. "Thank you for the dinner invitation."

With a heavy sigh, she wrapped her arms around his neck and squeezed him close. In his mother's arms, he might as well be nine years old again, brokenhearted after striking out in the last inning of the game. Whatever was wrong, his mother had always been able to make right.

"It's been too long, son. Don't stay away so long." His mother's pointed stare at his feet was accompanied by an almost inaudible sigh. "You came from work. The tie is nice, but it does not go with this jacket." She wiggled her arm through his and pulled him inside.

"I didn't sign up for a fashion show, Mom." Caleb smoothed a hand down the tie again, glad to have it, even if it didn't go with the jacket. Flannel and denim. That was his dress code. If Summit hit the big-time, maybe he'd transition to khakis and golf shirts with logos.

"Thank you for observing the bare mini-

mum," she said mildly before moving along.
"Your brother and father are in the office, no
doubt plotting world domination. Please tell
them dinner will be served in ten minutes."
She gave him a gentle shove toward Senior's
stuffy office and then disappeared behind the
swinging door leading to the butler's pantry.

"I should stand right here for nine minutes
and thirty seconds," Caleb muttered. He'd
expected more emotion from his mother. In
a battle between him and the other Callaways, she'd always landed in the middle, a
disputed territory until they negotiated a surrender. Her face had been serene, nothing
but happiness showing. "Maybe Senior has
forgiven me."

At some point, he'd stop squirming like a
kid at his stepfather's displeasure. He should
be immune to the unease.

Today was not that day, but he'd learned a
long time ago not to show nerves.

Senior had inherited power and wealth, but
what he'd built through guts, determination
and solid planning was a lot to live up to.

Caleb straightened his shoulders and
marched into the oppressively dark room lined
with bookshelves filled with leather-bound
volumes no one in the house had ever read.

This was an office, a study, an important room; it should have nice, expensive things, according to Senior. He was enthroned behind a grand desk, while Caleb's younger brother, Whit, paced in front of the fireplace. Before Caleb could say anything, Whit tossed the newspaper he'd been reading into the fire.

"Mom says dinner in T minus ten." Caleb paused in front of the desk. He remembered his spot on stage well. When they both turned toward him, it was impossible to ignore the overwhelming vibe in the room. Anger. Neither of them had forgiven him his part in stopping the lodge at the reserve.

"Good. Time enough to cover business and keep your mother happy with a nice family dinner." His stepfather braced his elbows on his desk. "You've dragged your feet long enough on the reserve's lodge project, Caleb. The new plans have been approved. Get your crews to Sweetwater. The sooner this is finished, the sooner we can all get past this… distraction."

Caleb stared at his brother. As usual, Whit was a member of the audience. Before Whit came along, Caleb and Senior had formed an uneasy relationship, but with the birth of his younger brother, the balance had changed. Whit was the favored son, even if Caleb reaped plenty of Callaway benefits. The urge to argue with Senior, or tell him the whole truth about Winter's role, was strong, but taking the credit for wrinkling the lodge plans was still the right thing to do.

Confessing that she'd been the one to alert the governor might change Senior's feelings a bit, but he'd still stepped in to save Ash's job.

And he'd made Winter a promise to keep the secret. A little family drama was no reason to break that promise.

Meeting Senior's stare was difficult. He'd always been a man to respect, at least until this drive to push Whit into the capital had taken over. Having his stepfather refuse to take his calls had shaken Caleb. He'd shove his way back inside this small crack.

"It's time to focus on rehabilitating the family image. The reserve is what caused the breakdown, so this lodge matters more than ever." His stepfather inhaled slowly. "What we need now is a way to save some face, make some money and regain the ground we've lost in this political race." He pointed at Caleb. "You did all this. Stop stalling and fix it."

He was responsible for *all* of it? No way. If either of them had listened to reason to begin with…

It didn't matter. They hadn't, but Caleb hadn't been much better. Sitting on all the boards required by the Callaway fortune was an obligation he did his best to shirk. Thanks to Winter Kingfisher's insistence, he now knew more about the nature reserve and his brother's election plans than he wanted to.

"He doesn't have anything to say to that." Whit shook his head and crossed his arms in a tight knot over his chest. The disgruntled grimace on his face hadn't changed much since he was twelve, but they'd outgrown the ability to wrestle away their grievances.

The tension between them was always there. Being an adopted Callaway meant Caleb had a later start than his younger brother on getting everything he wanted. Before his mother's marriage to Senior, they'd lived in an apartment and spent Sunday afternoons clipping coupons. At five, he'd loved scissors, and she'd always been smart enough to capitalize on the blessings that came her way.

"I'm waiting to hear the plan. I know you have one." Caleb pivoted to face his father. "*Dad* has a plan, I mean. Junior follows it. As always." He couldn't go for a headlock, so he'd use his words.

Whit scoffed. "Unlike Caleb, who doesn't need any help from anyone, ever. Right? Forget about the loans that started your business, the family connections that keep it afloat and the fact that you're never here." Whatever else he meant to say was swallowed whole, as his lips clamped tightly shut.

Why had he stopped? He was absolutely right.

Being unable to argue knocked Caleb off balance.

"I'd first like to hear some kind of explanation about why you'd foul up the *plan* we had in place," his brother snapped.

Caleb shook his head. "It was the right thing to do. That lodge, if we'd built it at The Aerie, would have destroyed so much of what makes the reserve important. Habitat, old growth forest, the history of the land there." He motioned widely, hoping they'd fill in the blanks. He didn't have a firm grasp of the importance of the land protected by the reserve, but Winter had convinced him saving it mattered. "You've always taken such pride in donating that land to the people of Tennessee. What I don't get is how you could have ever believed building there was worth everything you'd lose."

"I was in a hurry." His stepfather checked the clock, the lines around his eyes convincing Caleb he was exhausted. "Time is short. The election is many months away. We want the lodge story laid to rest. Ash Kingfisher has been working with the same firm that did the first environmental-impact study to evaluate the spot over by the old weather station. The board is pleased with the results. The architect's drawings have been modified to meet the demands of the report and the new elevation. We need this lodge finished, Caleb. I'll divert a Callaway Construction crew to join yours to speed things up. Whit will officially announce his run for governor there, but to do so, this project has to be fast-tracked. Now."

Caleb wanted to argue. He had his own business, built one project at a time, and was sitting on the edge of real success. The Yarborough luxury subdivision, Rivercrest, would keep him in business for years and allow him to build as he wanted. Was his company the size of Callaway Construction? Not yet, but taking this project would delay the growth a high-profile project in Nashville might bring.

Building the lodge would be trouble from top to bottom and beginning to end. Small-town Sweetwater would bore him to death. And then there was the proximity to Winter Kingfisher.

But he'd been on the outside with no way to even look in, and Caleb could acknowledge both Senior and Junior had good reason to demand payback.

"Fine. I'm the lucky guy, not a midlevel manager from Callaway Construction, who'll take over." Caleb propped his hands on his hips and frantically evaluated different objections. None of them would hold water. "What about my crew? Who is paying them while I'm doing this?"

"Bring them. Put your crew to work on the lodge. Callaway Construction will pick up the tab. Run both crews. Get this done. It's your mama's dream, too. For once, instead of wasting money on frivolity and fun little projects, help us. The timing is crucial. So is doing this the right way." Senior's lips disappeared in a tight line. "We need you."

They needed *him*? Had he ever heard that before? Not that he could remember.

"Dinner's ready. Tell me where we're going to end up with this negotiation." Caleb's vaguely guilty conscience was only going to push him so far.

"You got a promotion, son." His stepfather stood and hitched up his pants before settling his belt around his waist. "It's time you joined Callaway Construction as more than a name on the financial report. This lodge? It's your first project. You'll come in on time and under budget. And you're going to make sure those Kingfishers disappear. I don't want to hear one more word out of Sweetwater. Winter Kingfisher..." He grimaced. "She knows how to keep the news stirred up, and thanks to her job at the reserve, she has connections with all the news stations around the state capitol. If she's talking about the reserve lodge or Whit, you distract her."

Caleb waited for more direction. There had to be more, didn't there?

Senior waited for him to agree.

"I'm not sure how any mortal man is going to distract Winter Kingfisher if she doesn't want to be distracted." Caleb turned back to stare at Whit. "I mean, not even the golden boy here could hold on to her long enough to get her to say 'I do.'" And didn't it say a whole lot that no one in the room was plotting to win his ex-fiancée back to their side. Stupid mistake.

If Caleb had convinced Winter to marry him, she'd be priority number one in this recovery plan. He might be annoyed with her, but no one would doubt she'd been the brains in this political organization.

Standing his ground when Whit marched up to aggressively invade his space was easy. He had six inches and at least fifty pounds on Whit, not to mention right on his side. Caleb had his long-gone father's build: big, solid, ready to work.

His brother, who'd always given off the polo athlete vibe—rich, lanky and well-dressed enough to hide narrow shoulders—should be bearing more of the responsibility here. Caleb couldn't imagine Winter sitting silently by while the Callaways planned this lodge, but even if she had, Whit had still gone after her brother in a public way, with them both ending up on the front pages. Firing Ash Kingfisher, a man who'd never been anything but a solid champion of the reserve? Yeah, even Caleb knew there was no way

Winter could have let their engagement stand after that.

And instead of plotting to win her back, the Callaways were trying to keep her quiet.

"She was always too much for you, wasn't she, Whit?" Caleb asked softly, mad all over again at being the odd one out in this family. He took a childish pleasure in the way his brother stepped back. Whit wanted to fight. He'd never been able to best Caleb physically. Being his father's favorite had always been enough to get by.

"All my boys in one room." His mother was posing in the doorway again. "Dinner is ready. Come to the table." She tried a beautiful smile, but steel laced her words when she added, "Now. No fighting."

"Coming, Marjorie." His stepfather pointed with his chin. "One more minute. That's all we need."

She surveyed all three of them before turning and slowly walking away, the clipped steps of her heels echoing on the expensive tile of the hallway.

"Follow your mother, Junior." Caleb watched his stepfather and his brother argue without saying a word. Whit tucked his chin and marched after their mother. Every disagreement they had ended the same way—Whit followed orders.

Before he could tell his stepfather what he thought of the command performance, Senior held up a hand. "I don't want to hear it. Not right now. Your mother…" His stepfather stared down at the desk. "She needs us to get along right now."

The grim determination on Senior's face was nothing new, but his tone had changed. "What does that mean? Is something wrong?" Caleb crossed his arms tightly. What had he missed?

Watching Senior consider his words carefully was the scariest reaction Caleb might have expected. Whit Callaway, Sr. never hesitated. Worry punched a tiny hole in his resentment of the man.

"She's been having some forgetfulness." Senior rubbed his hand on his forehead, the fatigue on his face growing. "We've been to a couple of specialists, the best, but…" When their eyes met, Caleb understood. He'd heard so many stories of his grandmother and great-grandfather losing their fight with dementia.

"What's the diagnosis?" Caleb asked.

"Early stages of Alzheimer's." Senior met

his stare. "She's taking everything she can to slow this down and give it everything she has, but I don't want her upset. So you and I are going to get along." *Or else.*

Caleb understood the unspoken words and supported them.

He also wondered what would have happened if he'd skipped dinner. Would anyone have told him what was going on with the most important person in his world? Anger burned bright and hot before he squashed it.

"Go to Sweetwater. Take over the project. Show us what you can do. Get the lodge built. Distract Winter Kingfisher until everyone that matters has forgotten her." His stepfather clasped his hands together. "Easy enough."

Put your life on hold until it's done. His core crew would be working because he was definitely bringing them to Sweetwater, but finding new business for his own company would be next to impossible while he was stuck there.

Unless he pulled off a miracle, Mitch Yarborough and Rivercrest would move on without him.

"How long?" Caleb asked. He had four months to start the Yarborough project. This could still work. If he got the lodge off to a solid start, someone else could come in and finish.

"As long as it takes." Senior met his stare directly. He would accept nothing other than a yes.

"And that gets me what?" Caleb drawled. That had always been his concern—whether what his family offered matched what they demanded. He could live without their money. Missing his mother was almost impossible to comprehend.

"An open door." His stepfather's lips were a tight line again. "Whit and I will be busy, running his campaign. Your mother needs you, needs *all* of us right now. Knoxville is an easy drive from Sweetwater. She'll like that you're closer to home. To us."

The most effective leverage his stepfather had would always be Marjorie Callaway and it still worked.

"Check out the plans. I don't understand how you could say no. This place is going to amaze us all. It'll be the premier luxury mountain-resort destination in the south." His stepfather grabbed a long tube from the credenza behind him. "Take a look. Then come to dinner."

Instead of twisting harder, Senior offered him his hand to shake. Caleb stared hard at it before taking it. They'd never be warm and fuzzy, Callaway family dinners. They would almost always be businesslike. Until tonight.

"One more thing." His stepfather ran a hand over his nape. "Your mother…" He shook his head. "It's best not to mention the Kingfishers. All this circus about the canceled wedding gets her agitated. I haven't been able to keep all the news from her but…" He sagged against the desk before forcing himself to stand tall. "Try not to upset her."

When his stepfather left, Caleb tugged on his collar, ready for a shot of fresh, cool air. He'd had his doubts that Senior ever saw him as a son, but he understood the man loved his wife.

"I've been gone too long," Caleb muttered. The ticking clock reminded him he had to get a move on. "Let's see what we've got."

Caleb unrolled the architectural plans. He'd seen the early drawing for the lodge at a board meeting six months ago. As he recalled, it had been glass. So much glass. So modern, perched high on the top of the mountain. When board meetings came up, he usually found some other obligation that could not be avoided. Job sites were fun. Board meetings were not, so he avoided them.

As he studied the revised drawings, flipping slowly through the sheets of paper as he absorbed the large-scale plans, Caleb could imagine the final structure, the way it would blend perfectly in the broad clearing surrounding the old weather station, nestled in the shadow of the peak of The Aerie.

For this setting, the facade was wood timbers. Airy central spaces backed by a solid wall of windows that would frame a view of The Aerie, one of the highest and rarest points in the reserve. Instead of perching on top of the rocky mountain, a placement that would require high infrastructure work, the architect had situated the lodge in the shadow of the mountain. Small arms shot off the central building, where luxury rooms and small cabins spread out, up and down the sides of the valley. "They should fade into the background." And each one would have spectacular views. The Aerie. Down the valley. Old forest. And the shining water of Otter Lake, along with the morning mist, would attract visitors year after year.

If the Callaways had been hunting for a way to salt the family coffers, they'd found it.

Their first plan, to build on The Aerie to capitalize on the view, would have devastated so much of what made the place worth protecting. Ash Kingfisher's insistence that destroying The Aerie was the wrong decision had handed them perfection. The Kingfishers had done them a favor, not that Whit or his stepfather would ever acknowledge that.

He'd take the plans and turn them slightly, insist on Tennessee stone and timber. Summit Builders had always focused on that Tennessee connection. This could be a true art piece built from Tennessee materials and history.

"So much money." Caleb shook his head slowly. "How do they do it? Always land in the money."

And he was going to enjoy building the thing, so there was no reason to say no.

Except for the Yarboroughs and their beautiful site overlooking the river. With hard work, luck and no interference, the timing could still work.

But then there was Winter Kingfisher.

Keeping her interested in anything except

the lodge would be impossible, no matter what his stepfather ordered.

When she'd marched into his office, Caleb had been knocked sideways. She'd been as beautiful and put-together as she had been every time he'd appeared for a family photo opportunity, but she'd also been fiery and determined to save her brother's job and the reserve.

The comparison between her impassioned defense and his stepfather's reception was a stark contrast. In that instant, he'd been nearly certain that if Whit had managed to marry Winter Kingfisher, he'd have married up.

In terms of intelligence and strength of character, for sure. Now she owed Caleb and that was the only card he had that she might care about. Their maneuver meant a vindicated Ash Kingfisher was running the Smoky Valley Nature Reserve, all the while keeping an eye on the Callaways. Otter Lake was safe; Ash was Sweetwater's hero. Would gratitude or guilt be enough for Winter to agree to lay low until the election?

He'd try both angles. He needed her co-operation, a smooth build and an accelerated timeline. Everyone could have what they wanted.

Except Winter.

Her engagement was over, and she no longer had the job she loved.

Could he convince her that she was actually better off that way? Caleb squeezed his eyes shut. It was easy to imagine her negative reaction if he tried that.

Caleb slowly rolled the plans back up and slipped them in the tube before he walked into the dining room.

"I was beginning to worry you'd decided to make a run for it, after all." His mother's warm smile was sweet as she pointed at his usual spot. "Cook made prime rib. I know it's your favorite." It wasn't, but now wasn't the time to correct her, so Caleb nodded. When he sat at her right hand, she gripped his hand hard. She knew his stepfather had broken the news. As always, she was determined not to discuss something so unpleasant as an unfavorable diagnosis.

"Whit, remind Winter I need a phone call or a text or something to let me know when she's skipping dinner." She tsked. "The lady works too hard. I hope once the wedding goes off like a dream that she'll be able to slow down."

Caleb met his stepfather's hard stare and nodded. This was what Senior meant. His mother was mostly there with them, but she'd forgotten that the wedding was canceled. Reminding her would upset them all.

"Yes, Mama," Whit mumbled and shook out his linen napkin before taking a sip of the wine next to his plate.

Something, maybe the tension in the air, was enough to clear away her confusion. His mother straightened in her seat and cleared her throat. "Right. I forgot for a second. Winter is no longer part of the family." She forced a laugh. "That is due to having too much on my mind, gentlemen. There's no need for such solemn faces. Everyone smile, I command it." Her smile, Caleb noted, was genuine.

His mother motioned at them to continue their eating. "So, did you boys come to an agreement?"

"We did. I'm going to start the lodge, now that the plans are approved. Should be a fun build, with a few modifications." Caleb met his stepfather's stare. "Guess I better find a place to stay in Sweetwater."

His mother's frown seemed to be one of confusion, but eventually her smile returned. "Well, now, that lodge has been a long time in the making, hasn't it? Once you get it open way up there on the top of the mountain, that is going to be a nice place to stay."

Ever the optimist… For her, it was hard to imagine living outside of the comforts of home. Whit Callaway, Sr. respected Caleb's mom, loved her and worked hard to make sure she had every creature comfort.

For those reasons alone, Caleb would smooth things over with his family.

Building the lodge would be an interesting project.

Staying one step ahead of Winter would be a real challenge.

For his mother, he'd absolutely give it his best.

Winter had dragged him into this mess. The least she could do is keep a low profile until Whit was elected. Selling her that would be the biggest challenge of his life.

CHAPTER THREE

"WELL, NOW, A birdie told me you might make a visit today," Janet Abernathy said from her spot on the ladder's third rung. "Bright and early for a Monday, too." Winter eased closer as the ladder rattled, concerned her interview might be interrupted by her having to call for an ambulance. Janet was holding a framed painting with both hands, but Winter couldn't see either a hammer or a nail, so her purpose was unclear. The subject of the painting was enough to freeze Winter in her tracks.

Someone had captured the mist rising off of one of the valleys in the reserve at daybreak. The pink of sunrise tinged one side of the wispy smoke, while the other glistened. Somehow, an artist had managed to convey the beauty and the delicate details in vivid color. This special instant could never last, except in paint and brushstrokes.

Winter had no words to describe the techniques or the principles that made this painting art, but the emotions it provoked could be named: awe at nature's fragile, powerful beauty and love for the mountains that meant home. Neither Knoxville nor Nashville made her feel the same.

One painting had exactly what made these mountains like no other place for her.

"Pretty, right?" Janet said. At some point, she'd braced the painting against the wall and joined Winter in admiring it. Enthralled, Winter had missed the whole thing.

"Amazing. What's it called?" Winter inched closer, realizing there was no need to whisper. They were alone in the wide-open space of the gallery, but it felt right.

"*Painting number seven.* The girl has no poetry, even if she's brimming with natural talent." Janet sighed. "Or *this* is her poetry."

Drawn to the painting, Winter studied the darker corners, old growth forests making a frame for the airy center. "*Enchanted.* The title should have something to do with *enchanted*." Winter shook her head. She'd memorized her grandmother's stories before studying Cherokee folklore and history on her own, but not everyone else had the same interests. "Sorry. The Cherokee have a story about a secret lake that has restorative properties. A wounded animal could enter the lake and come out on the other side, healed. One day a hunter discovered it and was warned to never tell another soul. Humans being as they are, the hunter broke his promise and suffered the consequences. Now, the lake is hidden, but on cool mornings, the mist rises." Winter rubbed her forehead, aware all over again how a lot of people didn't care to hear her stories. Kids did. Adults, not as much.

When she turned to say something to get the job interview she'd planned back on track, Winter found Leanne Hendrix frozen in the roughed-in doorway leading to Sweetwater Souvenir. After all the renovation, the large open space was a perfect white backdrop, just the three of them and this art. Janet had propped one shoulder against the wall, her head tilted to the side. It seemed she was waiting, but for what?

Winter cleared her throat. "Who's the artist?" The urge to self-consciously fluff her hair was strong, but she fought it. Wearing one of the dark, perfectly tailored suits she'd chosen as armor while she worked in the district office of the reserve had been a boost to her confidence.

Or that had been the plan.

The silence in the room was chiseling away at it.

"I painted it. I didn't know the story. I just wanted to keep the memory of a perfect morning forever." Leanne shifted a step farther into the room with a nervous glance at Janet, whose face was slowly morphing into the Cheshire cat. She wore a grin so big it made Winter nervous. "I'm glad you like it."

"Me, too. I'm also pleased as all get-out that I'm right about Leanne's talent. Since it's one of the larger pieces we have, I'll hang it right there, where anyone walking down Main Street can see it and be drawn inside." Janet held up one finger, bright red nail polish flashing. "However, we're either going to have to put an astronomical price on it or mark it 'not for sale.' Otherwise, I'll have a big ol' hole on the wall the second day after we get these doors open." She tapped her chin. "What to do, what to do…"

Before Winter could bring up the reason for her visit, Janet had moved back into the souvenir shop on the other side. The musical bells tinkling signaled a visitor to Sweetwater Souvenir.

"She does that. It's like she has a sixth

sense when someone with money is about to walk in." Leanne shoved her hands in her back pockets and met Winter's stare. They both laughed and her shoulders relaxed.

"I wanted to talk to her about the part-time job." Winter waved a hand toward the open doorway. "But I have no money in my pocket. I might have lost my chance forever."

Leanne shook her head. "No, I mentioned you'd be by to ask about the job. She'll be back." She tapped her forehead with one finger. "Never forgets anything, Miss Janet."

They'd shared a burger, but other than stories other people told about them, neither she nor Leanne knew much about the other. They'd never been particularly close.

"I didn't know you were an artist. Why didn't you talk about this at The Branch?" Winter realized they'd been focused on her problems. How selfish and unacceptable. Compared to Leanne's life story, Winter's had been a charmed existence, but no one heard Leanne whining about shampoo. "What's the plan here?" Winter glanced around the large open space, the white walls crying out for something.

"I'm not sure I *am* an artist. That's all Miss Janet's doing. I wouldn't call myself anything but a…dabbler, but I have enjoyed painting. It keeps me busy, my mind occupied and out of trouble. Today, I've got to get moving on covering these walls. That's the plan. Local artists of all kinds. We'll have shelving, all painted white, for the smaller pieces, and there will be a small desk near the door." Storefronts on Sweetwater's main street all had history, thanks to more than a century of life, but the door's beautiful carved wood was another kind of art. If Leanne was capturing fleeting moments in paint, whoever had crafted the door showed art was meant to last. Coneflowers were carved into the heavy lower half of the door while morning glories twirled on vines around the thick, wavy glass in the top half. "I can show you the back room. Janet has asked me to work on setting up displays, but it makes me so nervous. There's a big difference between hanging key chains and folding T-shirts and arranging art, things people have poured their hearts into." Leanne motioned over her shoulder. "I mean, there are people who do this for a living, you know? Planners who set art installations for galleries. Me? I'm just…" She shook her head helplessly. "She's got faith in me, so I've got to give it a shot. Anyway, talking through it will help."

Winter watched her unlock several locks on the door. "Takes security seriously, I see."

Leanne held up her hands and made air quotes around "Art gallery," as she said it. She shook her head. "Since most of this is my stuff, I'm not sure who she's afraid will be breaking in to steal things. In another life that might have been me, actually, but I imagine Janet's the only one who can turn my work into money."

Winter glanced over her shoulder at the mist painting perched on top of the ladder. If she had a place, she'd spend money she hadn't earned yet to own it. "If they're all as good as that one, I get it."

Leanne's cheeks turned pink. "You're kind. I'll paint one for you. I loved your story." Then she motioned around the room. "Some of these you'll recognize. Kingfisher originals." She paused in front of a collection of Winter's father's woven, double-walled baskets.

"Yes, I've seen enough of these to pick them out of the crowd." Winter traced a finger around the mouth of a tall basket near the front. "My father's current claim to fame and favorite conversational topic. The tradition is to pass the knowledge from mother to daughter, but my grandmother had only sons. And my father? Yeah, he only does things wholeheartedly. He's experimenting with different materials and dyes. I'd say he needs a hobby, but this is it." She smiled at Leanne. "I'm so glad he's found somewhere else to store them. My mother is, too." She'd been so wrapped up in the drama with Ash and Whit and the lodge that she'd missed her father's exciting announcement that his work would be featured in a brand-new Sweetwater gallery, but her father had spent a lot of time since reminding everyone.

"Yeah, finding a place to put all my paintings in the tiny apartment upstairs was getting to me, too." Leanne chuckled, the sound melodic and unexpected. Both of them had grown up in Sweetwater. They'd never been friends, but in high school, Winter heard plenty of stories about how wild Leanne was. More recently, the story of how she'd stolen Christina's car and driven away in the middle of the night had made it all the way to Knoxville.

The rest of the story—how she'd done it to enter rehab to fight her addictions—hadn't made it quite as fast, but the people of Sweet-water loved a good story. If it had a mostly happy ending, they'd tell it over and over.

Leanne was making her second chance work. She had a lot to be proud of.

"I'm not sure paintings like that should be stacked on the floor, but…" Winter moved over to the canvases leaning against the wall. The first one was a large piece showing The Aerie. The heavy forests of the reserve yielded to an open area that seemed almost barren compared to the shadowy forest, but the view down the valley was inspiring. It had been years since Winter had made the climb up herself.

Now that she had time on her hands, she should correct that.

"That's one of my favorite places in the reserve. I have a few of them. It's so easy to breathe at the top of the mountain." Leanne cleared her throat. "We've got some jewelry pieces that should go in the window, and later today, the most talented stained glass artist is coming in." Leanne nodded. "The collection will be strong—Janet has a good eye, even if she's pushing for my stuff to be the centerpiece."

Winter studied Leanne's face. There would

be zero chance Leanne would be comfortable as the center of attention. "Lucky for you, my father will steal any sort of spotlight in any room anywhere," Winter said, laughing. "That has been true my whole life. I love him, but the guy is ten pounds of personality in a five-pound bag."

"Your father is a blessing, for sure." Leanne waved her toward the door. "Just like I know your help will be when we talk Janet into hiring you. I'll be happy to have another set of hands here."

As she smiled, Winter realized she'd missed this, the comfort that came from being proud of her family connections. When she'd moved to Knoxville, her plan had been to conquer the city first. She'd always intended to follow the steps all the way to Washington. With Whit Callaway, the boy she'd met in a college accounting class. Winter wasn't the charming one; winning people over was his job. Instead, she was the strategic one. Her whole life, she'd been able to see several steps ahead.

Neither one of them had developed much love for debits or credits, but they'd instantly clicked by rolling their eyes at the professor's snide comment about young people who refuse to choose practical careers.

She and Whit had been determined to be more than practical. They'd wanted to do something important.

Friendship was easy between them because Whit had agreed with every one of her ideals. They'd dreamed of the same thing: a career of public service. If she'd married him right out of college, that might still be the plan. Instead, she'd been determined to conquer Knoxville on her own through a job working for the reserve's district office. She'd proven herself there and the wedding had been next. In Knoxville, everyone knew the Callaways. She was Whit Callaway's fiancée. Here? Kingfisher was not a political name or a wealthy name, but it was respected.

"Can you help Leanne get this place set up?" Janet asked. "It might take all three of us, since we ain't none of us done this before, but then I figure the three of us together could bring about world peace or put a person on Mars." She shrugged. "Depending on our whims. Leanne does not have the confidence to sell her own work, but, Winter…? You could sell every one of those paintings she finishes with stories like that, no matter what price I talk her into, leaving me plenty of time to do other things." Janet clapped her hands. "Everyone does their part. Everyone makes money. That's my plan and I'm sticking to it."

"I've got a job?" Winter asked, all the questions she'd carefully prepared about how many hours and when she might be eligible for a raise and whether or not there was a bonus for good sales tumbling around in her brain, and absolutely none of them coming out of her mouth.

"We're focusing on local artists. Can't imagine anyone else better prepared to tell and sell the history of Sweetwater, these mountains and the people who lived here than you, Miz Storytellin' Kingfisher. I can't wait to welcome the crowds we'll draw. Minimum wage per hour. Thirty percent commission on anything you sell." Janet's sly smile was scary. "I expect you could be a real sales genius with the right incentives."

Thirty percent? She'd been prepared to argue for fifteen. She'd never done this before, so Janet was taking a chance on her.

"That's acceptable, although at the end of three months, I'd like an opportunity to sit down with you to discuss growth potential." There. That sounded as though she knew her own value and Janet would be a fool to argue.

Janet's amused chuckle was disconcerting, but she offered her hand for a shake. "Soon as you're ready to move out of Mama and Daddy's house, you let me know. I'm in between renos right now, but I've got my eye on a cabin in desperate need of a redesign. Rent would be cheap." She shrugged. "If you do as well as we both expect, could be we'd need to expand our horizons, though. This month and next might be slow, but once summer rolls in, I expect we'll all enjoy an income boost."

Winter wanted to dance in place, but she would keep her feelings under wraps. "How soon do you want to open?" Crossing her fingers would reveal too much, but Winter couldn't help sending positive energy out into the universe. *Please let it be soon. Please let it be soon.*

Janet shook her finger at Winter. "I like you Kingfishers. Your brother has always been one of them enigmas, but my boy Sam admires him, and that's good enough for me. Your daddy? He's charm personified, and your mama…" Janet stared out at the street for a second. "Gotta appreciate a woman who holds her ground. Plus, she's got good instincts. That night out at the reserve's ranger station open house, we talked about the skeeves and how that Callaway boy had always given 'em to her. She was pure joy when you pushed him in the water. In my book, the Kingfishers are quality people. Untangling yourself from the Callaways'll take some time, but you let me know how I can help." Janet clasped her hands in front of her. "Get to work right now if you'd like. Got a carpenter coming to put up some shelves and a party planned in two weeks. Let's say twenty hours a week for now. I'd suggest you ladies get a move on getting us ready to open."

"I will." Winter smiled serenely, but inside her head a loud parade had formed because she'd be working again.

Janet tapped the Choose Duncan Again button that Winter had been faithfully wearing. "Lose this. Say what you want, but no wearing politics while you're working here, especially not that guy. I still work at the school three mornings a week and the teachers would never let me hear the end of it."

The celebratory parade ended with a sad trombone. The button was Winter's single, constant, pitiful effort at impeding Whit Callaway, Jr. Twenty hours a week. She could take off the button for twenty hours a week and a paycheck. That meant Winter had to find something more effective.

Janet glanced at her watch. "If you want to make yourself scarce, I'll understand, but I got an important client coming. Regina, my business partner and best pal, usually negotiates all the contracts, but she's over in Cherokee doing some gallery scouting. Woman's a pure genius for scouting, I tell you. Got a line on a computer system that'll make tracking our inventory and sales a snap." The musical bells rang and Janet turned. "Just one second, Mr. Callaway. I'm finishing up some business."

At some point, the name *Callaway* better stop showering her with cold anxiety and then hot rage, but Winter wasn't there yet. She had no real interest in talking to any Callaway.

Janet leaned forward. "Caleb Callaway. He's hoping to rent a place close to the reserve. Got some business here in town for about six months. Guessing construction of that lodge is about to start." She winked. "His money's the same color as everyone else's, so I figure, why not? The man did put a stop to destroying The Aerie, something this town was firmly behind."

She waited for Winter to argue.

The town of Sweetwater had initially squared off against her brother, the only man determined to save The Aerie, a rare habitat in the reserve, from development because the town needed the business the lodge would bring in. Ash had been Sweetwater's Most Wanted for a minute.

And that had been Winter's fault, even though she knew Ash would agree she'd done what she needed to do if he ever found out. Slipping the governor a way to take down the Callaways in order to protect the reserve? Less noble.

The Kingfisher way was to stand up bravely to do the right thing. Her attempt to save her engagement by sneaking around? That had been a mistake. If anyone ever found out she'd been the anonymous source, instead of Caleb Callaway, Ash would forgive her. But Sweetwater would take longer to forgive and forget.

Caleb had taken the credit and the heat for pulling in the governor.

At her request.

He'd taken the heat for her.

Of all the Callaways, he was the one she was least prepared to face at that second.

When he paused in the open doorway, his jeans and rough denim coat a far cry from his brother's polished loafers and wool sweaters, a hard knot formed in her stomach.

He hadn't expected to find her standing there, but the serious expression on his face was fair warning that their business was not finished.

She'd begged him to confess to leaking the environmental-impact report to the governor's office and take the heat off Ash. Telling the truth, that she'd been the one to sneak the report in during a random visit to the education coordinator at the capitol, would have done nothing to save Ash's job.

Caleb Callaway, the family playboy who'd built a reputation for solid building practices and being at odds with his brother, had been the only answer at that time. When she'd evaluated her options to save Ash's job and The Aerie, Caleb Callaway's intercession had been her only choice.

She'd done what she had to do to get the Callaway playboy to show up for the board meeting and throw his support behind Ash.

He'd done it. He'd confessed to leaking the report. Caleb had helped her, going beyond her request to make certain Ash kept his job, had gotten Ash's idea for the new lodge heard and had gained a seat on the Callaway board of directors.

Caleb had given her more than she'd expected, including a promise not to tell anyone about it.

Guilt triggered a small panic attic as tingling heat spread up the back of her neck. He was here in Sweetwater as a result of helping her. She just knew it. From the expression on his face, he wasn't pleased about it, either.

What would he ask for in return?

CHAPTER FOUR

AFTER A WEEKEND spent scrambling to get the plans in place to start the lodge on his stepfather's accelerated timeline and move his crew to the reserve, Caleb was rushed, frustrated and annoyed that he hadn't skipped dinner on Friday night. This time frame set by Senior was ridiculous. The only way to make it work would be to spend nearly every minute at Otter Lake. He'd end up swinging a hammer himself.

Then he remembered his mother's confused frown and determined smile.

Senior was worried. Even Whit had been subdued. The family dynamic had changed. People were depending on him.

He could do this, even if he'd rather not be stuck in Sweetwater. Proving that and meeting Senior's deadline would go a long way to smoothing over family tensions. It was worth the sacrifice.

Thanks to an unexpected phone call from

Mitch Yarborough, who was ready for a builder's signature on the dotted line in order to get his Nashville subdivision underway, Caleb was thirty minutes late meeting Janet Abernathy, Sweetwater's charming kingpin of rental properties. He was also completely unprepared to run into Winter Kingfisher then. As soon as he'd entered the cute, cluttered tourist trap of Sweetwater Souvenir, he could hear the murmur of womens' voices, but when he'd paused in the open doorway to the other side of the shop, he'd slammed on the brakes.

Retreat was not a good option, and then her eyes met his. He couldn't have turned his back to save his life. Why did she seem scared when he was the one having trouble catching his breath?

"Here's a Callaway I'm prepared to welcome to town." The woman marching toward him crackled with energy, even if her voice had pieces of slow Southernness to it. "I'm Janet Abernathy. We've spoken on the phone, but I don't remember meeting in person. You don't get to town often, as I understand it." She smiled slowly as she offered him her hand. "I count that a real shame. We're gonna fix it, though."

Charmed and caught off guard at a warm welcome, Caleb relaxed a fraction as he shook her hand. "Right. Sorry I'm late. I had a...thing." He shrugged. No one cared that he was scrambling to make sure the projects he had in the works stayed on track or that Missy Yarborough had had a restrained yet intense fit when he'd told her he'd be living in Sweetwater until he could get the project up and running.

In fact, he'd be surprised if anyone in the room actually wanted to greet a Callaway at all that morning.

Besides that, Callaways didn't make excuses and avoided apologies when they could.

Ever since the Kingfishers had routed his brother and father so soundly, he had the feeling Callaways were no longer greeted as wealthy benefactors in Sweetwater. Before his previous quick trip to town, how many years had it been since he'd visited? Five years? Was that how long it had been since he'd fished Otter Lake?

"Sure. You had a thing. It happens. We busy corporate moguls have to schedule full days." Janet tapped his arm. "Let's get you out on the road. This first place I have to show you..." She held up her hands and gestured as if she was pushing open the curtains on a grand vista. "You won't need to waste a bit of your time with any others."

Caleb ran a hand down his nape and wondered if Winter would say something. Anything at all would be good.

Then he realized how little her opinion should matter. She was a part of his mission here in Sweetwater. As long as she wasn't organizing press briefings or rallying the town against him or his family, his job was going to be easy.

"I'm surprised you have it available to rent, then. Because it's the slow season?" Caleb asked as Janet waved her hands.

"No, it's not a renter, it's a buyer, but for you, I'm going to make an exception." She nodded around the room as if everyone had asked a question. "Regina and I bought it because we wanted to try our hands at a vacation rental." She pursed her lips. "Well, that's not entirely true. I wanted to decorate something other than my own living room, but then we decided to hold it instead of reselling it. We weren't sure why then, but smart businesspeople follow their hunches." She clapped. "And it's all working out."

Caleb raised his eyebrows at Winter. She

was a hometown girl, had probably known Janet Abernathy her whole life. Surely she could follow the conversation better than he was managing. She shook her head, but her lips curved as if there was a smile waiting.

Seeing her again like this, looking a lot like her old self with the suit and the heels, but different, too... Softer...

Then he read the campaign button pinned loud and proud to her nice suit. That, they would have to talk about.

While he was trying to come up with an answer for her, Janet breezed past him. "Let me get my pocketbook and away we go."

The petite blonde who followed him was shaking her head, but she didn't pause to greet him.

That didn't happen often—women passing him by instead of making a point to introduce themselves.

The fact that he hadn't noticed her until she passed under his nose might be the reason.

Winter was in the room. She would draw attention no matter how many women were there.

"Caleb." She tangled her fingers together in front of her. "You're going to be in Sweetwater for a few months." The way she fidgeted and refused to meet his eyes convinced him she was as pleased with the notion as he was.

"I won't be stuck here any longer than necessary, but yeah, until I get the lodge construction up and running, I'll be in town."

Her eyebrows rose. "Stuck, huh? Like it's a punishment."

"Isn't it? My stepfather's decree—do this and all is forgiven. Given another option, I'd be eating a nice lunch right now. Instead, I'm in Sweetwater." He pointed at the window. "Home of…a coffee shop." Irritated all over again but aware he'd made his own decisions, Caleb held up his hands. Why did she give him the kind of jitters he hadn't experienced since prom night? "Never mind about restaurant recommendations. I can find the only one in town by myself. Let's talk about how my visit is going to play out. Between us."

Her eyes shot up, and this time she met his gaze directly. There was no way to miss the sharp intelligence there. She'd make a much better ally than enemy, something he'd always understood even if the rest of the Callaways had forgotten.

"What does that mean?" Winter shifted

a step closer to him. "As long as you keep your promise not to tell anyone the truth, why would there be anything between *us*? You'll do your job, dismiss the people in this town, which seems to have become the Callaway way of life, and hit the road again. Nobody is looking forward to that as much as I am." The corners of her lips turned up, but not into a genuine smile. "Maybe you'll even learn to cook while you're here. Wouldn't want to take your chances eating anywhere with less than four stars, am I right?"

The urge to defend himself was strong. Holes-in-the-wall, fine dining and everything in between were his kinds of places. His point had been about limited selection, not that it was beneath him.

But the hard glint in her eyes convinced him to drop that piece of the argument.

"I've got a short time frame for construction and other work that has to get done. I don't need a circus going on while this lodge goes up." Caleb remembered standing across from his stepfather as he'd delivered the news about his mother's diagnosis. The tension. The fear that neither one of them wanted to acknowledge and his determination to repair the bridges he'd burned. "You've spent a lot of time in the center ring, grabbing the front page. Now, you'll need to…stop. The lodge goes up. Ash has his job. Kingfishers and Callaways go along their separate, sometimes parallel, but never overlapping, paths and we all win. No bad press. This all works out for everyone." Except for her, if she was still brokenhearted over the engagement ending. Whatever. She'd land on her feet. People as determined as Winter Kingfisher didn't stay down for long.

He braced his hands on his hips. This was how he did business. He was up-front. Blunt. She'd appreciate that. "No campaigning for Richard Duncan until the lodge is finished." There. That was clear.

Winter blinked slowly, the small frown of concentration suggesting she was evaluating his words carefully. "You're building the lodge. Not Callaway Construction." She pursed her lips. "That's a good optic, plays better for all the papers covering Whit's political run. Your company has a much better reputation. It's so small, compared to the far-flung projects Callaway Construction has. Less destruction and legal fines, that sort of thing. The family unity is always nice, even if you have a reputation for being the least Callaway of them all."

Watching her pace was almost like tracking a tennis match. Then he realized what she'd said. The least of them all. Even knowing her current opinion of his brother and stepfather, that stung.

"Caleb, daylight's wasting. You ready?" Janet stuck her head into the large open space. "Time enough to talk to the pretty women later. Let's find you an address to call your own."

Caleb nodded at Janet but made sure he caught Winter's stare one more time. She hadn't agreed to anything. This was the trickiest piece of the puzzle, figuring out Winter's next step.

The fact that she robbed him of IQ points simply by standing opposite him increased the degree of difficulty.

"We have a deal. I might be stuck here, building this lodge I don't care about in a place I don't know because of you, but I'll keep my promise as long as you'll help kill this story dead," Caleb said. "The less time that takes, the better chance I'll remember my promise. No more circus, Winter."

The firmness of her jaw suggested she didn't appreciate his honest terms.

"It must be nice." Winter walked slowly toward him. "Being able to dismiss the battle to save a place I love as a circus. Your family is about grabbing headlines. Your brother is about publicity at all costs. Your stepfather and brother were happy with my circus when I was setting it up for their benefit." She sighed. "Having me fade away would be convenient for the Callaway political team. I guess we'll have to see which ringmaster wins, Caleb."

Calmly laying down the gauntlet had been a mistake. Instead of agreeing out of gratefulness or even sympathy, Winter's stubborn expression indicated the battle was still on.

And she was more prepared to fight than he was. After wasting precious seconds trying to come up with a better parting line than hers, Caleb turned and followed Janet through the souvenir shop. Regrouping at this point might be weak, but it was the only choice he had.

"Follow me." Janet jingled a key ring. "I'm bringing a contract because I know you're going to love this place." She turned and pointed at a white SUV. "We're headed to the base of the reserve—can't beat the commute out to the old weather station."

Caleb slid behind the wheel of his truck and eased out onto the main street behind Janet while he cataloged the changes in Sweetwater. As long as he'd been a Callaway, they'd made infrequent trips to the town and the reserve. Nothing changed quickly here. Businesses came and went but the small town seemed timeless, especially compared to the tourist explosions that had taken place in Gatlinburg and Pigeon Forge.

And as he drove out of town, he wondered how anyone lived there happily. Where were the restaurants? How did they entertain themselves? During the day, Otter Lake could offer fishing and all kinds of water activities. Hikers would enjoy the reserve, but what about everyone else?

Caleb tried to figure out how he'd fill in that blank. He worked. He went to parties to build relationships and find more work, and ate out and… What else did he do with his time?

"It's a good thing you like to work. Getting this lodge built and open is going to be a full-time obsession, no doubt," Caleb muttered as Janet turned off the two-lane highway in front of him. They'd passed the small apartment complex where some of the reserve's rangers lived, as well as the road that led up to the campground and ranger station. This was new territory for Caleb.

The old pines lining the road cast a dark shade even in midmorning and it was the kind of forest that faded into darkness and seemed secretive. In less than twenty minutes, the neat civilization of Sweetwater was gone and it was easy to imagine life before the reserve and development.

"Virgin Callaway territory. Who knew it still existed in this corner of Tennessee?" Caleb rolled to a stop right behind Janet's SUV and watched her climb the steps to a large wraparound porch. Native stone and wood made up the facade of the two-story house. It could have been built decades ago. At first glance, the house made him think of pioneers and wagons and hard living. What did that say about the interior and modern conveniences?

It couldn't be any more different than his modern Nashville town house, which had a view of the city.

"Now, don't go jumping to any conclusions. It's the view from the back deck you gotta see." Janet motioned at him to hurry up and moved to unlock the door. While he waited, Caleb surveyed the exterior. Everything was in good shape. Tearing it down to start over would have been a bad idea. He admired the craftsmanship.

The quiet hush around them would take some getting used to. In Nashville, traffic noise was a constant backdrop, whether he was working or playing or sitting on the balcony at home. He told himself he liked the energy of the city. This place had none of the noise or traffic. Everything was still.

"Come on in, hon." Janet's heels tapped ahead of him on the hardwood floor. The stone and wood carried on inside to a great room that opened wide off a short foyer. "You shoulda seen the furniture we carried out of here. Plaids. All of it covered in some sort of plaid." Her nose wrinkled. Janet didn't care for plaid. Judging from the replacements she'd chosen, she preferred light fabrics, furniture built for comfort and a minimal style. He liked it. Shadowy sunlight filtered in through large glass doors filling one wall.

"Want to explore the kitchen?" Janet pointed at the right side of the open room, where modern appliances gleamed. "All brand-new."

He hadn't expected that or the brief flash of the picture of a family seated around the large island.

Caleb shook his head. Who was he imagining gathered around for a nice dinner? Not his family. Formal dining at the Callaway home required multiple courses and professional staff.

Learning to cook for himself had never been a priority, either. Those appliances should still be good as new when he moved out.

Janet pointed up the stairs. "Five bedrooms. Hardwoods. The Heathcotes lived here before selling. Had four kids, but they all moved away. Not enough work here to keep them. When her husband died, Mary sold this place and moved down to an assisted-living facility in Knoxville. Hated to see them go, but you understand if you think about it hard. Still, when you go, I'm going to hunt up the right couple or family for this place. You can tell the Heathcotes loved it while they were here." She brushed her shoulders. "Prettiest bathroom I've built yet, if I do say so myself. Got one of them rain showerheads.

Separate bathtub with jets." She motioned over her shoulder that he should follow her, so Caleb obediently trailed Janet through three bathrooms and five bedrooms. This house was nothing like what he'd describe as his perfect home, but when he stepped into the master bedroom, a space all done in smooth lines and calm colors, he could appreciate how Janet had taken the house's history and turned it into a modern, comfortable space.

"I'll take it." Caleb held his hand out to take the small stack of paper Janet immediately shoved in his direction. It was more house than he'd need, especially since they'd be running extra crews to get the lodge built quickly. He'd never be home.

But when he was home, this was where he'd want to spend his time.

"I was saving the best for last," Janet said over the hands she'd clasped together under her chin. "In case I needed to justify the price tag, but…"

Caleb studied the agreement he'd scrawled his name on in an uncustomary rookie mistake. He should have negotiated. "Rent's higher than I expected." But the place was worth it, so he offered her the signed contract back.

Janet smiled broadly. "Sure, but you didn't expect this, either." She moved over to the French doors along the side of the bedroom.

Caleb expected a small balcony, something too small for practical use. That was his experience in the Nashville rental market.

Instead, he followed her out to a wide space that ran across the full length of the back of the house.

"Two stories. Bottom level is a kind of wraparound porch," Janet said. "And for good reason. Soak in this view."

Caleb eased into one of the chairs Janet had picked out and contemplated the deep, dark forest standing guard around the small clearing. Through a small break in the trees, he could see water. "Is that Otter Lake?"

Janet nodded. "In summer, when the trees fill in with leaves, that'll disappear. Whoever buys this house could do a little more clearing, with permission of the head ranger at the reserve, of course, and open that up." She sighed. "Gonna make a fortune when I sell this." Then she turned to look at him over her shoulder. "Of course, my buyer better get on well with Ash Kingfisher. This isn't technically a piece of reserve land, but it's surrounded on all sides." She smiled slowly.

"Well, I wouldn't say I'm on the best terms with any of the Kingfishers, but Ash does owe me his job and this lodge." Caleb stood slowly. There was also the fact that Callaways actually owned all the reserve lands. He should be able to do anything he wanted here. "We might be able to negotiate something."

"If you were buying the place." Janet smiled sweetly. "Not renting it." Then she tilted her head to the side.

Almost as if she was waiting for him to make an offer. He hadn't expected much in the way of business savvy from Janet Abernathy.

He'd been misguided, obviously.

"Good point. Renter here." Caleb inhaled slowly. It was all in his imagination, of course, but the quiet stillness here made him want to slow down, take it all in.

"I like to point out all the possibilities in every business relationship, Caleb." Janet braced her hands on the balcony railing. "Life changes quickly, even here on the edge of nowhere. Never know when the lightning bolt hits and a renter changes his mind, finds a place to put down roots."

He couldn't see her face. Was she referring

to him? Roots here. Caleb shook his head but bit back the snort that was his first response.

"Sunrise will be a true blessing, Caleb. You wait and see. Hard not to greet the day with enthusiasm when you can watch the sun break on Otter Lake." Janet patted his arm. "It'll cure whatever ails you, I guarantee."

His mother. This job. What to do about Winter Kingfisher. The list was short but overwhelming.

"Well, now, I'll get out of your hair. You take a minute or five right here. Work can wait that long." Janet offered him the key ring and waved. "Next time you're in town, stop in at the souvenir shop and let me know if you have any problems. Bring me a check. I'm easy to track down."

Before he could get a phone number, something that might come in handy for a landlord, Janet was gone.

"Guess I'll be making another visit to Sweetwater Souvenir soon." Caleb stretched out his legs and focused on the peekaboo view of shining Otter Lake. Why hadn't he spent more time in Sweetwater? Resting his head against the back of the chair was nice, but his eyelids grew heavy. Something about the place was sapping his restless energy. He should get up.

He should do a lot of things, but the truth was that work could wait. His problems would still be there after a short nap.

CHAPTER FIVE

ON WEDNESDAY MORNING, Winter hit the snooze three times, a new personal record. Two had become her normal routine after a lifetime of waking up five minutes before the alarm went off and bounding out of bed, her mind already on everything she wanted to accomplish.

As she stood under the hot shower, her smuggled bottle of the good shampoo cradled in her arm, she realized how low this week had already brought her.

It had started out well, with a reinvigorated effort to get so happy and fulfilled with her life that Whit regretted ever attempting to take on the Kingfishers.

Her solid start had taken a slight downturn after Caleb weakly threatened to expose her secret unless she gave up on her plans to help Whit's opponent.

Then reading the story about Governor Duncan's appalling stance on the state teachers' union wanting to negotiate higher salaries for the coming school year had dimmed her positive attitude further because his quotes were... Winter winced as she tried to imagine standing at a podium and spinning anything so bad. Did he have no one with any media savvy on his staff? Worse, was he raised by wolves? "Shooting himself in the foot and on the record."

At least she wasn't facing the news media after that mess.

Winter had been able to shrug off the gloom for the most part. Working at Sweetwater Souvenir might not mean power suits and power players, but it was challenging. A different kind of challenging than what she was used to.

And planning with Leanne had been so much fun.

While they moved artwork around and considered the layout, Leanne had told Winter funny stories about her kids. When they evaluated Leanne's canvases to decide which ones they should hang first, Winter told Leanne some of her favorite Cherokee stories, including the tale about Rabbit, the trickster, mostly passed down from her grandparents while they hiked or fished at the reserve.

Leanne had done a small canvas featuring a rabbit with fur so fine that Winter had almost touched the paint, expecting soft warmth. "If that doesn't sell the night of the opening, it's mine." Thanks to Janet Abernathy and Regina Blackburn, none of the other paintings would be in her price range until commissions started coming in. Leanne was lucky to have them representing her. Otherwise, she'd be giving away her talent for far too little.

The first paintings they chose would set the tone for the shop, so they'd deliberated carefully. Selling the collection Janet had put together should be easy once the number of tourists rose in the spring.

Even with the minor dark cloud of Caleb's arrival, Tuesday had been a good day until she'd driven into Knoxville to volunteer at the closest office of the governor's reelection campaign. Caleb's ultimatum had increased her desire to do *something*. Richard Duncan wasn't accepting her phone calls. Fine. Campaigns could always use volunteers, and she'd wanted to get involved so that when the prime months before the election hit, she'd have demonstrated her skills.

She could man a spot in the phone bank, sure, but she could do so much more.

Walking into that cramped spot in the strip mall had been an exercise in humility.

"Why am I having so many of those lately?"

Instead of greeting her warmly because she recognized the true gifts of Winter's experience and talent, Duncan's east Tennessee volunteer coordinator had stared her up and down before asking what she wanted. There was no doubt in Winter's mind that Monica Hill recognized her, but instead of welcoming her in, suspicion had been thick in the air.

After a tense exchange, where Winter did her best to communicate that she was committed to Duncan's campaign, Monica had finally given her a short list of businesses that had supported the governor's previous campaigns. To make phone calls and network? No. To address and stuff envelopes with campaign materials.

And that was it.

Before she'd gotten back in the car to return to Sweetwater, Winter finagled two campaign signs from Monica.

All that had happened before she'd spied the newspaper her father had left folded on the kitchen table with Richard Duncan's angry face and a jaw-dropping bad quote.

"Your campaign to keep Whit out of the capital is failing, thanks to a bad candidate making it impossible to support him." Being against Whit wasn't the same as being for Richard Duncan.

She'd courier a letter and résumé to Duncan's attention. With a better advisor, he could improve his positions. He wouldn't be the first politician to have an abrupt change of heart.

"Why would that work, Winter? Calls haven't. Neither have emails." She closed her eyes against the water and did her best to drown out the self-doubt. "When plan A doesn't work, you better have a plan B."

After she got out of the shower and dressed, she straightened her shoulders and headed for the kitchen. No good would come from letting her parents know that she was struggling. Every time she saw her mother, Winter had to ignore the expectant waiting in her eyes. Her parents were as anxious for Winter to get herself together as she was.

"Good morning," Winter said as she marched toward the refrigerator. *Pretend everything is fine. It is fine.*

"Those signs are not going up in my yard," her mother said from her usual spot in front of the stove. In a world of instant oatmeal and drive-thru biscuits, her mother was firmly in the "breakfast is the most important meal of the day" camp. She got up early and cooked, and had for as long as Winter could remember.

Winter stopped behind her mother and propped her chin over her shoulder to stare down at the Western omelet Donna Kingfisher had expertly turned. "I've got to put the signs up, Mama. I have to do something."

In the big picture, the signs were nothing. Why did they seem so important now?

Her father folded down one corner of the paper. "No signs. Richard Duncan might not be a Callaway but he's also not getting our vote." The edge of the paper popped back up. The governor's face was frowning back at Winter, too, but from her spot, she couldn't read the headline. "The man has never met a teacher, obviously."

When her father had a negative word to say, and this was as close as he got, things had gotten real.

"I want to hit the craft store in Knoxville early." Her mother plopped down the plate on the table. "You're getting enough rest, eating well for once, and I don't want to hear another word about skipping breakfast or signs. Eat."

Arguing would be a waste of breath. Winter took her usual spot at the table but paused when she understood what her mother had said. She was sleeping and eating better than she ever had in Knoxville. There, the pace of life, on top of work at the reserve, had kept her running all the time. Here, rest was a guarantee.

Had her mother worried about her health while she was living in Knoxville? Winter had never given it a second thought. Independence and accomplishment were her mother's values. Winter's, too, for that matter.

Being at home like this, with her mother's concern so easy to see, wasn't easy, but the brush of her mother's hand on her shoulder as she put more plates on the table was nice. Sweet. Comforting.

This time over the breakfast table was important.

A campaign sign wouldn't solve the problem, so why argue?

Skipping this meal?

That would be a criminal waste of eggs and precious breakfast food. Winter picked up her fork and took a bite.

"Fresh orange juice." Her mother slid a glass toward her. "And water. Drink them both, please." Her mother put down the second glass with emphasis before delivering the same setup to her father. "You can take a mug of rose-hip tea in the car. I made you both to-go drinks."

Her father immediately folded his paper and followed directions.

When Winter had eaten as much as she could, she leaned back. "Thank you, Mom. That was good."

Her mother nodded. "I know. And you have a big day and a lot of work to do. We all do. Your father is teaching a weaving class at the seniors' center." She waved her fork at her husband. "And since I have this place to myself all day, I'm going to work on my projects. Create a new soap, new lotion, a bath bomb or two." She ran a hand over Winter's glossy hair while Winter squashed the urge to wiggle with guilt. "I've been doing some tinkering with my shampoo formula." Her mother leaned over, scooped a glass jar off the counter and held it proudly. From Winter's spot, she would call it gray goop instead of shampoo. "My current formula is for my hair, which needs extra oomph—" she pointed at the blond curls tamed by a messy braid "—but for yours, I've been playing with oils. You like glossy. Give this a shot." She smacked the jar on the table. Winter assumed her face had betrayed her misgivings about putting gray goop in her hair because her mother waved. "I can make it pretty later, add some scent. What's your favorite?"

Winter tried to imagine what scent would match gray goop. Didn't matter. She was going to have to give the gray goop a shot. To make her mother happy. "Anything flowery. You know I like flowers."

Her mother pursed her lips, clearly unconvinced that Winter was on board.

There was no way the gray-goop conversation would drop until Winter used it, so she resolved to enjoy her only good hair day for a while and nodded. "I'll try it tomorrow."

"Retirement is the promised land and don't let anyone tell you any differently." Her mother had sold her law practice as soon as she turned sixty and had been making full use of every day since. She'd always loved her greenhouse and gardens, but with the extra time, her mother had become an inventor. If her father's new obsession was baskets, her mother's was all-natural beauty products.

Winter envied both of her parents. They'd worked hard. Now they were reaping the benefits and living every day better than the last. The fact that they were both building hobbies into something more, brand-new ventures that hadn't been a part of their Monday-through-Friday, "go to work every day" lives, was impressive.

She'd moved back home and had a part-time job.

Yay, her.

"Even if you aren't voting for Duncan, we could still put the signs up."

Her mother spluttered for a few seconds. "Lie? No, Winter Rose Kingfisher. We don't lie. The idea of the man gives me the skeeves. Those signs go up and there's not enough lavender in my garden to burn to clear this place of bad energy. No. We'd never recover."

Winter glanced over at her father. At a family dinner when they'd been plotting Ash's comeback from the Callaways' scheming, her father had admitted how he'd contributed to his mother's beliefs that the skeeves were a valid thing, rooted in intuition. In this effort he had perpetuated the longest-running lie that Winter knew of and included the salvation of a schoolyard bully who was now a thriving pediatrician thanks to her mother's burned lavender, but more to her father's schooling about fairness and hard work.

Neither one of them would disabuse Donna Kingfisher of the idea that she'd changed a life.

Her father gave a tiny shake of his head as he stood to clear the table. The sound of running water was loud, so Winter decided to wait until the dishes were done to try again. She dried while her father washed. When everything was put away to her mother's satisfaction, Winter slumped against the counter. "I tried to volunteer at their Knoxville office last night. The signs were all I could manage and..." They weren't enough.

Especially if they were going to be hidden in the garage somewhere.

"Is there no other choice? No one else we can vote for?" her mother asked dramatically. That was her default. Drama. Winter remembered the restrained dinners at the Callaway table. The food had been less inspiring there, but the atmosphere had fit Winter perfectly. Polite conversation. Moderate tones. Hardly any emotion leaking around the edges. Soothing.

"No. Duncan is the incumbent and no one else is mounting a campaign against him.

Only Whit. Only the Callaways stand any sort of chance against him. They have the resources to do it right." Winter closed her eyes as she remembered the dinner where she and Whit had gone back and forth over whether it was a good time to make the run. He'd been serving in Knoxville and they'd enjoyed that.

But Callaways were impatient and they didn't lose often.

Her mother crossed her arms over her chest. "Hate to say it, but we may have to vote for a Callaway."

Winter thumped her head on the wood cabinet behind her.

"It's like you and your fancy shampoo." Her mother sniffed. "Mine's better for the environment, but you have to be you. We have to vote for the best choice, even if it's Whit Callaway."

Winter rolled her head from side to side until she felt her father's hands on her shoulders. "Hair looks good, Winter, but this desperation to elect *anyone* else? I don't know if that will work out in the long run. Getting even? It's a bad look and a worse life choice." He pressed a kiss on the top of her head.

Since that was the realization that she was

coming around to on her own, slowly, Winter leaned against her chair.

"Is Whit Callaway husband material?" Her mother tapped her fingers on the counter. "No, ma'am. He is not. That man would have gotten on your nerves in a heartbeat as soon as you two were living together. Nobody wants to credit my intuition, but I will." She pressed her hands to her chest. "He's wrong for you. A mother just knows. There is something better for you, baby, than marriage to a man you don't *love* love. None of those Callaways measure up to Kingfisher standards. Can he at least do some good in Nashville?"

Winter wanted to argue about loving Whit. Neither one of them had been *in love*, but they cared about each other and…

When the silence stretched out, Winter tilted her head to the side to consider the right answer.

"I'm asking. Can he do any good in Nashville?" Her mother held out her hands, ready for a response.

"Absolutely. No doubt in my mind." Winter shook her head. "But what about me?"

When she heard how pitiful the words sounded, Winter desperately wanted them back. All of them. She'd rewind the whole day and start over with only two snoozes and gray goop from a jar.

Her father reached over and wrapped his hand over Winter's forearm. "Baby, you're going to be fine. You just need a minute."

Winter and her mother could argue about whether the sky was blue, but it was almost impossible not to trust her father's faith in her ability. "I should get to the shop." She trudged over to pick up the signs. "You're sure about this?"

Her mother shook her head. "Never been more certain of anything. Kingfishers don't put Duncan signs in their yard." She walked over to Winter, wrapped her arms around her and squeezed tightly. Lavender and rose and warm kitchen all tangled together into her mother's signature scent. Winter rested her head on her mother's shoulder for a second before standing tall. "What Kingfishers do is the right thing. You'll find it. No doubt in my mind. If your grandmother was here, what would she say?"

Donna Kingfisher had admired her mother-in-law above all other people. Instead of quoting international peacekeepers or Nobel Prize winners or catchy self-help slogans, her mother would rely on her mother-in-law's wisdom.

"Make him pay?" Winter knew a joke would only exasperate her mother, but she didn't want to be wise about any of it. Her mom's long-suffering sigh was expected.

"You need to spend some time near the water. It will settle your brain, refill your soul," her mother said and squeezed Winter tightly.

Einisi might also have been convinced that she had one foot in the grave because she heard a howl hoot before sunrise, but Winter knew her mother was right, and her grandmother, too. This conflict inside needed some resolution. She'd always think better next to Otter Lake.

"Peace comes from the flow of water. Try to find some peace." Her mother bent her head down, the long, fuzzy blond braid draping over her shoulder. "Now get out of my house. I have some soap to make." She waved to Winter and made a "hurry up" motion to Winter's father, then the two of them walked out with their arms intertwined, her father swinging the signs.

"My mother was smart, baby. Yours is, too." Her father propped the signs up next to the garbage can. "To get what you want, you're going to have to let go of whatever you're holding on to."

Winter inhaled slowly, the cold air clearing her mind. "Right, but I don't have to make any decisions today. Today, I have to go arrange baskets created by a local artist. His talent is impressive."

Her father's chest puffed out and he brushed both shoulders off. "I know that guy. He's good."

He saluted her before sliding into the truck he'd packed with all his provisions so carefully the night before.

"Those seniors will be making double-walled baskets in no time," Winter murmured as she carried the signs to the station wagon. They'd be in the trash can before she got home if she didn't take them with her. The car started faithfully, as it always did, and she made the quick turn through town to park in front of Sweetwater Souvenir. When the tourist season hit, these spots would be few and far between.

She had one hand on the door when her phone rang. The display showed the name of a reporter from Knoxville, Bailey Garcia. *Of course. Just what I needed.* The calls used to be fun, a battle of wits to test how much information she could cram into a passing conversation. Now? Only a determined "making the best of it" would do.

Ignoring the call would mean fewer calls in the future. Winter was tempted to decline.

But Bailey had been so helpful in the battle to save Ash's job that Winter had to answer. "Hi, Bailey, I haven't been out to the lodge site, so I don't have any news to report."

Bailey laughed. "Direct. To the point. That's why I always enjoyed your press events, Winter. We didn't waste time with pleasant conversation."

Why did that sting?

It was awfully close to the conversation she'd had at The Branch about friendship and sharing. Winter could name a long list of acquaintances like Bailey, people who'd been helpful along the way, but none of them had spent time on "pleasant conversation."

"How can I help you? I have a nice new art gallery that I'd be happy to give you a tour of." Then and there, the inspiration hit. If she could get news crews to Sweetwater for the gallery opening, Janet would have so much good press that she'd be an instant success. Did she still have the pull to manage that?

"I was hoping for a quote about Whit Callaway's new relationship." Bailey paused. "Have you heard?"

"Why would I care?" Winter drawled while she mentally flipped through all the news stories she'd seen. She would remember a new name linked with Whit's.

Wouldn't she?

"Gospel singer out of Nashville. Candace Hawthorne. They've been seen all over Knoxville and Nashville for the past three weeks. Speculation is he's hunting for the first Mrs. Callaway. Well, a *replacement* first Mrs. Callaway." Baily added, "We got some footage of them at a fund-raiser last night. If I had to guess, I'd say they're discussing wedding rings."

Winter watched the front window of Smoky Joe's, Sweetwater's coffee shop. If she had a meltdown on the street she'd have an audience, so she forced herself to take deep breaths.

But nothing worked. He was moving on with his life and with much better strategy than Richard Duncan. Whit was smart. This was a solid move to cast himself in a much better light and to throw a few shadows Winter's way.

And his actions made it even harder to present herself as anything other than the jealous ex to anyone who might benefit from her political and media savvy.

Candace Hawthorne could have him, with Winter's blessing, but the voters in the state needed some good advice.

"If that's the case..." Winter cleared her throat. "Listen, it wouldn't be the first time Whit Callaway has pulled a stunt like this. I hope every news story is about how that kind of maneuver, rehabilitating a rotten image by pairing it with a squeaky clean one, is one of the oldest tricks in the public-relations handbook. Anyone who falls for it deserves a governor like Whit Callaway." *What does that even mean, Winter? Smart? Determined. Committed to improving education and the support programs for Tennessee's people. Ready to sacrifice a lot to lead the state.* Winter clamped her jaw shut, paused and then asked, "Anything else, Bailey?"

Winter could hear the rustle of pages. Was that pen scratching across paper? Before

Winter could tell the reporter not to use her words in a story, Bailey said, "If you have any pull with Caleb Callaway, could you get him to return my calls?" Then she laughed. "I'm guessing you don't have anything to do with Caleb Callaway at all, do you, Winter? Never mind."

Winter closed her eyes. She was never intended to be the go-between for Caleb Callaway, but if Bailey could get to him, maybe she would forget Winter's comments about Candace Hawthorne.

"I'm sure Caleb's on the job. You want to talk to him, go to the old weather station." Winter ended the call because she wasn't going to help anymore or dig the hole she'd stepped into any deeper.

What had she done? She and Whit had negotiated a marriage contract, one intended to cement his win.

But neither one of them had ever wanted anyone else to know that or to make it anything less than a true marriage for the best reasons. It would have been. Eventually.

Would Bailey put together what Winter had almost admitted? That Whit's new relationship was not that far from the one they'd had, a performance meant to garner followers?

Except Winter had believed the decision to be smart and sound for both of them. What if Candace Hawthorne had another agenda or no agenda at all? What if she and Whit were falling in love? Real love?

The hard knot in her stomach was impossible to ignore. Every time she messed up, that knot made an appearance.

But every good PR person knew the best way to cover a bad story was to make a bigger, badder story.

She'd have to do that. If she could manage to swing good publicity Richard Duncan's way, too, she could kill two birds with her one stony hard knot.

Janet waved at her from the window so Winter got out of the station wagon. On her way in, she paused on the sidewalk. Her mother didn't want signs in the yard. Why drive a station wagon if you couldn't turn it into a rolling advertisement to bring down your enemies? Winter stretched into the back and stood the signs carefully so that anyone passing by could read them. She shoved aside the junk her mother stored in the back to wedge the signs in place and then sighed happily. It was only a little something, but it was something.

Then she realized Caleb Callaway was standing on the sidewalk in front of Smoky Joe's.

His angry jaywalk across the empty street was fast and Winter was frozen in place.

CHAPTER SIX

CALEB'S WEDNESDAY GOT off to a late start thanks to an overcast sky, which meant he'd overslept because no natural sunrise alarm had poured in through the skylights. When he'd discovered his coffeepot was cold and unresponsive, he'd taken it as a second sign that he might be able to take his time getting to the job site that day.

For him, the kind of bachelor who did not cook, life in Sweetwater had meant surviving on frozen dinners and cereal. And slim pickings if he wanted to eat out. However, coffee was critical to his success. In Nashville, he could drive five blocks in any direction and find a place that served coffee through a to-go window. In Sweetwater, not so much.

Then he remembered passing the coffee shop as he'd been driving through town, and the world had stopped spinning in a caffeine-withdrawal-driven whirl.

One plus for Sweetwater? Parking was a snap. That morning, the street was deserted.

Because everyone had already beaten him inside Smoky Joe's.

Standing in line to get a cup of coffee was uncomfortable when the rest of the coffee shop crowd was dead silent. No one stirred while Caleb waited. That gave him plenty of time to mentally list all he had to accomplish to catch up. While he was in town, he could leave a check for Janet at Sweetwater Souvenir.

He'd also have a chance to remind Winter of what she owed him. Anticipation added an impatient tap to his boot as he waited.

She was a worthy opponent. Working alongside her would create an unstoppable team. What had Whit been thinking? A smart man would never have disappointed her enough to drive her to drastic measures in the first place, much less end their relationship.

Admiring his brother's ex wasn't going to make it any easier to manage her reaction.

Eventually, the man in front of him stepped aside, his hands filled with a tall, steaming cup and a plate holding a large, single slice of homemade banana-nut bread.

Battling with Winter required fortification. He deserved a piece of that bread. "I'll have the same thing. To go."

The elderly woman behind the counter narrowed her eyes at him. "Oh, yeah?" She raised her chin. "Do I know you?"

Confused, Caleb paused in the middle of pulling out his wallet. What did that matter? He was a customer. With money.

Then he realized in small-town Sweetwater, everyone knew everyone. That made it easier to close ranks against the outsider. Repairing the Callaway reputation here would need to be accomplished by someone on the inside. Since the Callaways lacked any inside source, he'd have to wiggle his way under the town's defenses.

This woman and the crowd watching their conversation could be his first attempt.

Caleb offered the woman his hand and prepared to shake gently, since she looked like she'd evaporate like a vampire in the sun if he pressed too hard. "Caleb Callaway." He didn't have to say anything more.

Biting back the wince that wrinkled his lips when she squeezed his hand took some effort.

"Call me Odella." She tapped her name

badge. "This is my shop. I don't have to serve anyone I don't want to." She raised an eyebrow. "Do I want to serve you?"

Caleb took a twenty-dollar bill out of his wallet. "I can pay you. Coffee and a slice of that bread. Please."

"Well, now…nice manners." She pinched his money between her finger and thumb and rubbed it as if she was testing to make sure it was real. "Good enough for me." She made change and then took the bag and cup the younger girl behind the counter had handed to her. "You'll be back, too. This could be the start of a long-lasting friendship."

Caleb sipped his coffee and considered how long she expected this friendship might stretch. How old was she? At least a hundred.

Then he managed a bite of the bread and realized that their friendship was going to grow deep and quick. "Odella, I came in today because my coffeepot isn't working."

"But you'll be in tomorrow because…" She smiled patiently.

"Because I'm smarter than I appear. And this is the best banana-nut bread in the state." Maybe it was some special ingredient, but his overwhelming frustration at being stuck in

Sweetwater lessened. He should have come in here before confronting Winter.

"Coffeepots are easy to come by." Odella pointed at the bread. "That you cain't find anywhere else. It's the secret to my success and my longevity."

His mouth was full so Caleb held up a finger. "'Nother slice, please."

Her creaky chuckle suggested she didn't use it much, but her smile was contagious. She slid the bag across to him and then cleared away the money he'd set on the counter.

"Keep the change." Caleb saluted her with the second bag and then headed for the door.

"And a generous tip. Callaways'll surprise a person now and then." Odella's voice carried well enough to follow him out onto the sidewalk. There he spotted Winter Kingfisher crawling around in the back of an ancient station wagon, a campaign sign displayed in the window.

And he remembered his intention to settle this. He shoved what was left of his breakfast in the Callaway Construction truck and marched off across the street.

"Shouldn't you be out at the lodge already?" Winter asked. "The day's disappearing as we speak."

Caleb slammed to a stop in the middle of the street. Why would he care if she questioned his routine?

Unfortunately, the tone she'd used, which questioned why he was wasting time in town, reminded him of someone else. Normally, it was his stepfather's voice demanding he explain himself or do better.

"You want me out of Sweetwater. *I* want me out of Sweetwater." Caleb covered his heart with one hand. "Honest. We both have incentive to make the lodge build go quickly, but here you are making a statement with your signs. Why can't you let this go?" He motioned at her station wagon. "Is this your car? I mean, did your parents give it to you at birth?" He shook his head. "Never mind. Forget that."

"What's wrong with my car?" Winter crossed her arms over her chest as she moved to stand in front of it protectively. Or aggressively. One or the other. "And what is wrong with Sweetwater? I love this place. You're lucky you get to spend every day out at The Aerie, Caleb. But like the rest of your family, you don't appreciate what you have."

He admired a woman who came out swinging. That was part of his problem with Winter. He admired her too much. She had an impressive uppercut.

"Lucky we have Winter Kingfisher to tell us where we're wrong." Finally, a good line. Caleb propped his hands on his hips. "You can't let this go, not even for me and our bargain. What will happen if I tell everyone I know that you're the one who slipped Duncan the report? And almost lost Sweetwater the lodge? And almost got your brother fired? And that I, a lowly Callaway, did the heroic thing? And all because you asked me to?"

Why was she fighting this so hard? Because Whit had broken her heart? This dogged insistence was coming from somewhere besides a true commitment to politics or the governor. Had to be. No one in their right mind would work so hard for Richard Duncan. Caleb had been forced to make dinner conversation with the guy more than once, and he had the depth of a mud puddle. Conviction wasn't driving Winter's determination.

So if it was hurt over Whit, what could

Caleb do about that? Tell her she deserved better. True, but not really helpful.

"Go ahead and tell everyone you took the heat for me. People will understand that I did what I did because I love the reserve." Winter squared her shoulders. "Do your worst. So will I."

"My worst? Like turning the first station wagon that ever chugged off an assembly line into a rolling billboard?" Caleb studied her face as she smoothed a hand over the glossy fall of hair. Something, anger or nerves, made her lips tighten, and she instantly glanced away from him. Was she bluffing? "You don't think I'll do it, do you? You don't believe that I'll tell your secret, even to make my family forgive me or to get public sympathy." He mirrored her stance, arms crossed and feet braced. "You trust that people in this world still have enough integrity to keep something so flimsy as a promise, when it would be to their personal gain to do otherwise. And from a lousy Callaway, no less." Amazing.

"I want to. I want to believe that people keep promises. Your brother let me down," Winter answered softly. "We were partners, but he turned on me and my family in an instant. You aren't going to do that, are you?"

She was right about that, but he'd never understood why she'd done what she'd done. "Why an anonymous report, Winter? Didn't you break a promise you made to Whit? Like, loving and cherishing promises, forsaking all others?"

"We weren't married yet, Caleb." She rubbed a hand across her forehead and studied the ground for a second. "Whit and I did make promises to each other. We were partners. Our goals were the same. We were working together for our future and for Tennessee."

"So, what changed?" Caleb asked. She had never struck him as the type to hide her activity. Why had she tried to go around Whit instead of loudly and proudly facing off against him.

Love. Had to be.

"Whit let me down." She shook her head. "And I love this place more than all our plans."

Where did Whit fall in that? Between Sweetwater and their plans? Shouldn't she love her fiancé more than a piece of land? Wouldn't Whit be her first priority if she loved him enough to marry him? Her words rolled back through his brain and snapped into place.

When Winter talked about his brother, she never mentioned love.

"You and Whit, this was a marriage of... What? Political dynasty or something?" Caleb asked. No one did that anymore, did they?

Her stiff shoulders convinced Caleb he was on the right track with...something.

"My being disappointed by my best friend was one thing. Whit and I would have recovered from that, but Whit and Senior turned on my family, too." Winter shook her head. "He let me down. Please don't do the same, Caleb. Your promise matters."

Did she believe that? That a promise meant something to Caleb Callaway?

Here, facing off with him in the street like Old West gunfighters, he was convinced she did.

Winter trusted he'd keep his promise to her, no matter the incentive to tell the world.

Even after the other Callaways had fought hard and dirty.

Her faith robbed him of the ability to ever attempt the bluff again that he'd tell her secret.

He wanted her to trust him, admire him.

Why? Answering that honestly would take some consideration. Examining it too closely was a bad idea.

"This? It's a couple of political signs." She smiled at him and shrugged. Her whole demeanor had transitioned from "I will go toe to toe with you" to "Me? I'm harmless."

Her charm was nearly irresistible. Senior's frowning face in his head was the antidote.

"Low profile. I get in and out. Take those signs down." Caleb's lips were a grim, tight line. "I expect you to do the right thing here." He turned around and crossed the street.

Refusing to glance back to see if she was watching him was difficult, but he pulled it off. Then he headed for the old weather station, prepared to put her out of his mind.

But the idea that she and Whit had been more about a marriage of convenience than a love match explained why it had seemed easy for them both to walk away. Why did that bring a ray of light out on an otherwise gloomy day?

WATCHING CALEB STALK AWAY, a cloud of suspicion or confusion or even disappointment drifting behind him, was hard. That had always been Winter's weakness—a fear of letting people down. She excelled. She underpromised and overdelivered in order to keep people raving over her abilities. Always.

On top of that, his brother had put her in this spot in the first place.

How unfair.

"I will always do the right thing for Sweetwater, the reserve and my family," Winter muttered. Of course she would.

When he pulled out of the parking spot without acknowledging her, Winter added, "Look at what I've given up. You don't even know this place, the town or the reserve. If you loved Otter Lake and these mountains the way I do, you wouldn't forgive Whit as easily. If you knew how hard Ash has worked to protect the history of this area, you would be angry at the Callaways, too. That kind of anger can make a person brave. Don't fool yourself that I'm intimidated by you or your family."

In a huff, she climbed back inside the station wagon, yanked down the signs and broke them over her knee. Then she realized she might still have an audience and glanced over at Smoky Joe's. Yes. Plenty of diners were watching. When she turned to march down the sidewalk, she realized Janet Abernathy and Leanne were staring out the window of Sweetwater Souvenir. Fab. All that was missing was her mother.

Mad enough to kick rocks, Winter forced a smile to her lips and walked inside the gallery. "Morning."

Janet sniffed. "Not a 'good' one, though, I take it." She shook her finger at Winter. "Girl like you knows better'n to run headlong at an opponent. I'm surprised you aren't finessing this situation better."

Winter inhaled slowly and then exhaled, hoping that it would settle some of the nerves shaking her. "What do you mean?" Did that sound angry? By Janet's raised eyebrows, Winter would guess yes. But she was angry.

"Couldn't tell if y'all were about to kiss or kill each other. I figure where there's some kind of smoke, there's bound to be a fire. I'm saying you better not miss out on something good because you're focused on that bad thing in the rearview mirror." Janet tsked.

"Caleb Callaway is not my future, Janet." Winter was taken aback at her suggestion. Who would think she'd ever get tangled up with the Callaways again?

"Fine. Not your romantic future, but bad mornings could be better by making him a friend." Janet turned to Leanne and muttered, "But he's a handsome man, and it seems a waste of them fireworks, you know?"

Speechless, Winter held out both hands. What was she supposed to say to that?

Janet angled her head forward as if sharing a secret. "Okay, plain talk. One thing I know about brothers is that there's always some competition. You would know in your heart whether Caleb and his brother are friendly or not."

They weren't. At dinner, conversation had been stilted anytime Caleb made an appearance, and Whit seemed to both admire his brother and make a point of beating him at races Caleb didn't know they were running. She'd always attributed that to being the youngest. She and Ash were locked in battle, and her brother was oblivious. That's what made losing to him so hard.

"Okay, but what does that have to do with me?" Winter asked.

"Be easier to have a friend than an enemy is all I'm saying." Janet nodded. "If you could show Caleb what you love about Sweetwater, talk to him about why you're campaigning the way you are, he might be easier to handle than shouting in the street." She held up her hands. "Flies, honey, vinegar—catching what you want is all about your choices is all I'm saying. You know how it goes." She checked her watch. "Gotta run. Regina and I are headed for lunch down in Knoxville. Got some strategizing to do and then I'll pick up the new hangers for our framed pieces." She wagged her fingers, picked up her purse and sauntered out the door.

The silence left in the large gallery was tense until Winter checked to see what Leanne was doing. She was chewing her lip nervously and had made a tight, controlled knot with her arms.

"What a day." Winter paced in a small circle as she rolled her shoulders. "A few campaign signs. How was I supposed to know they'd cause such an uproar?"

Leanne wrinkled her nose. "Uproar is your goal, right? That's the way you want to get even?"

Hearing it stated so baldly like that twisted the knot in her stomach tighter. "Sounds childish when you say it that way."

Leanne shrugged. "Or it sounds reasonable. Normal. Like what most people want to do when they're hurt." She patted Winter's back before quickly stepping back.

"Thanks for that. It's nice not to hear how I should be better, do more, put this behind me and rise above it." Winter closed her eyes as she realized that she was the one who'd been telling herself all those things. Her father was sure she'd be okay. Her mother had supported every decision she'd made except for backing a bad candidate.

Even Caleb was sure she was better off after Whit than before.

So what was her problem?

"I haven't been in a position to do a lot of forgiving," Leanne said slowly, "but I've had to ask for it over and over. Alcohol erased my memories, but no one else's." She wrinkled her nose. "I've gotten good at it, but I've learned something, too. Letting go is the only path to moving forward."

Winter let out a gust of air and realized she'd been holding her breath. The tension in her shoulders was tight enough that she heard a snap. "That is the message I keep getting."

"Yeah, I've had those messages, too, the

ones you turn away from and smack right up against a second later."

"So, in my spot, what would you do?" Winter asked, desperate to have help getting out of her hole.

Leanne held out her hand to tick off points on her fingers. "Forget Whit. He's the past. Figure out what you want. If it's a career in politics, push to get what you want, but make sure it's what you want, not something you're settling for. And three, win over Caleb Callaway." She nodded as Winter shook her head. "Yep. He's here in town. Make him love Sweetwater and Otter Lake and the lodge he's building. How nice a revenge would it be to send Caleb Callaway home singing the praises of this place and Ash Kingfisher and Winter Kingfisher. Whit would realize how he messed up."

When she put it like that, the payoff for winning over Caleb Callaway was nice.

"All I'm saying is that this place is easy to love." Leanne pointed at the stack of paintings resting up against the wall. "Want to help me frame these? Janet brought us one of these." She pointed at some kind of gun resting on the desk. "Shoots these little thingamajigs in to attach the frame to the wood in the canvas. How hard can it be?" She waggled her eyebrows.

"Why is it that a shiver of dread just went down my spine," Winter murmured.

"We live dangerously, the single ladies of Sweetwater. I'll let you have the first turn." Leanne picked up the smallest easel, the one of the rabbit Winter had been coveting since she'd seen the painting, but rebelled at the price tag.

"The next time you go up to The Aerie, you want some company?" Winter asked as she took the gun and studied the end of it. If they messed this up, Janet would not be pleased.

But maybe there would be a discount on any mangled painting.

She didn't notice the silence until she turned to ask Leanne how long it would take to replace the canvas if they needed to hide the evidence.

Leanne was blinking quickly, almost as if she was hiding tears. "What's up?" Winter asked.

"I'm so glad you came to work here, Winter." She laughed and wiped under her eyes. "You make me believe that things can change. For me. I've been worried about that."

Winter stepped closer and bumped Leanne's shoulder with her own. "Stop worrying. You've got this."

Her watery grin was cute. "Yeah. I've got this."

"It's nice to have someone to talk to about this." Winter rolled her eyes. "I sound like a middle-schooler, don't I? It's hard to make friends. We owe Macy a thank-you for pulling us together."

"I know what you mean. Working with you has been more fun than I expected." Leanne raised her eyebrows while Winter considered that. "You're so intimidating. You know that, right?"

Winter gestured down at her too-tight jeans and the bright T-shirt that was the uniform of Sweetwater Souvenir. "It's because I'm so cool." Pretending she didn't understand what Leanne meant was tempting. Macy had said something similar in the booth at The Branch. But it was time to be honest. That's what friendship would take. "Pretending to have it together is easy.

Now that you know the truth, what do you think?"

Leanne pointed at the weird framing tool. "I'm letting you play with the toys first. That's gotta mean something."

Relieved, Winter said, "Yeah. I wish I'd been nicer to you in school." Or outside of school.

But she'd been a Kingfisher, charging on to big things.

"Eh, forget thinking like that. Unless you really believe you're better than me and most of the town of Sweetwater." Leanne was watching her closely. "You don't, do you?"

Winter ran her fingers through her hair, dismayed that there'd been a seed of that opinion in her brain. She was determined to do great things for Sweetwater, but did she honestly think she was the only one capable of achieving that?

"Sorry. Maybe I did." Winter rubbed her forehead hard, dismayed at all the weak points this trip home had exposed. "But I'm not. You've been kind to me. Helped me get a job. Made every day better."

Leanne shoved Winter's shoulder. "Oh, come on, Winter. Nobody's perfect, especially in the past, you know? Forgiveness. Give it a shot. You need some practice, so start with yourself. We're friends now, so this is what matters. Next time I go up to The Aerie, I'll see what you're doing. Every artist needs someone to do the heavy lifting."

Winter flexed her arms, amazed at how easy Leanne made friendship. Why had she made it so difficult her whole life? "I have no artistic ability, but I'm strong enough to handle that." And she'd love to see Otter Lake again. With her friend Leanne.

Leanne bent her head to catch Winter's stare. "You *are* strong enough. You're going to figure this out."

Winter pursed her lips and then nodded. "I am." She was.

And it didn't make sense to antagonize Caleb Callaway. Flies, honey and vinegar, as Janet said. Converting him should be her goal.

Right after she and Leanne framed all these canvases or returned from the emergency room with multiple bandages, thanks to a failure to operate the tool properly, she'd figure out the first step.

She and Whit Callaway had clicked immediately.

What she felt when she faced off against Caleb was different, and she'd never had to charm anyone into liking her. Could she do it?

It was time to find out.

CHAPTER SEVEN

SKIPPING A DRIVE into Sweetwater on Thursday morning had been a decision he regretted all day long, so on Friday, Caleb got up and headed into town, determined to pay his rent, speak rationally to Winter if she was at Sweetwater Souvenir and get his day started correctly with a visit to Smoky Joe's. An uncontrollable yawn hit just as he parked in front of the coffee shop, so Caleb made himself a promise to knock off early and get some rest. The drive into Knoxville on the weekend would be tough if he was on the verge of nodding off.

At least small-town life made one easy thing: no traffic. When he made it back to Nashville, he'd have to remember how to negotiate the rush hour.

He'd eaten his first slice of banana-nut bread before he made it out of the coffee shop, but he was surprised when Winter met him in the middle of the street again. He glanced up and down the empty road. "We've got to stop meeting here." He sipped his coffee and wondered what the chivalrous thing to do in the situation would be? Offer her a sip, a bite, an escort out of the street?

When her lips curled up into a slow smile, he took a step back. He wasn't ready.

"You're right. Were you coming into the store?" She motioned with her head before shoving her hands in her pockets. Was she nervous?

"I was. I wanted to leave a check for Janet." He sighed. "And I wanted to talk to you."

She shuffled her feet. "Me, too. Not the check part, but the rest."

He should let her go first, but she was in no hurry so he blurted, "I was hoping to see you." Desperate to smooth over his awkwardness, Caleb added, "Because I've decided I don't know this place as well as I should."

Her eyebrows shot up. She hadn't expected him to agree.

"You decided after I told you that." She blinked innocently. "That seems about right."

She had a good point. Arguing with women never got him very far. They'd use logic to work circles around him and then trip him with his own shoestrings.

"We need to renegotiate." Caleb led her over to the sidewalk, one hand resting between her shoulder blades. Almost like it belonged there. "I don't want things to be nasty between us."

Winter sighed. "You're right. We're both here in town for a while. We should get along. No more signs, but I can't promise I won't work against Whit."

Interesting wording. "So it's *against* Whit, not *for* Duncan because you strongly believe all teachers can be replaced and they should celebrate their jobs, not strike." To occupy his hands, he held out the bag of banana-nut bread. There had been more. Odella would sell him more if Winter accepted his offer.

"It's a rare person who would share Odella's baked goods. You're a true gentleman, aren't you?" Winter grinned and the shot of warmth that washed over Caleb stole his breath.

How did she manage to do that so often? What would his brother say if he knew Caleb was… How did he feel about Winter? If he was still fifteen, he'd call it a crush. He was in trouble.

"Not every day I'm accused of being a

gentleman, no." He shuffled his own feet. Like a schoolboy. How embarrassing. "But I appreciate it."

"Let's leave the politics question alone for a minute." Winter tangled her fingers together. "How about we talk about Sweetwater instead. I can help you see all the great things about this place. That way it won't seem such an imposition to build this beautiful lodge. When you're finished here, it will be nice to know that the reserve has another fan on the board of directors. Ash will be there, thanks to you, but if I knew he had an ally in the Callaway family, I would be relieved. That used to be me. You're stuck here, but here is a great place."

He wanted to explain that being stuck here wasn't the issue—missing out on opportunities in Nashville, jobs that would help him stand apart from the Callaways, was. Then he realized that Sweetwater no longer stifled him like a heavy quilt. Instead, new benefits to being here popped up every day.

Like the chance that he might run into Winter Kingfisher in the middle of the street.

Telling her that would be a mistake, but he wanted to confess everything that he was worried about: his job, his business, his mother. Why did he care that Winter understood he had his own plans for the future?

The troubling thrum of excitement at the promise of time with her couldn't be ignored. He'd been wishing for a longer look at Otter Lake. No one would be a better guide than Winter. "You'll show me your favorite spot on the lake?"

"Ash would be a better guide. Head ranger and everything." Winter raised her eyebrows. "I could set that up."

When the excitement immediately dimmed at the prospect of following grim Ash Kingfisher down a trail, Caleb knew he was in trouble. Big trouble. Falling for Winter was not an option. The Callaway family would explode in a fiery boom.

Did that matter? He'd done something similar when he'd taken credit for stopping the lodge for a whole lot less.

"The last time we negotiated, it was about Ash and Whit. This time, let's leave them out of it." Caleb shoved his hands in his pockets. "You and me. Tomorrow. I'm giving all my crews the weekend off to go home. I have plans on Sunday, but Saturday would be a nice day for a hike." The Callaway Sunday dinner would require a satisfactory performance report, but Caleb would be able to deliver it if all went according to plan that day.

That meant he had to get to work.

"I know the perfect place." Winter's smile hit him full force again. "If you're struggling with a decision, this is the spot you need to see. It'll help clear your mind so you'll make the best choices."

Shock froze his boots to the asphalt. Did she know he was pushing to get this project done so that he could get on with his own company's business? As each day closed, he was less sure he could knock out the lodge in time to have both things he wanted: his family's approval and a new contract with Mitch Yarborough.

And now Winter was skirting along the edges of all that, something else he might want but that would definitely derail his hopes for the other two.

Could he even commit to that much time locked down in Nashville if his mother needed him at home? Anything more with Winter was so far out of the question, he should ignore it completely. He hoped Winter's hike could cut through some of his confusion. Nothing else was working.

If this place could clear his head, he

needed to go there. "Give me your phone." He held out his hand.

Without hesitation, Winter offered it to him. She watched him put in his contact information. "Text me when you figure out what we do next."

Caleb wrapped his hand around hers. Warmth spread from that contact and it was difficult not to jerk his hand away. He slipped the phone inside her hand. Words would not come until she stepped back. The urge to follow suit, turn tail and escape to his truck was strong, but at the last second, he remembered the check in his pocket. "Hey, Winter…" His words stumbled to a stop as he realized she hadn't moved. She'd been standing there, watching him the whole time. "Can I leave this for Janet? It's the rent check."

She carefully took the envelope, being careful not to touch his hand. Had she been as shaken by his touch as he'd been by hers?

He hoped so, but he had to figure out why he felt that way. Some other time. He'd already exceeded his boyish awkwardness. *Get it together.* He turned back to the coffee shop, where the group of people with their noses pressed to the glass disappeared in a wave.

Caleb had been in town long enough to know that they were still watching, even if he couldn't see them, so he raised a hand to acknowledge them as he turned away from Winter and slid into the truck, pleased with the morning's progress.

He'd found a haven in Smoky Joe's. Convincing Winter to show him her highlights from the Smoky Valley Nature Reserve would go a long way to remind him of the importance and beauty of the land he'd barely set foot on in years. Was any of that his thing? A little, but it motivated the Kingfishers. Understanding Winter Kingfisher was a powerful incentive.

The only piece of the reserve he knew well was the lodge's site in the shadow of The Aerie. Day and night he'd been there working, and he was now beginning to catch up.

If he had one talent, it was the ability to track different pieces in different stages in his mind.

"Not exactly worthy of a cape, hero." Caleb took a bite of his bread and consoled himself that he'd still managed the right thing, even if he wasn't sure why.

One last check of the sidewalk where he'd left Winter showed she was standing in the same place, tapping the envelope against her hand and watching him. That made him more reluctant to leave, for some reason, but daylight was burning so he eased his foot on the gas.

Since he'd been in Sweetwater, he'd gotten up with the sunrise, thanks to the skylight in the master bedroom, and rushed to the job site to beat his crews there. Driving the curving road up toward The Aerie that morning was different. Nice. Some of the peace he'd only found at the end of the day as the sunlight was dying on Otter Lake filtered in. Many more moments like this and he'd understand why people like Winter Kingfisher battled to save it.

The banana-nut bread was gone by the time he bumped down the gravel road to the old weather station. Under normal circumstances, the road was clear all the way up to the site, where the men and women working on the project parked their cars and trucks in a scattered fashion. His first clue that something was different was the sight of a news van blocking half the road near the gate.

The second was the fact that every person on both of his crews was standing in a circle around a news reporter as she... What exactly was she doing? Taping a story of some kind.

And grinding work to a halt.

He'd hoped that the Callaway Construction foreman that Senior had sent along could eventually be proven capable of completing the lodge, leaving Caleb free to return to life in Nashville and the Yarborough development.

Today's work stoppage indicated that was a foolish dream. Ken Lowell was front and center, the confused furrow of his brow proof that he had no clue what to do. He worked hard, followed procedure to the letter, but couldn't solve a problem to save his life.

Carlos Lopez was shifting back and forth near the rear of the group, clearly antsy to get back to the job. He understood the reason they were working as hard as they were and he had a seven-year-old outside Nashville waiting for her daddy to come home for the weekend.

Frustrated that this very important project hadn't rated an A-team crew, Caleb made up his mind to let Senior know exactly what he thought of Callaway Construction's junior varsity.

Even better, this little break has been

caught on tape, to be broadcast right into Callaway Central. Senior will blow a gasket. Blaming his stepfather for the crews he'd provided would be Caleb's only defense. His very weak defense was more like it. He hoped Lowell's consternation made it into the broadcast.

Caleb slammed to a stop in front of the group and watched the cameraman turn toward him.

Everybody's watching. Play this right. Caleb paused to grab his hard hat and buy a minute to calm his nerves, then slid out of the truck. Charm was the name of the game with the press. He'd learned that early on. He used to be good at it, but never had he felt this amount of anger. "Morning, folks. What's going on?" Friendly. Casual. Completely unconcerned about the daylight and money they were burning.

"Bailey Garcia, Channel Six News from Knoxville." The reporter marched forward, her hand extended. "I've been unable to get a phone call through to you, Mr. Callaway, and Winter Kingfisher suggested we stop in to check the progress of the lodge ourselves. Viewers in east Tennessee are concerned that the reserve's management keep its promises, you see."

Hearing Bailey use Winter's name hit him like a punch to the gut. He'd tried to build a bridge, daydreaming about being friends with Winter or whatever, but she'd been laying dynamite right behind him. Still, there wasn't a thing he could do to address that now.

Bailey Garcia moved back in front of the camera and motioned for the guy to pan slowly. Since there was a large group of construction workers blocking her view, Caleb wasn't sure what that would accomplish. Nothing. It would do nothing but delay his progress.

"As I'm sure you're aware, there's been speculation about Callaway business practices. The original plan to build this would have required expensive site preparation that would have destroyed important habitats and the cost could only be offset by…mediocre materials. Has this new plan changed that? Care to give us a tour?"

Speculation about Callaway business practices. Mediocre. Senior would lose his cool for sure.

And he had Winter to thank for all of it.

Caleb smiled slowly, a trick he'd learned to buy precious seconds.

"We aren't prepared for television crews today. I'll have to ask you to return to your van. This is a hard-hat area." He motioned around the group at all the people there wearing the required protection. "It's for your safety. You can get your footage from there, but we've got to get to work. We're on a tight schedule."

"No tour. Fine, although I have to wonder what you're hiding. A quick on-camera interview, then. I have only a few questions. Has Ranger Kingfisher been cooperative with your project, Mr. Callaway?" She shoved the microphone under his nose and Caleb calmly held a hand out as if he was ushering her back toward the van. "What about Winter Kingfisher? Anything you can tell us about her efforts to prevent your brother from landing in the capital? I asked her for a quote about Whit Callaway's—"

"I have no comment. The Smoky Valley Nature Reserve staff will field all your calls. Please contact the ranger station for progress reports. I have my job to do here. For your safety, all visits will stop at the gate." He tried his charming smile. It had always worked, and this time, Bailey Garcia's progress slowed. While she was confused, he turned on his heel and hurried back to his crews.

Then she called, "Do you have something to hide, Caleb? It looks like you have something to hide." Ignoring that challenge was difficult. Then she added, "We'll come back tomorrow or the day after. While Whit Callaway is running for governor, our viewers will be interested in the lodge's progress. Don't you want to put any suspicion to rest?"

He did. He honestly did, but nothing he would say today or even the next would accomplish that. Proving himself—that would support the Callaway family and reputation. Only getting the lodge up, on time and on budget, with the proper materials and minimal impact would answer all the reporter's questions. That couldn't happen while his crews were busy being background extras instead of hammering and plastering. "We don't get paid to stand still. Everyone, move. Double time. Daylight's burning. If we want a weekend off, it's time to get to work."

Caleb watched his crews scatter, shook his head at Ken Lowell, who held out both hands helplessly, slapped on his hard hat and picked up a hammer. Banging in a few nails might make it possible to hold a normal conversation by lunchtime.

Then he remembered that unless he did something, Bailey Garcia would be back. His team might be less like statues on her second visit, but there was no way they'd work at full speed with the distraction of a camera around.

And when Bailey Garcia made her report, there was a good chance other stations or newspapers might decide they needed to come mess up his plans, too.

Caleb shoved the hammer through the loop in his tool belt and dug his phone out of his pocket. A quick search turned up the Otter Lake ranger station phone number.

Was Ash Kingfisher any more reasonable than his sister? It was time to find out.

"Thank you for calling the Otter Lake ranger station. How may I direct your call?" a young woman asked after the first ring. She sounded efficient. Kingfisher had struck him as a guy who ran a tight ship.

"I need to speak to the head ranger. This is Caleb Callaway." Throwing around his last name was a last resort, but he had to get to Kingfisher quick. Bailey Garcia didn't seem to be the type to give up. He checked over his shoulder. She was still down near the gate, and the camera was rolling. As soon as she wrapped that up, Caleb would bet all the money in his wallet she'd shoot down the hill and back up to the ranger station.

When he heard the beep for an incoming call, Caleb pulled the phone back to check the display. Melissa Yarborough. Of course. Two nights ago when they'd talked on the phone, she'd been impatient for his answer on whether he'd be coming to Nashville that weekend to sign the contract with her father. Missy didn't like to wait. Normally, she didn't wait for anything.

"Ash Kingfisher." The gruff voice matched the stoic facade Caleb remembered from his last meeting with the head ranger. "What can I do for you, Callaway?"

Call off your sister. Make her back down. Neither Kingfisher would appreciate the sentiment, but Winter would make him sorry he ever said it. Ash wouldn't have to move a muscle. His younger sister fought her own battles.

"I'm giving you a heads-up. Bailey Garcia, the news reporter, is here at the job site, getting in the way, slowing down work."

From his perch on the second-floor framing, he could watch the news team loading up in the van. "When she comes to you for a quote, make it clear she's trespassing on private property and she has to stay out of the construction zone. I'll put up a sign." *Note to self: have a sign made.*

"Why?" Ash asked.

Few words. Normally, Caleb appreciated that. Today, he was tired of being stonewalled by Kingfishers.

"Because I can't afford to lose another half day escorting nosy reporters out of harm's way," Caleb said, ignoring the slight exaggeration. "This project is important to you, too." Caleb stared out over the site from his bird's-eye view and tried to ignore the silently ticking clock. He had to get back to Melissa Yarborough.

"Dealing with the media gives me the nervous sweats. A reserve public information officer… It's too bad we don't have one of those right now," Ash drawled.

You owe me your job. Caleb bit back his angry response and rolled his head on his shoulders slowly. Ash believed Caleb had been the one responsible for the political frenzy surrounding him and the lodge in the first place. Winter had sent her brother out of Caleb's office when she'd made her passionate plea to Caleb to take the heat. The pinch of the promise he'd made to keep her secret helped him focus.

"Because the sooner this lodge is open, the sooner Otter Lake has a state-of-the-art showpiece to attract visitors. Considering the sluggish drip of tourists I've seen in town lately, you and Sweetwater could both use the new attraction." Caleb cleared his throat, aware that his tone was rising. "It's good publicity for the reserve. Helping me control access to the site and the story being told about it helps the reserve."

"And the Callaways." Ash said nothing else, but Caleb could hear the rustle of paper. "Fine. I'll try to manage the news exposure for now. Put up your sign. We can work this out together. For the reserve."

Before Caleb could come up with a response, the call ended.

The attitude communicated with that gesture surprised him, but Caleb had to laugh. These Kingfishers made their opinions known.

He hit redial on his missed call and raised a hand at the foreman waving to get his attention. He pointed at the trucks lumbering down the gravel road. The first was loaded with plywood for the roof sheathing. Once the roof was on, interior work would go full force. The second was more lumber. Caleb made the signing motion so that his foreman would go on and receive the truck deliveries.

If he wasn't here, the man would step up without being told to.

Wouldn't he?

"Caleb, I was hoping you would call me back quickly," Melissa Yarborough said smoothly. "The time to make a decision is drawing near. What should I tell Daddy about your commitment?" She sighed. "I mean, to the project, not to me. No man committed to me would stay away for so long. I'm certain you've already moved on, as have I."

Even seated on a roof truss in the middle of nowhere, in east Tennessee, it was easy to picture Melissa's trendy office in the middle of downtown Nashville. Ice was forming on his phone even as they spoke. All that remained between them was saying the goodbye words.

And she was right. It had come time to make a hard decision.

He'd hoped once he got this project to a

certain point, a Callaway Construction foreman could complete it.

Today had proven him wrong.

"Missy, I'm sorry. This project is going
to take longer than I expected. Tell your father I appreciate him approaching Summit
Builders for Rivercrest, but I won't be free in
time. I have to finish this project for my family, and I'm too early in the process to guarantee a start date on anything new." There.
That was a plausible reason to bow out of
the project that didn't make him sound like
the dabbling son of a rich man or someone
who'd forgotten the size of the opportunity
Yarborough offered. Maybe he could make
it out of this with his reputation intact.

The delicate pause spoke volumes.

"I might convince him to wait another
month," Melissa said slowly, "for someone
who was about to join our family, Caleb."

It was tempting to tell her what she wanted
to hear. He wanted to build Yarborough's
project and the next one and the one after
that.

But not enough to string along Melissa.
Her, he was prepared to say goodbye to.
They'd been about nights out on the town,
not the difficulty of long-distance dating.

He'd been confused by the suggestion that what Winter and Whit had had been about convenience and power, but here was the same kind of offer. He could have everything he wanted. All he had to do was give up on the idea of marrying for love.

Joining two wealthy families to make more wealth was an accepted practice. It made sense on paper. In a flash, he realized Senior would happily bankroll an investment if it led to powerful connections in Nashville, Whit's future home.

Why had it seemed so disappointing when he thought of Whit and Winter making such an alliance themselves?

Before that second, he'd have said he was capable of doing that, the rational thing, to grow his business. Now he knew better.

"Imagine the possibilities, Caleb," Missy said softly. "Come to Nashville. We can discuss our expectations for the project and a match. You'll see the benefits."

The weird reaction he'd had to Winter was proof enough that he needed to cut the ties to the Yarboroughs. Now that he'd faced off against fiery Winter, it was harder to remember what he'd enjoyed about conversations with Missy. Was he angry at Winter King-fisher? Oh, yeah, now that she'd sicced the media on him directly, they'd need to talk. Again. But he was more excited about that coming argument than he was by anything Melissa offered.

Besides, Caleb already had one wealthy, demanding family to deal with. No intelligent man would choose to add another. "No, the Yarboroughs should move on without me. Find a replacement." Was that clear enough?

"Fine. Goodbye, Caleb." The absence of static on the line was clear-cut proof that Missy was done with the call. The frost in her tone confirmed she was also done with him.

And for some reason, when he ended the call, instead of being weighed down by losing the project he'd been daydreaming about for months and the woman he'd been half-heartedly dating, Caleb was relieved.

Letting go of that was the right thing to do.

As if the universe was waiting for him to wise up, his phone dinged with a text.

From Winter.

Ash called to tell me about Bailey Garcia's visit to the site.

Caleb stared hard at the phone. Surely she had something else to say.

Yeah. I decided to go with the reasonable Kingfisher this time.

Her instant response convinced him she was waiting anxiously for his reply.

I had nothing to do with that.

Caleb shrugged his shoulders to try to get rid of some of the tension.

Really?

Could she convince them both of that?
The pause this time was much longer, but eventually she answered.

Okay, I suggested this visit as a way to end a call with her, but it wasn't a premeditated move. I was having a bad day and needed a way out. Solid PR move.

That he did believe. She'd explained. Would she apologize?

Lost a half day of work. If that happens often, this is going to turn into a bigger problem for all of us.

Why would she care? That played into her plans.

It was an accident. I'm sorry. Let me work on this. There's a way to make sure this doesn't happen again.

Caleb waited to see if the dots appeared to say she was still typing. After a minute, he texted Thank you?

This time, he'd bet on an eye roll.

Ash will also start fielding progress calls and will visit the site enough to know how to answer them. It should be something the head ranger can do.

That had been his solution, too. Caleb's eyebrows shot up as he read the last sentence. Was that a change of heart? Or the smallest seed of the beginning of an attempt to let go of the past?

Does Ash know he's doing all this?

He had a difficult time imagining her older brother had a lot of extra time for media relations. The reserve needed a public-information officer. Why hadn't one been hired to replace Winter?

Caleb imagined it would be hard to fill her shoes.

Not yet, but he will do it. No need to threaten to tell my secret again.

This time she included an emoji: thumbs up.

She was helping but she wasn't a pushover.

When we hike on Saturday, you're going to fall in love. You'll understand why I did what I did.

The kick of anticipation in his chest was surprising, but Caleb didn't question it. She meant he'd fall for the reserve and Otter Lake. He was ready to spend time with her. She robbed him of breath and knocked him off balance. Winter didn't do anything he expected and he was learning to expect that.

Good. Where?

He stretched in the warm sunshine as he waited for his answer. Was he behind schedule here? Yes, but things would work out.

The Aerie trailhead parking lot. Bring water.

Caleb didn't answer but he fought the urge to salute. Glancing over his shoulder at the bare peak above the job site, he decided it might be nice to have an even better bird's-eye view.

The urge to send a flirty emoji was strong, but what?

Then he realized he didn't have the time to waste with flirting or daydreaming about things that should never happen. Had he lost his mind?

Now he had a date with Winter Kingfisher and a lot of work to get done before that.

"All right, crew. Everybody's working hard. Efficiently. There's time for R and R this weekend." Caleb navigated the beam down to the ladder nearest the location, where the roof sheathing was being offloaded. "Start bringing those materials up."

He had a hammer. Better yet, he pointed at Carlos and the nail gun. Power tools. Nails. And a deadline. It was time to get to work.

CHAPTER EIGHT

SLIPPING HER PHONE in the pocket of her jeans was easy.

Convincing herself that texting with Caleb Callaway and setting up a date for Saturday was more difficult.

"Not a date. An appointment. That's all." Winter had one hand on the door to Sweetwater Souvenir when her phone rang. Her first thought was that Caleb wanted to continue their conversation. Why did her heart skip at the suggestion?

When she read the display, her heart sped up faster than its normal rate. Who would be calling her from Nashville?

"Hello?" She waved in the window at Leanne and pointed at her phone to explain the delay.

"Could I speak to Winter Kingfisher?" The smooth male voice was pleasant, but Winter had no idea whom it belonged to.

"I'm calling from Governor Richard Duncan's office. He'd like to schedule a meeting, but unfortunately, his time is limited. Would you be available to meet with the governor at one o'clock today?"

Winter blinked rapidly and tried to do time math calculations in her head. That would leave her just enough time to go in and explain to Leanne, race home to change clothes and then hit the highway. Capitol parking was a nightmare, so she'd need a few minutes to find a place.

It would be tight, but she had to give it her best shot. "Definitely. I'll see the governor at one."

The call ended before she could ask or say anything else. This was a job interview, wasn't it? What else could this be?

After she stumbled through a weird explanation to Leanne, then raced home and changed, and cut short her mother's questioning, Winter hurried back to the station wagon, wearing her trusty dark suit and her best heels. Her hair? Gray goop was surprisingly effective, so she wasn't forced to choose between good looks and good relations with her mother.

Snapping at her mother would leave a guilty mark in her brain.

Leaving Leanne with her jaw dangling open wouldn't be easy to forget. They'd made plans to finalize all the shelving displays. Winter was deserting her when she needed help. Another regret.

But what else could she do? When life handed her an opportunity, she had to seize it. As long as it paid off, she could make amends later. She'd make it priority number one.

Now all she had to do was figure out how to convince the governor he needed her on his team. She could do that.

She'd been peppering his office with phone calls and emails ever since her spectacular breakup with Whit had made the news, and she had gotten no response.

"So what's different now?" she muttered to herself as she inched into one of the rare open spots marked "visitor" in front of the capitol building.

The long drive should have given her plenty of time to rehearse what she'd say, but she was as off balance when she located a parking spot as she'd been when she hit Sweetwater's town limits going five miles over the speed limit.

"You're going to be right on time. No need

to sweat." Winter put the car in Park and then inhaled slowly. She held the breath and then exhaled, hoping it would calm the fast beat of her heart. "No need to sweat *anymore*." Irritated with herself, she yanked her purse out of the passenger seat and rummaged around to find something to knock the glow off her forehead.

Presenting a strong, capable facade to the governor mattered. If he was searching for a new press secretary, she had to be fully prepared. Winter put on lipstick, ran a hand over her hair and made another mental note to get to the salon ASAP. None of that mattered now. She could handle anything the media threw at her, and to get a job doing what she was good at on a large stage like this could reset her whole life.

"Just do what you're good at, Winter." She met her stare in the mirror, checked her lipstick, craned her neck to check out the news van she could just see out of the corner of her eye and then slid out of the car. "Great. News reporters. At the capitol." Why hadn't she expected that? "Hope I'm not the subject of the story." Even joking about it reminded her of the bad days of watching Ash sweat in front of a pack of reporters. But it was a joke. There was nothing for news reporters to *report*. Not about her.

The heels she was wearing were beautiful. They were completely wrong for hiking from the worst parking spot in the lot up past security to the elevators, but she would pretend none of that bothered her.

Stepping off the elevator in front of the glass doors leading into the governor's office took a minute. The lurch of her stomach made her curse the nerves that had never bothered her before. Why didn't this feel right?

Representing the reserve in front of audiences big and small made her feel strong. Invincible. Powerful.

Today she was half a second from running for her life.

Winter straightened her shoulders, winced at the blister forming on the back of her heel and marched inside the governor's office.

"Good afternoon. How may I help you?" the young man seated behind the desk asked, the earpiece he was wearing giving him a slightly robotic air. Winter recognized his voice. He was meant to talk on the phone.

"Winter Kingfisher. I have an appointment to meet the governor." She shifted the portfolio she'd grabbed at the last minute from her right hand to her left and pretended to wait patiently while he ran a finger down a list of appointments.

"Yes, here you are." He waved gracefully toward a small seating arrangement of a couch and two obviously uncomfortable antique chairs. "If you'll have a seat, I'll let the governor's assistant know you are here." Then he tapped the earpiece. "Governor Duncan's office. How may I direct your call?"

Winter perched on the edge of one of the seats. Standing gracefully would be possible from the chair, even if the couch would be distinctly more comfortable.

She expected to wait a bit. That was a common power move, especially from someone as important as the governor, but his assistant materialized almost immediately.

"Winter, it's good to see you." Nia Greene held out her hand. "It's been too long."

"Nia." Grateful for a friendly face, Winter shook her hand easily. "I'm so glad you're still here. I was hoping to have the chance to say hello."

Nia gestured forward. "Follow me. The governor finished up a conference call so he has a small window. So glad you could make it on such short notice. Everything is going to work out fine. Traffic must have been good. You can never tell what it'll be like over there toward Pigeon Forge or Gatlinburg. That's where you're coming from, right? Guess it's a good thing it's the off-season."

"Sweetwater, which is pretty close." Winter considered that as she followed Nia down the hall. "I thought I had an appointment. To discuss employment."

Nia paused and wrapped her hand around Winter's arm. "Well, now, about that…" She slowed her pace, so Winter matched her step for step. "I open all the governor's mail. I found your résumé, read your letter and realized how lucky Richard Duncan would be to have someone like you on his staff." She bent her head down and smiled. "And I was pretty sure all you would need is a chance to sit down to discuss your experience with him in order to convince him of that, so here we are. I had Terrell call you to set something up, and I know you'll make the most of whatever time the governor can give you." She blinked excitedly as she waited for Winter to acknowledge the truth of her statements.

Instead, Winter wondered if it was possible to actually make a run from the office. Would the governor's security detail stop a woman in a dark suit from running for the elevator? What if she kicked off her heels to increase her speed and comfort?

But Nia was watching carefully, so Winter nodded as she mentally scrambled to switch gears. It had been a kind gesture.

It was one thing to present herself well to a potential boss when the boss knew that he or she was hiring.

Selling her skills to a man who had no need for them was a much bigger task.

She should have stayed home in Sweetwater. Working at the gallery never made her want to run and throw up at the same time like this did.

Nia squeezed her hand. "You got this, girl. The Winter Kingfisher I now handled scarier challenges than this before breakfast." She held up a hand. "Wait here. I'll make sure the governor is available."

Impatient with her unexpected nerves, Winter wiped both hands on her skirt. Sweaty handshakes were pretty much the first warning she'd gotten in her first PR classes in college. No one wanted a share of her sweat.

This was the opportunity she'd told herself she needed, just the slightest door ajar that she could push wide open. Why was she so nervous?

Nia stepped back out and then motioned her inside.

When she crossed the threshold, Nia said, "Governor, let me introduce you to Winter Kingfisher. I had the pleasure of working with her on a project when I was still over at the agriculture department. If you've never been to Sweetwater, Winter can make you believe it's a slice of heaven."

"Oh, I've been to Sweetwater," Richard Duncan said loudly as he rounded the desk, his hand outstretched for a shake. "Had a real nice visit there when I was on the campaign trail for the first time." Winter held on tight as he shook forcefully.

"Yes, sir, I was there. You wanted a chance to view Otter Lake. With otters." And when the otters were otherwise occupied doing otter things instead of performing for dignitaries, Richard Duncan had reacted like a five-year-old.

A *spoiled* five-year-old.

Why hadn't that weird visit stuck out in her memory more? It was while she was there, in his office, that she remembered chauffeuring Duncan and his demanding entourage through the reserve, all while Ash grimly glared at her from the back of each photo opportunity.

That was not a reassuring memory.

"Well, it seems I'd remember a lady as pretty as you are." Duncan returned to his desk chair and pointed. "Have a seat. I confess, I'm not sure what's on the agenda for this meeting. Nia had to remind me you were here. What did you want to talk about?"

Winter eased down in the leather armchair and wondered if she was prepared to do this, to make the case why he should hire her. This was her chance to make it or break it.

"Well, Governor, I was hoping to convince you that you needed my services as a media advisor. My experience at the reserve has prepared me to stand in front of your public to answer all questions about your policy and stance on the issues facing Tennessee today." Winter slipped a résumé out of the portfolio she was clutching like a security blanket and placed it carefully on his desk. "My credentials are outlined here, but you will not read the passion for Tennessee's history and future in black and white. I have been living that my whole life." Sometimes less was more. Before she went too far, she needed to pause to reassess the situation.

Richard Duncan gave her a grin and picked up her résumé. Would she call it sincere? No. But maybe that was the closest his face could get to honesty anymore.

Immediately, she was irritated at her own cynicism. It stopped her in her tracks. If she believed that he was incapable of honesty or true caring for the people he represented, what was she even doing in this seat? If that was the way his brand of politics had to be, she needed to move on to a new life. Life was too short to be living the biggest part of every day surrounded by people she didn't trust.

Why hadn't she ever felt this while she worked with Whit?

Because they'd been on the same page every step of the way, until Senior started pushing so hard. *So* hard. Then they'd decided to get married, since Whit's chances of being elected were better if he was part of a couple. A large society wedding would cement their happy, stable image and invite large donors to connect with the Callaway family.

The sinking feeling that she hadn't been so far above the muck herself made it difficult to sit across from Richard Duncan.

"Can't say that I'm hiring any new staff." He tilted his head from side to side. "But the campaign is ramping up. Whit Callaway's making more progress than I like, even after the whole lodge story." Duncan leaned back in his seat. "If only I had another story like that one to lift the sails of this boat." He tangled his fingers together and studied her face.

Was he waiting for her to produce a story like that?

There was no sense beating around the bush. At his warm reception and Nia's welcome, Winter had wondered if Duncan knew who she was and her former connections.

But, of course, he did. Studying the opposition was the first step in any campaign and the most important.

"Sir, I don't have a scoop for you." Winter mirrored his pose, determined not to be intimidated into backing down. That was no way to get what she wanted. Did she want to work with Richard Duncan? She wasn't sure. Did she want a job offer? Yes. So much yes. Her pride needed a boost like that. "But I can help you strengthen your position on any number of issues. It would be a privilege."

"Hmm," Duncan said as he tapped his fingers on the desk. "A woman scorned does bring some awesome power." He leaned forward. "When my wife is angry, I do my best to find the right gift for her. Don't need an enemy with her kind of knowledge out there in the world. She's a real good partner, but it doesn't do to lose sight of everything she knows. You get what I'm saying. If you don't, Whit Callaway surely does by now."

Before Winter could tell him exactly what she thought about that, about how his wife deserved more than insincere gifts from a man who'd taken vows, he slapped his hand on the desk. "All right. You talked me into it. You want a job, you got it. On a trial basis. We'll do this for a month and regroup before we go into the election prime time. Maybe you take over communications. Maybe you don't. We'll see. In the meantime, you can work with the volunteers. Either way, I know I want you working for me, not against me. I can afford to pay an extra salary to better my odds. How's that?"

It was the offer she'd hoped for since she'd been plotting from her old bedroom in

Sweetwater. She could prove herself and rise quickly to an important position in time for the daily reports nearing the election.

But it was all wrong. It was about the threat of what she might know, not the chance to show what she could do.

The idea of working for him had replaced the hard knot of nerves with the nausea some people experience when they've made an epic mistake.

And now she had to extricate herself from the situation.

"Your offer is interesting." Why wasn't she saying no?

Because she'd worked so hard to land right here. It wasn't in her to give up easily.

"Would I be serving in an advisory capacity?" What did she want his answer to be?

Duncan's lips turned down as he considered that question. "Well, now. You think your *guidance* could improve the campaign?"

"I'm not sure who your top advisor is at this point," Winter said politely, "but some of your stances might be improved with softer language. For instance, the teacher's union and their plans to strike for higher salaries. The truth is that most people will vote for anything, even higher taxes, when they believe it is good for their kids. Instead of saying teachers are lucky to have their jobs, you should stress how raising their salaries will impact other programs because you're committed to a balanced budget." Winter knew what she was saying would work, but figuring out how she'd come to be on the side standing against teachers would take some soul-searching. Or not. Not even the boost to her pride would be worth it.

Education had been the cornerstone of every program she and Whit had pursued. Richard Duncan would tear it down to save a buck.

He sniffed. "Don't need an advisor for decisions like that, hon. I make my own decisions, shoot from the hip and let the chips fall." He tapped the nameplate in the center of his desk. "Voters liked that well enough last time. I'm gonna let that bet ride this time around."

So, *no* was the answer to her question about serving as an advisor.

Which meant she'd be facing the firing squad over and over, trying to spin whatever nonsense he'd spouted while he was "shooting from the hip." At least Whit and Ash, the two men she'd spent most of her life coaching on what to say, listened when she talked.

Richard Duncan seemed half a second from patting her on the head and sending her on her way. Regardless, it was definitely time to go.

"Thank you for your kind offer, Governor Duncan. If it's okay with you, I'd like to give this some consideration. I'd hoped to have a chance to affect policy." Winter realized as she said the words that it was the truth. That's what she was missing. With Whit, the two of them had discussed issues and every decision had been based on careful judgment and weighing the benefits versus the costs. With Richard Duncan "shooting from the hip," nothing would be studied the same way. Every issue would be decided based on emotion and prejudice and which group yelled the loudest and longest. "My version of politics is about service, not being served. That's what I could bring to the right campaign."

Richard Duncan tipped back his head. "Oh, you're one of those. An idealist." He nodded slowly. "Of course you are. Talking your way into a meeting with the governor." His eyes were big. "That's the kind of thing only young people or foolishly passionate

people will attempt." He pointed at Winter.
"On you, it looks good. When you're ready
to get real, you give me a call. We can work
something out. What do you say?"

Winter was so surprised by the soften-
ing from his initial bluster that she wasn't
sure what to say. She offered him her hand
again. "Thank you for your time, Governor.
I owe Nia a big thank-you. This meeting has
cleared up some things for me."

He narrowed his eyes. "That Whit Callaway must be a fool. The boy had a good thing
going and threw it away for what?"

Flattery. And even though it was coming
from the worst kind of public servant, it still
felt good. What was wrong with her?

"One thing you're forgetting, Governor, is
that you weren't running against Whit Callaway last time. He's smarter than you give
him credit for, with or without me. He made
a mistake, focused on the money instead of
the promise. You're making the same mistakes." Winter met his stare head-on. There
was no need to sugarcoat it. Richard Duncan,
the career politician, would appreciate Whit's
motivation. And there was zero chance he
was listening to her free advice. "It'll take
a lot to bring down the sitting governor in

this current climate, but the Callaways aren't afraid of playing and they have the big budget to back that up."

He whistled. "Now, you said a mouthful there. I've got some good fund-raising, but who can match a family with enough money to go their own way. No lobbyists or special interests required. It's a true luxury to be able to make a platform without those burdens." His assessing study convinced Winter that he was smarter than his front-page coverage indicated. Duncan could be shaped into a winner with the right policy adjustments.

But did she want to take on that job? Did she want to make a reasonable, rational, likable human being out of the guy who'd just acted and sounded like that?

Lipstick on a pig came to mind.

The fact that she could hear it in her mother's voice was almost all the confirmation that she needed to escape far and fast.

"Governor, I should be going. It's a long drive back to Sweetwater." Winter stood and turned toward the door without offering him her hand. That should be enough of a signal to him that she'd already decided.

"Don't forget to give Nia a call when you're ready to join a real political campaign, even from the sidelines. She can patch you through to me." Richard Duncan didn't stand or follow her to the door. He was lounging in his seat, a man comfortable with his place in the world.

His relaxed posture made her want to poke some holes in his campaign or…him. It was a terrible sign.

Leaving without speaking her mind was hard, but seeing Nia's friendly smile made it easier. How did she stand working next to Duncan? "How did it go?"

Mindful of the kindness Nia had done in order to help an acquaintance, Winter answered, "The governor and I had a good talk, really cleared some things up for me. I can't thank you enough for giving me this shot to speak to him in person. This has been a big help." It had.

"You moving to Nashville, then?" Nia asked. "I'd be happy to help make some calls to find places close to the capitol."

The suggestion almost shocked Winter into recoiling.

That knee-jerk reaction was enough to convince her that whatever she decided to do, it would happen in east Tennessee. Nashville wasn't home.

"I'll be in touch when I know something certain." Winter patted Nia's shoulder and waved toward the elevator. "I better get on the road if I want to make it home before dark. Thanks again."

She was careful to greet everyone she passed with a smile. The way politics worked was that friends and enemies lurked in plain sight, but it was almost impossible to tell which was which without the benefit of hindsight.

Carefully ducking the news crew gathered on the steps took some maneuvering, and Winter was happy to make the long trek back to the car. The more distance she put between herself and Richard Duncan, the better she felt.

That was why she and Whit had been so good together. He'd trusted no one while Winter was careful to give almost everyone the benefit of some doubt.

Giving the report anonymously to Richard Duncan had been an example of hoping the man in charge of Tennessee's government actually cared about the things he said he did. He'd cared enough to have his campaign photos taken at Otter Lake. He'd also cared enough to take up the cause of halting destruction at The Aerie, as long as it benefitted him.

Whit might have done the same thing if she'd been able to phrase the argument correctly.

How hard had she tried?

Deep in thought, Winter barely noticed that she'd trudged back to her parking spot. She slipped the too-tight heels off with a sigh and then started the car. The drive back to Sweetwater would be long enough to figure out what she wanted, but the truth was she didn't need time. If she trusted her mother and her philosophy about the skeeves, she already knew her decision. She'd been right about the gray-goop shampoo.

And Winter was pretty sure she was right about Richard Duncan.

Not that she'd tell her mother that without being tortured or the threat of returning to the original lavender-scented messy hair.

"So instead of worrying, turn up the radio, Winter Rose Kingfisher." That sounded a lot like her mother's voice, too. Again, she was perfectly correct, so Winter found a classic-rock station and gave the volume knob a twist. She'd sing at the top of her lungs and the trip would fly by.

As she pulled into town, Winter noticed the lights were blazing at Sweetwater Souvenir. Leanne was seated behind the counter at the cash register. She'd made it back to town ten minutes before closing time.

And she didn't want to go home to tell her mother how right she'd been about what a waste of time and miles the drive to meet with Richard Duncan had been, so she parked in front of the store.

After four hours in the car each way, not even the nice lunch she'd enjoyed could lift her spirits.

The bright space of Sweetwater Souvenir might do the job.

"Well, if I didn't know better, I'd say you didn't get the job." Leanne was leaning against the counter, what appeared to be a stack of catalogs at her elbow. Even after a full day at the shop all by herself, her smile was warm and welcoming.

"How did you know it was a job interview?" The better question was how did she know Duncan had offered her the job she'd been strategizing to get ever since she'd pushed Whit into a puddle of water in front of the town of Sweetwater.

Leanne raised her eyebrows. "Come on,

Winter. Don't play dumb. And I know you got an offer. The man would be a fool not to make one. What I can't tell is how you responded? I don't see a happy glow."

Winter was certain her face was grim with more grim piled on top. She stepped out of her heels with a sigh and wished for a comfy chair. "You ever had the experience where you fight and you fight to get what you want and then someone is prepared to hand it to you, and everything about the situation feels too wrong to accept." She ran her hand through her hair, pleased at how well her mother's goop was holding up to a long day. "Taking means you win, of course. If you can ignore the wrongness. And the fact that the person you're defeating never stood a chance. Should I hope that I can turn things around?" She'd been able to guide Whit into agreement. For some reason, she was certain the tactics that worked with him would sail right over the head of Richard Duncan. "Or admit defeat."

At this point, defeat would be a gift. She wanted to sleep for seven full days and wake up a new person.

"What does losing look like?" Leanne asked. "Sometimes it's the best thing that can happen, you know?"

"True." Winter covered her face with her hands, determined to gain some control.

Leanne reached across the counter. "You're tired." Her lips curled but her eyes were filled with compassion. That compassion made it twice as hard for Winter to stand on her own two feet, so she gripped Leanne's hand. Hard. "You don't have to do anything tonight, do you? No big decisions required?"

Winter shook her head, her throat working against ridiculous tears. What would crying serve? Even if she was facing the end of her hopes for political service for at least the near future, crying about it changed nothing.

Leanne squeezed her hand. "Here's the good news. I have been where you are. I once worked hard to get a good man to marry me. Schemed. I did things I shouldn't have, but I got exactly what I wanted." She bent her head down. "And then all that scheming and bending myself into corners I should never have been in blew up in my face. More than once, because after you compromise on what you know to be true, you have to continue making bad choices or whatever you're holding on to is going to fall to pieces. I was lucky to survive it, but I'm telling you, I will not make that mistake again." She huffed out an exasperated breath. "I have so many other mistakes to make, why cover old ground?" She waited until Winter laughed. "Come on. I'm not as good at this as Macy or Christina, but that was a pretty funny piece of commentary."

Winter nodded. "It was. And you're not doing so bad this go-around, are you? That mistake brought you two great kids that you can't stop talking about. And you're about to be a famous artist, after all."

The smile instantly disappeared and Winter regretted teasing Leanne. She didn't want to be in the spotlight.

"Well, locally famous." Leanne cleared her throat. "Although Miss Janet is a powerhouse of creative sales ideas. I could be looking at a worldwide tour unless I figure out how to throw on the brakes soon." The color in her cheeks was impossible to ignore. "I hope no one who gets behind me regrets it. I meant what I said. I'm not through messing up."

"I know what you mean." Winter understood her fear. If she passed on this job, her parents would be happy, but what about when she never found another way to prove herself? How long would their happiness last when she was living at home and collecting her pitiful reserve retirement check? "I don't want to go home. Where can we go for dinner?"

Leanne perked up immediately. "I'm so glad you asked. I was mentally exploring my empty refrigerator and trying to convince myself that I didn't need to order a pizza from The Branch." She waggled her eyebrows. "But if I were entertaining, I'd have to do that. Because the cupboards are bare. I hate grocery shopping so much I'll eat green beans and scrambled eggs for dinner to put it off. Different story, of course, when I have my kids." She raised both hands at Winter's gagging expression. "I know. It's so silly, but after so many years of never being able to afford to buy what I wanted, I am overwhelmed by the choices. When we were married, Brett got so tired of inching along the aisles that he took over the shopping. I made lists. He followed them." She sighed. "That was one of those benefits of married life that no one tells you about."

Winter was trying to frame a delicate question about whether Leanne missed that kind of life or Brett, the man. It was delicate because Christina, Leanne's best friend, was head over heels with Leanne's ex.

Leanne hooted a loud laugh. "If you could see your face."

Winter immediately straightened and decided it was none of her business how Leanne felt or what sort of soap-opera shouting might happen behind the scenes.

"The thing about falling out of love with someone is that it doesn't always have to be full of bitterness and hate." Leanne closed her eyes. "Okay, maybe for a minute or two, it has to be, but then you understand that he's a good man who loves his kids and deserves to be happy. If he's also the kind of lucky rat that picks the one woman in the world you'd go to war for, it takes another minute to wrap your head around it, but forgiving is easy when you love someone." She crossed her arms. "That's my story, anyway. Do I forget my highly evolved feelings? Every now and then, but nothing would let me hurt Christina because of it. We've been through too much together for that, and she'd die for my kids. That matters."

Winter wondered if she'd be able to move on the way Leanne had. The hurt she was nursing over Whit, a man who'd never been what Brett had to Leanne, seemed petty.

They'd been friends, nothing more, and he'd made a mistake.

For that matter, she had, too. Underhanded tactics were never the right decision.

"There's life after divorce." Winter nodded slowly. "And stupid, public breakups. Good to know."

"Am I helping?" Leanne flexed both arms. "I'm actually helping! It feels good. Like you have no idea how good. For a long time, I was a bad mother and a bad friend. I was forgiven. Now I'm going to go around preaching the message of second chances. And it feels go-o-ood." She drew out the last word.

"You have helped. You're a go-o-ood friend." Winter mimicked her delivery of "good" while Leanne preened and laughed. "Tomorrow, I'll be better. Forget Whit. Forget Richard Duncan."

Leanne held up her hand for a high five. "In your situation, it's the only way to win. It's not easy. You don't just make the decision once. You gotta do it every day, every minute the urge to settle into hurt or anger or bitterness hits. Shut it down and skip away. I'll remind you because I am a professional at forgetting my own good advice but I'm learning to enjoy telling other people how to live their lives. You do you and let the jerks of the world regret their choices, you know?"

That was the piece she was missing: repetition. She'd already told herself to do everything Leanne said, but then she forgot. Lighter and freer at the suggestion and Leanne's promise to help, Winter pointed at the clock hanging behind the counter. "Closing time."

Leanne snagged the keys off the counter. "I'll lock up. Then we'll call in an order and ask Astrid if she wants to join us for a dumb television movie. I'm thinking car crashes or alien invasion, a nice 'end of the world by ice age' flick. What do you say?" She didn't wait for Winter's answer but trotted around to the front door. "You're in. I can tell."

Leanne bent to pick up her shoes and studied the scuff marks on the bottom. She'd done some important walking in these shoes.

They weren't going back to the capital, not while Richard Duncan was there, anyway.

That meant letting go of her revenge plan completely. Didn't it?

Whit Callaway was twice the man his opponent was, even if his blind allegiance to his father led to some spectacular fails.

And Caleb Callaway had treated her with

respect and rescued her when she needed it most, after she'd made the cowardly decision to fight anonymously. His help had stopped a bad situation from getting worse, and she'd always appreciate what he'd done. Tomorrow she was going to make a turnaround. Instead of leaning on Caleb to put everything right, she was going to pitch in. This lodge had to be finished. Even from her spot outside the hustle and bustle of a campaign, she could help. It would be easy enough, but she was the only one who could fix the mess she'd created.

She might not understand how Caleb could dislike Sweetwater so much, but she knew him. Not the outside picture of the rich guy who dabbled in work, but the man who'd stepped up when he was needed, over and over.

Callaways weren't Kingfishers, didn't share the same ideals, but they weren't afraid to lead in tough situations. That was admirable, no matter what else was going on.

At this point, getting even with the Callaways seemed like a stupid idea in the first place. They had money and power, and if she was honest, the right ideas on their side.

Where did that leave her?

Struggling in Sweetwater.

"I have sweatpants you can borrow. That suit is making me uncomfortable." Leanne pointed at the hidden staircase behind a white panel door. "Let's go?"

The struggle could wait for sunrise. Tonight, Leanne, greasy Branch pizza and aliens at the end of the world were going to save Winter.

CHAPTER NINE

CALEB WAS RUNNING about twenty seconds late when he drove into the parking lot at the bottom of the trail that led up to The Aerie. Since he'd never been much for hiking and it was the steepest, rockiest climb in the reserve, he expected a workout and only caffeine and Odella's baked goods would pull him through.

When his phone rang as he pulled into a parking spot, Caleb shifted around to locate his cell.

Senior was calling.

Early on Saturday morning.

That could only mean one thing: he'd seen Bailey Garcia's report and he was displeased.

Declining the call would not go well.

Winter was leaning against the station wagon, no political signs in sight. A backpack was slung over one shoulder, and she was bundled in layers. Of the two of them, no one would have any difficulty deciding who the expert was.

He held up one finger and pointed at the phone to ask for a minute. She nodded, but he wasn't sure she was fully there. Her expression was distracted or thoughtful. Maybe she needed caffeine, too.

"Yeah?" Caleb said by way of answering the call.

The silence on the other end suggested his stepfather was seething with impatience. "Answer the phone politely, Caleb," Senior snapped. "The news updates aren't quite matching your status reports. Why are you letting reporters on the job site? I shouldn't have to tell you—"

"Ash Kingfisher has agreed to handle all calls from reporters. There was nothing in that report that was untrue, and it did match my status reports. I told you—next week, we'll turn the corner. We'll be caught up by then, and weather permitting, we'll move ahead."

Why did he always struggle like a twelve-year-old called to the principal's office in the face of Senior's displeasure? Because his good opinion mattered and Caleb had never quite met the criteria.

"Fine. Why do I suspect Winter Kingfisher had something to do with this reporter?"

Because she had, but only indirectly. He wasn't going to get into that.

"Bailey Garcia was heavily involved in the battle over the lodge. It makes sense she's not ready to let the story go, but Ash and I will handle it." Caleb hadn't yet followed up with Ash. That was on his list of things to do, though. Telling Senior he was going to go for a hike before he negotiated an agreement with the head ranger would not go well.

"Fine. I don't care what you have to do, but get the stories coming out of Sweetwater locked down. Whit's not making any gains right now, so this is critical." Senior sounded tired. "And your mother..."

Caleb tipped back his head. "Mom's okay, right?"

"She's fine. I just..." Senior's pauses had always heightened Caleb's concern, but when they were centered on his mother, his anxiety rose. "I'm more aware of time and how it passes now. Do you understand me?"

The lump in his throat was instant. "So she's not fine."

"Today she is, but days go by so fast. She has dreams for her sons. We're going to make them come true, you hear?" Senior cursed under his breath. "I need you for this, Caleb. Whit needs to win *this* election, not the next one. We have no guarantees for the next one."

Caleb bit his lip. The urge to ask what his mother was dreaming for him, her first-born, was stuck there, but he was afraid of the answer. What if the answer was nothing? Maybe he'd wasted too much time playing at what he enjoyed or his goals were too silly.

But Senior was right. He could help Whit.

"I'm about to meet with Winter now, Senior. I'll make sure nothing else is coming out of Sweetwater, or it if does, it's the story we want to tell." He wasn't sure how he'd manage it, but something in him wanted to exceed his stepfather's expectations.

"Good. Good. Thank you. You've stepped into a difficult spot here, so I appreciate your hard work." His stepfather cleared his throat. Since that was the most emotional conversation they'd shared in a while, Caleb understood the urge. "If orders and threats don't work, try charm. That's something I never learned to use successfully." His stepfather's voice was gravelly. "Heaven help me."

Caleb blinked once or twice before he

grinned. "The Callaway bar for charming is set pretty low, is that what you're saying?"

Caleb could hear a smile in Senior's voice as he answered, "I'm saying you got charm from your mother. Both of my sons did. I definitely married up, convincing a woman like her to take a chance on me, but I'm smart enough not to let her ever regret it. Take my advice. Smart is good. Smart and charming is better."

They laughed together until Caleb said, "Gotta run. I'll update you with the progress on everything tomorrow. I'm looking forward to seeing you all at dinner." He ended the call and stared at his phone, gripped so tightly in his hand that the bite of the edges distracted him. Should he skip the hike and head home immediately? Senior sounded strained. Caleb missed his mother. Even talking to Whit seemed like a nice idea.

But they'd asked him to do *this*, to keep an eye on Winter. Threats hadn't worked. Neither had reason. Senior was right. Charm was a last-ditch solution but he'd give it a shot.

Winter hadn't moved from her spot in the sunshine next to her beat-up car. Which would be harder, climbing a mountain or charming Winter Kingfisher?

No matter how hard the climb was or how completely unprepared he might be to keep up with her, he wouldn't complain. His pride wouldn't let him.

Caleb grabbed the knit hat he'd tossed into the SUV at the last minute, his single concession to coming prepared, before picking up both cups of coffee and getting out of the truck. His breakfast was long gone, but he'd gotten the biggest to-go coffees Odella had. "Morning." He offered her a cup and waited to see if she'd accept it. Any thawing of tensions between them would be nice.

"I needed this." Winter accepted the cup and sipped. A long, happy sigh was her response. "I don't know how she does it, but Odella makes coffee like no one else."

"If you could find a way to bottle it, Sweetwater would rival Seattle as the home of good coffee." Caleb sipped and held out his hand. "I'll carry the backpack."

Winter snorted. "It's mine. I'll carry it."

So, no thawing then.

"Discovering Odella, her coffee and her baking has been the highlight of my stay in town." Caleb smiled at Winter, ready to win her over.

Her sniff was a cold answer. "The campground diner has a breakfast to beat any restaurant you've ever eaten at in Nashville. Burgers at The Branch are solid. The pizza tastes good, but be prepared for heartburn the next day." She covered her heart with her hand. "The new sandwich shop opening up on the corner of Main Street has bread that will make your mouth water. There are plenty of highlights." She shifted the backpack and turned to stare up at the mountain.

That was a literal cold shoulder.

He couldn't give up.

"All I need is a friendly guide, someone prepared to help me make the best of Sweetwater." Caleb sipped his coffee innocently when she swung back to face him.

"In my experience, those are hard to find when you make it clear that your visit is a punishment," Winter said sweetly and raised her eyebrows.

Had he done that? Caleb considered the question as he cradled the warm coffee with both hands. Maybe. He certainly had viewed this assignment as a sort of sentence and hurried to reduce time served through good behavior, tight schedules and pushing his crews.

Unsettled and a little guilty at the reminder of the men and women who were there to do a job, not prove a point or get out of jail quick, Caleb straightened. On Monday he should reevaluate his timeline.

She finished her coffee and shifted restlessly. Winter had always struck him as a woman in constant movement. In Knoxville, she'd juggled the demands of the reserve, Whit's campaign appearances and wedding planning. Then it had all stopped at once. How was she handling the town's slower pace?

Asking her that outright would only confirm her suspicion of his opinion of her hometown.

"I've never been to the top. Is the climb tough?" Surely he could do it. He worked in construction. Sure, so many days that meant long meetings instead of physical labor, but he couldn't let Winter show him up.

"It's not bad. The trail is in good shape all the way to the top, but it gets rougher there, lots of bare rocks that can trip up the unsuspecting or inexperienced, but that's not where we're going." She pointed at a smaller opening at the base of the parking lot. "Buckeye Cove is where I want to take you. This trail ties The Aerie to Yanu Falls by skirting the edge of Otter Lake. It was originally a piece of a long trail the Cherokee used for summer hunting. Not even a century of forest growth has completely eliminated the trail worn by the hunters who traveled through here. Try to keep up."

Those were the last words she said before she stepped off the pavement onto a rough trail that wound through old-growth forest. If not for the sheer face of the mountain creating a natural boundary, clearing some of the spots on the trail would be impossible, but coverage of trees and warmth of the sun on the rock face of the mountain created a cozy pocket that meandered all the way down toward the water.

If he could have managed to make conversation at that rate of speed, Caleb might have remarked on the pretty weather or the soft light breaking through the trees or the occasional birdcall that made a faint musical sound as he and Winter walked.

But he could not.

Talking would have required stopping and gasping for air for a minute.

Winter seemed to have no time for that. At one point, he lost sight of her on the trail and realized this might be the place to commit the perfect crime. She could lose him in the wilderness to be eaten by hungry bears and not a single person would doubt that the city kid deserved what he got.

Then her gleaming dark hair popped back into view. Over her shoulder, the ripples of a quiet cove of water gleamed.

"Buckeye Cove. Named for the trees. My grandfather brought me and Ash here every summer to get us out of my grandmother's hair." She glanced over her shoulder at him. "My grandmother always made room for us at her place when school was out because both of my parents worked, but going from no kids to two, one of whom wanted to watch *The Princess Bride* on repeat, got old quick." She yanked a tarp out of the backpack and spread it. Instead of inviting him to sit next to her, she plopped down and he got the impression he could do whatever he wanted. Stay or go. Winter Kingfisher didn't care.

"Let me guess. Ash was the one with an affinity for Princess Buttercup." Caleb eased down beside her and crossed his arms over his bent knees.

"You know *The Princess Bride*?" She was watching him closely. "I find that hard to believe. Ash wouldn't even claim to know it and he can recite whole sections word for word."

Caleb tilted his head to the side as he tried to imagine dry, stone-faced Ash Kingfisher reenacting a scene from the movie. He couldn't do it. It was all too easy to imagine a young Winter as Princess Buttercup. Would she throw herself down a hill to find her true love? Not so much, but she would battle alongside him.

"I have a good memory for trivia." Caleb smiled at her. "Movies on repeat must be a universal way to torment older brothers."

Winter crossed her legs. "Maybe so. Did Whit do that, too?"

"My last summer at home, definitely." Caleb knew how well this was going to go over, but he had to say it. "*Dumb and Dumber*. That was the movie."

When she didn't immediately answer, he turned to see her trying to hide a smile.

"The jokes write themselves. I can't make this up." Caleb leaned back on his hands.

"That explains so much." She laughed. "*Dumb and Dumber*. How did I not know that?"

That reminded him of his suspicion about their pretend engagement and marriage plans. Was he brave enough to ask the question?

He'd never know until he asked.

"It does seem like something a true love might know." Caleb shrugged. "Or even a best friend."

She slowly turned her head to stare at him. "What does that mean? You're questioning our friendship? Whit and I almost failed accounting together. That forms a bond real quick."

Why did the answer to the question in his head matter so much?

"It isn't the friendship I'm questioning." Caleb held her stare for as long as he could. Then glanced away. "Are you determined to stop Whit because you don't like his politics or because you're heartbroken?"

Winter huffed out an irritated sigh. "What difference does it make to you?"

Good question. The only way to answer that truthfully was to say more than he should.

"I don't want you to be heartbroken. That's why." Satisfied with his answer, Caleb inhaled and exhaled slowly. Why did this feel important?

She picked up a small pine branch and twirled it between her fingers. "Fine. I was hurt at Whit's refusal to listen to me and angry at the way he turned on my brother. I lost my best friend in this and the career and the service I'd planned for my life. My heart is broken, but I'm not pining for your brother, if that's what you're asking. I want my old life back."

"Friends. Not true love, then?" Caleb asked, his voice low because this was a question no one else needed the answer to. "But you were engaged." Why did this feel like a plot Senior might have pulled the strings to bring about? A masterful arrangement of two people for the best appearance. Whit had gone along with it, as always, and now Winter was the one putting her life back together. She deserved to be angry.

"Friends who would have made marriage and mission work." Winter broke off a small piece of the branch. "That's more important than love."

Caleb knew his eyebrows shot up. He knew she was smart and capable, but he'd never expected to hear something like that. "Then why do we spend our whole lives searching for love?"

Winter tossed the branch, but she didn't answer. He should let the sunshine work its way back between them, buy some breathing room. This was the most beautiful place he could remember. Sitting here with her was comfortable, relaxing. His whole mood improved.

"I gotta say…" He'd been experiencing the same relaxation every night while he stared out at the lake. Was this the place to confess it? "I can't remember another place where I've felt this peaceful. Otter Lake has some kind of mystical reputation for peace, right?"

Instead of answering, Winter rummaged in her backpack and pulled out a bottle of water. She offered it to him. "I knew you wouldn't take my advice."

Caleb shrugged. "I would have if I'd had any water bottles. You're the expert here, so I trust your advice. I also hate going to the grocery store. Janet's kitchen came fully equipped, but filling the refrigerator is still up to me."

Winter pointed at the distant falls. This morning, they were a sluggish roll as the temperature warmed, but in the spring and summer, Caleb guessed they were a beautiful attraction. "My mother and father married at the top of the falls." Then she turned and covered her eyes to stare in the other direction. "The reserve's biggest success, the growth in the population of river otters, is thanks to all the work the rangers have done protecting habitats on Otter Lake. I could tell you about endangered species and federal studies on the park's populations of bats and woodpeckers and bear and trout and…" She glanced over her shoulder to make sure he was following her.

"I get it. The list goes on." Caleb rolled the water bottle in his hands.

"The list goes on. The land the Callaways have protected here is important because of all that, but that peace you mentioned? The healing that comes from quiet and Otter Lake? I don't have facts and figures to prove that. You have to experience it. Like Cherokee hunters once did. Like my family has for generations."

"You have a connection to this place." And she was amazing. Winter Kingfisher was the kind of spokesperson that lived and breathed the area. On this sunny, cool day, fresh-faced and with her hair gleaming in the light, she could be the photographic representation of health and peace, surrounded on all sides by the reserve's blessings.

"The thing about Otter Lake is that everyone can have a connection. Families return again and again, and the people who work here all contribute something of themselves to that." She sighed. "I don't know about mystical properties, but there's something about this place." She tilted back her head to expose her face to the sun. "My grandmother used to tell me and Ash, when we were worried about something or uncertain, to go to the water. This place. Things would get clearer."

Caleb sat up next to her, their shoulders rubbing, and he studied her face, her closed eyes and the small curve of her lips.

"Got any worries, Callaway? Give 'em to the lake." She didn't glance at him, so Caleb faced forward. "Let's give it a shot."

Meditation wasn't his thing but something about the golden ripples of water settled him.

And her company...

Here, like this, he wanted to talk to Winter.

"I was rushing to get the lodge set up because I had a chance to build a cool set of luxury homes, all the bells and whistles, lots of positive press coverage that would establish my company in a new circle. I was in a hurry. Impatient to prove myself. Sweetwater seemed to be too slow for comfort, but now..." Caleb watched the ripples. "I can only do one project. I was mad about having to let that other one go."

"Because of me, it has to be this one." Winter crossed her arms tightly over her chest, shoulders hunched.

She didn't turn toward him so it was impossible to guess how she felt about that.

"Not exactly. And I've already made up my mind to make this mine. Materials I want to use, Tennessee stone and timber. The house Janet renovated is proof that Tennessee stands the test of time and the right touch can blend yesterday and tomorrow." Did he honestly believe that?

Yeah.

"I'm going to be proud of this when it's done." He would be. And if Senior wasn't, then...

"Then what's the worry?" she asked softly.

Caleb considered the question as ripples faded on the shore in front of them.

"I guess…" He leaned back again. "When this lodge is done, I have nothing behind it. Nothing to keep my crew working. What will I do next?"

When he turned his head, he realized Winter was watching him. "Caleb…" She stopped and shook her head. "That, right there. What will I do next? If you could sum up all my worries in one question, you hit it. All my life, I've known the answer to that. That's what I'm angry about, more than anything. Whit ruined my plan." They were both quiet as they stared out at the water. The branches above them stirred but everything was silent. "I have to find the solution to let all that go."

This was where he should argue, cajole, use his leverage. A grimace twisted her lips.

The more he considered this match she and Whit had made, the angrier he got. She'd risked so much to stand for the reserve and her family, while his family had been happy enough to profit from both. Winter deserved better.

"My grandmother would have said troubles come to bring growth. Through them we learn what's important." Winter's grumpy sigh teased a smile from Caleb but she missed it. "So what is important?"

Caleb tried to exhale to match hers. This time she chuckled. "My family. That's the only explanation why I'm here instead of Nashville." He shook his head. "After years of putting as much distance between me and them as I could, everything is different."

"That I did not expect." Winter patiently waited for him to explain.

Telling her a Callaway secret was a mistake. Winter Kingfisher could use it against them in her drive to settle the score.

But as he met her stare, got caught in her warm eyes, he knew she wouldn't. Charming her hadn't worked, obviously, but that didn't mean they had no connection.

Why was it so important to share with her? Because it had been worrying him. Because they might be the only two people in the world right here. Because she was ready to listen.

"My mother is..." Caleb cleared his throat. "She's being treated for dementia." There. That sounded clinical. It was easier to think of it that way. "I want to be closer to her, to home."

Winter's grip on his hand surprised him. She hadn't hesitated, either. "Caleb, I'm sorry. That's hard. I love your mother. Tell me everything."

Instead of glossing over the details in order to protect the Callaway reputation if he was wrong about Winter's trustworthiness, Caleb told her everything he knew. All the phone conversations he'd had with her since he'd been in Sweetwater, some easy and light, some frustrating and worrying.

"Until now, I've been able to do anything and everything I wanted." Caleb rubbed his free hand over his forehead and tangled his fingers through Winter's. "Now, I understand she's not immortal. Neither is Senior. Even Whit needs me more than I realized. It's like my whole world jerked to a stop after this lodge thing, and now that it's spinning again, it's wobbly."

Why did it feel so good to unload all that?

"Anyway, tomorrow is Sunday dinner in Knoxville. You remember those." Caleb managed to turn away from Winter's sympathetic face and drank in the sight of the water. "I'm glad to have had this chance to reorder my thoughts before I do."

Her thumb trailed over his knuckles. Did

she know she was doing that? He hoped she never stopped.

"Me, too. I understand things better now, too." Winter rolled her eyes. "You aren't going to believe this, but it was the whole *Dumb and Dumber* comment that helped me."

Caleb bent his head down as a surprised laugh escaped.

"I know. The thing is that Whit is not dumb. He never has been." She grimaced. "Well, about this lodge project, he was. About attacking Ash for being the leaker with no proof, he definitely was, but as far as what he wants to do for Tennessee, he's smart. His taste in movies is appalling. Always has been, though." Her lips were twitching. "My next fiancé will be a Bruce Willis fan instead of Jim Carrey."

Caleb wondered if he should tell her how many times he'd watched the entire *Die Hard* franchise.

She let go of his hand and Caleb felt the loss. "I hope you'll tell Whit and Marjorie that I'm thinking of them. If I can do anything to help your mother, please let me know." Then she leaned her head to the side. "I walked right into that one, didn't I? This is where you say, 'Well, it would be helpful if you'd stop talking trash about my family.'" Winter covered her face with her hands. "Fine. I will."

Relieved, Caleb stood and picked up the tarp. Winter had brushed off her legs and moved to the edge of the water. Strong and tall and...*strong*. All she had to do was work things out for herself. She understood family.

"You're one of the touchiest subjects at the dinner table. She forgets you're gone and then it all comes back. She misses you." He understood that. Winter would have added verve to every family meal.

"Well, I want to send along a gift for Senior and Junior. I can't build the lodge. A truce, of sorts." She blew out a violent gust of breath, then jammed the tarp into her backpack. "I'm going to set up a media day for the lodge. I'll work with Ash at the ranger station to develop press releases, coming from him, not me. We'll invite Bailey Garcia and others from Knoxville and Nashville. Richard Duncan, too, although I'm hoping he won't come. We need to say he was invited, because Whit Callaway is going to present a trustworthy, welcoming picture to those reporters and we're going to put this lodge story to rest while cementing the Callaway reputation for preserving Tennessee history." She offered him her hand to shake.

Surprised, Caleb slipped his hand in hers.

"You build that lodge with the bells and whistles you wanted to put into that other project. This lodge could be the keystone to business opportunities you haven't dreamed of yet." Winter smiled slowly. "I'll use my powers for good instead of evil. And the Kingfisher-Callaway feud is put to rest. The Callaways win."

In one flash, he could imagine her idea in bright, bold color. It would do more to enhance the Callaway reputation than this whole battle had done to harm it.

"Why would you do that?" he asked. Did it matter? For some reason, it did.

"Coming down here made things clearer." She shrugged. "My hurt is one thing. This place is another. Whit Callaway will do more for Tennessee than Richard Duncan. If I get out of my way, I can see that."

Caleb reached over to wrap his arms around her, the weight rolling off his shoulders at her words. A spontaneous hug was a risk, but he settled his chin against her soft hair. "Thank you, Winter. Everything has been a mess. This is going to put things right. I feel it."

She was stiff in his arms but she didn't step back. "I hope so. How soon do you want to plan all this?"

With the memory of Senior's phone call and Whit's falling poll numbers fresh in his mind, Caleb was certain there was only one right answer. "As soon as possible. We could do one this month and announce the date of the lodge's completion with another conference scheduled. Would that keep reporters out of my way in the meantime?" And would it mean that Winter had to remain involved with the lodge? He wanted that to be true.

She squeezed him tightly. "I hope so. I need to get a move on. I have some planning to start." She studied the ground. "I'm going to regret this and if you say yes, you'll regret it, too, but... Do you want to come for dinner at my mother's house? Ash will be there and we can make some preliminary plans."

Did she know her hand was tangled in his flannel shirt? Together, right here, they clicked. He didn't want her to realize it and step back, so he blurted, "Yes. Of course. It's frozen dinners for me otherwise, but... Why will I regret it?"

Each tiny movement shifted her closer to him. He could stand here, with her…forever. "Well, two reasons. First, my mother insists on making everything from scratch. Her tortillas are…hit or miss, mainly miss." She smiled along with Caleb and then straightened to move away. "Second, she's not an easy person to convince. You'll be coming in with some Callaway baggage, but if you can win over Donna Kingfisher, Sweetwater will slowly turn in your favor, too."

"I'm in. I'm brave. I can do this." He could. Bad food was one thing, but a tense atmosphere was nothing. He'd learned to travel through that early. Caleb stepped back. "I'll follow you, then? Try not to lose me on the way back. The trail is tricky."

She grimaced. "I don't know if you noticed, but we were moving down the whole way here. That means to get back…" She pointed straight up.

The trail down had been no walk in… the park. Getting back up to the parking lot would be a challenge.

Then Winter Kingfisher took off at a steady jog, her giggles trailing behind, and she cleared the first turn before he got his feet in motion.

If he survived the climb back up to the parking lot, he had some thinking to do.

Winter Kingfisher was special. She shouldn't be the only one to lose in this mess. What could he do to make that right?

CHAPTER TEN

CALEB HAD BEEN lucky enough to eat in the finest restaurants in Nashville, Knoxville and cities here and there. He'd managed to network in rooms filled with working-class ranchers and builders and businessmen, and had meetings with millionaires like Mitch Yarborough. Never in his life had he struggled to find appropriate conversation the way he did while he was seated around the family picnic table at the Kingfisher house.

If he could have described a setting as far away from his family's formal dining room, it might have been Winter's mother's greenhouse on a cold March day. The windows were steamed with the heat they generated. Here and there, white twinkle lights sparkled in the glass reflection, casting twice the light, some inside and some out. The situation might have been festive. An impromptu taco party with margaritas.

When they'd walked in together, Winter

had tried to smooth over the awkward silence by asking what the celebration was for.

Her mother had snapped, "Saturday," and marched back inside the kitchen.

When he'd turned to ask Winter if he should beat a hasty retreat because he had no time for food poisoning, Ash's girlfriend had wriggled in between Ash and Winter, her hand extended. "Better find a spot at the table, Callaway. Damage has already been done at this point. Only way out is through." She'd smiled up at him, the only person in the room who'd done so, and added, "Call me Macy. I'm not a Kingfisher, either."

Her grip had been impossible to shake so he'd followed her out on the covered patio and gawked at the greenery exploding inside. It was almost enough to distract him from the angry whispers going on inside. Ash and Winter's father stood between two arguing women. He couldn't make out a single word but it was impossible to pretend he didn't know the subject.

"Don't you worry. Winter's pretty tough." Macy angled her head closer to his. "I would not want to square off against Donna, but if you can make her a friend, she's the kind you'll never shake." She tapped a finger on the table. "I'm hoping someday to be a Kingfisher, because you can't beat how they stick together, but while you're on the outside staring in, they're kinda daunting."

Caleb understood what she meant. From here, he could watch Winter's face while her mother's braid swayed back and forth, a blond ticktock punctuated by the occasional point in his direction. "Did she say skeeves?"

Macy sipped her margarita. "Don't believe there's any alcohol in this but you should try it. It's good." Then she sniffed. "Yeah, the skeeves are a Kingfisher thing, too, sorta like the creeps, but related mainly to weaselly men. Like Whit Callaway." Her eyes sparkled as she watched him.

At some point, he'd mull over why he felt no need to jump to his little brother's defense. "Even before the breakup, Whit wasn't popular here, huh?"

"No, sir, he was not." Winter's mother dropped a basket on the table and plopped down across from Caleb. "He's a liar. That's why. Always pretending to be one thing and on the inside, being something else." She tilted her head to the side. "I don't like that."

Caleb carefully set down his margarita glass, the soft breeze next to him reassuring. Winter was there. If her mother lost control of her temper, she could save him. *Would* save him. He turned to acknowledge her presence, saw the frown of worry between her eyebrows and bumped her shoulder with his. "Don't worry. You did warn me."

Her lips were twitching. "I did, but nothing I could say would prepare you. I'm not prepared for this myself."

Macy giggled on his other side. "First time I came over, Ash said the same thing. There was no way to tell me what to expect. He was right, too." She picked up her glass and offered it to Winter's mother and waited patiently for her to return the clinking glass. "Luckiest night of my life, being invited to a Kingfisher dinner."

Watching Winter's mother unbend was amazing. If he'd been afraid she would murder him with a broken margarita glass, the look she gave Macy was pure light and sweetness. It was easy to see where Winter's passion came from.

"Mrs. Callaway, I'm sorry to have arrived without a hostess gift, but thank you for sharing your hard work with me. Making everything from scratch is impressive in this day of prepared meals. Winter and I wanted to get Ash's opinion on some lodge business, but I shouldn't have come without an invitation." There. That speech would have fit in any number of dining rooms he'd visited with his parents.

Donna Kingfisher's loud scoff would not. "Please, don't you try to pull the wool over my eyes with nice manners. I've already met your brother." She tapped the table. "Why are you bothering Winter? Hasn't she put up with enough from you?"

The urge to tell Winter's mother how he'd come to be dragged into the whole situation was strong, but he wouldn't do that. Not now, since he and Winter were working together for the first time.

"Have a taco." Winter slapped one down on his plate and then did the same with everyone at the table. "Eat. No conversation. I don't want to hear another word until every taco is gone."

Caleb picked up his food and chanced a look at her father. He'd imagined Martin Kingfisher to be the meek sort, but the way he was choking back laughter as he focused on his taco suggested he was a man who'd long ago figured out how to live with two fierce women. Caleb turned to see what Ash was doing. He had his head down, food going in as ordered.

So he took a bite of the taco, amazed at the way spices filled his senses. Was the tortilla less than refined? Yes, but this was a home-made meal and he loved every bite. As soon as he finished the first one, he checked the platter and wondered what his chances were of getting a second helping without having his fingers snapped in half.

"You like my cooking?" Winter's mother asked slowly, her eyes narrow, dangerous.

Caleb cleared his throat, uncertain why his fight-or-flight reflexes were clamoring for flight. "Yes, ma'am. I don't get much home cooking so…I do. Thank you for preparing them."

She didn't relent, her stare boring a spot right between his eyes, until she nodded at the platter. "Well, go ahead. Have another. Winter is going to tell us why you're really here."

Caleb picked up the platter and remem-bered his mother's teaching. "Would anyone else like another?" He served everyone at the table first before taking a taco, then put the platter back in place before glancing at Win-ter's mother again. She'd raised her chin but some of the murder had faded from her eyes. Her evaluation wasn't complete, but he was inching away from the danger zone.

"Two things." Winter squirmed next to him. "First, I have a confession. You know how, in the movies, the terrible villain threatens to tell all your secrets to the world?"

Caleb froze, taco halfway to his mouth. Was Winter about to tell her family how he'd tried to use their history to keep her quiet? He'd never make it out of there alive.

"Well, in case I ever run into a bad guy who wants to hurt me, I'm going to share my secret with everyone at the table." Winter poked his leg under the table and rolled her eyes at him. She could read his mind. "I never once believed you were going to, Caleb," she whispered, the brush of her hair against his ear sweet and exciting. She cleared her throat. "Caleb is not the person who leaked the report to the governor. I did. I never expected Ash to get caught in the middle. There was no reason for Ash to get caught up in it. When he did, I had to scramble to find some way to protect his job without ruining everything, which then fell spectacularly apart, anyway. A friend has told me that the worst way to live my life is making new decisions based on old, bad choices. So... I'm the reason the lodge blew up. Not Ash. Not Whit. Me."

Caleb chewed as he studied the faces gathered around the table. If he had to guess, Winter's mother and Ash's girlfriend were the maddest.

"I'm sorry, Ash." Winter shook her head. "I shouldn't have kept it a secret."

He reached around behind Caleb and patted her shoulder. "I said it at the time, but I'm sorry it never occurred to me in the first place. I would have done the same thing and felt no regret." Ash bumped Macy with his elbow. Did the petite firecracker know she was breathing so heavily? "There's no harm done. In fact, I'd say I'm better off now that I was before. I've got my job, a spot on the board and a great woman to guard my back." He seemed to be waiting for Macy to turn toward him. "Don't I?"

"Always," Macy said immediately. "But I don't understand why she'd let you face off against them alone."

"I was never alone." Ash shook his head. "Never alone. You were there. Brett. My parents. And Winter navigated the whole situation, remember?"

"That she created," Macy said loudly. "I want to know why."

Everyone at the table swung back to Winter, and Caleb wanted to wrap his arm around her shoulders. He'd been in her spot often enough, as the person everyone was watching as they waited to hear an explanation. "She wanted to protect the reserve without losing everything. How can she say it any plainer? She had her own plans, a wedding, a job. She wanted to keep those things. If you can't understand that, then you need to consider long and hard," Caleb said and leaned back from the table. It was a risky position to take, surrounded by the family, but she shouldn't have to face all this alone.

The risk was doubled when he realized Winter had never asked him to stand up for her. She wasn't the kind of woman who'd shrink away. He turned to defend his actions, but under the table, Winter reached for his hand and tangled their fingers together. All right. She didn't need him. But that wasn't the same as having an appreciation that he would stand by her.

He got that. He was the same. Could he fight his battles? Yes. Not having to do it alone was sweet.

Macy smacked a hand on the table. "Oh, okay, if you want to go and make a sensible case or something." She crossed her arms in a huff and then collapsed into Ash's side as he wrapped an arm around her shoulder.

"That's not the Kingfisher way, sneaking around like that. Face your fears head-on. Do the right thing without hesitation." Winter's father had braced his elbows on the table and rested his chin on his hands. Caleb wasn't going to do it. No one in this family would be happy if he made any move to touch Winter. He didn't want to add fuel to the fire, but when her shoulders slumped under the weight of her father's words, he wrapped his own arm around her shoulders. Instead of shrugging him off, Winter straightened. "I know. I'm sorry."

Her father waved his hands. "Then we're done with that. Now we make it right."

How the tense silence started to ease away caught Caleb off guard. At the Callaway house, Senior's frown would continue, unabated, until some other infraction took the pressure off the previous offender. Here, everyone settled into their seats, ready to move on to phase two—making things right.

Caleb shook his head as he sipped his margarita.

"I have a plan to get everything back on track." Winter gulped her own drink. "Caleb needs to finish the lodge on time and ahead of schedule. He's giving up a lot to be here in Sweetwater when he needs to be in Knoxville building his own business. He's doing that because he agreed to take the heat off me. So, we're going to dissolve the media interest in the lodge." She shifted forward to meet Ash's stare. "Media days. Once a month until the lodge is complete. I'll give you a list of contacts and create the press releases. You send everything out so it's nice and official. If you're being completely transparent about the lodge and the progress, then there's no need for reporters to ambush your crew, Caleb." She smiled.

"We're going to invite Richard Duncan to the first media day, though urge him with all our mental strength not to show, because Whit Callaway will be there, grinning happily from behind the podium. Ash Kingfisher, Whit Callaway, everything aboveboard. There is no more story. There is only positive publicity. The Callaways will return to the public eye and that should return some of Whit's momentum." She tapped her chin, the wheels turning quickly in her mind. Caleb had always loved watching her think. It was beautiful, and any moment now, she'd surprise them all...

"The other thing we could do," she continued, "is make sure Sweetwater is on board with the Callaways. The first step involves the gallery, which Janet will love, but I have to make sure it's right for everyone before..." She trailed off as she considered all the options.

Caleb glanced at each of them. Ash shrugged. "She does this. It's like her brain moves ahead while the rest of her has to catch up. Scary, but you get used to it."

The laughter around the table felt so good. Comfortable. Like a family might.

Then he noticed Winter's mother watching him again and remembered that his arm was still around Winter's shoulders. Should he move it or no?

"A Callaway who did the right thing when the cameras weren't rolling." She pursed her lips. "Interesting."

Caleb nodded. "Callaways don't always make the right decisions, but even we get lucky sometimes."

Her mom's lips curled and Caleb was certain he could run all the way to the top of The Aerie without dying. That's how strong he was in this moment.

Then Winter squeezed his hand and smiled up at him. "You just have to find the right Callaway."

After a lifetime of being the "least of" the Callaway family, it was a new experience to get respect, and from such a tough crowd.

"Well, Caleb," Winter's mother said slowly, "I underestimated you. That doesn't happen often, I'm happy to say, but I appreciate your patience. Thank you for helping Winter when she needed it and Ash when he didn't even know to ask. That's the kind of thing family does. You're invited back for dinner. Tomorrow we're having tofu, my weekly attempt at convincing my family that vegetarianism is an option."

"Not for me." Ash shook his head slowly.

Macy shrugged. "I only know how to cook eggs. I'd starve, Donna."

Winter's mother turned back to him, her eyebrows raised as if she was expecting him to make a flimsy excuse.

Thankful to have one and a *real* one, Caleb pointed at the remaining tacos. "I'd be happy to give it a shot, Mrs. K…" He waited for her reaction. Her twitching lips were a positive sign. "But I have Sunday dinner at my mother's. I'll be making the drive to Knoxville."

She relaxed a bit. One mother could appreciate a son going home, obviously. "Is your mother a good cook?"

Caleb paused to consider that. It had been so long, he wasn't sure. "We have a cook. Marcus is a great chef, but sometimes I miss family favorites. You know?" He met her gaze and something clicked. In that instant, he was afraid she could see inside his heart. He missed sitting at a table with his mother, cutting coupons and being easy and comfortable. Everything at the Callaway house was formal. Stiff. Easy to skip because it was less about family and more about obligation. Did that make his mother happy?

"Well, I guess you're in for another surprise. Here, in my house, the cook doesn't clean." She picked up her plate and handed it to him across the table. "Under normal circumstances, I'd say guests don't, either, but…" She studied Winter for a second. "You're not a guest, are you?"

Caleb took the plate, happy to have a job,

something he could perform, check off a list and expect reasonable results.

"I'm happy to clear the table." Caleb stood and took Winter's plate.

"Ash will wash. You can clear and dry," Donna Kingfisher said cheerfully. "Martin, you just…go, too. Okay?"

Caleb laughed. He couldn't help it. The Kingfisher and Callaway dinner tables couldn't have been further apart in terms of style, but one thing was absolutely the same: Mama made the rules.

"Yes, dear," Martin Kingfisher drawled as he picked up the platter.

"And make sure to pack up the leftovers for Caleb to take home. I like his appreciation, thank you very much." Her cheerful voice was such a difference that Caleb paused in the doorway.

"Come on, son, there's no sense in trying to puzzle it out. Been married to the woman for forty years and I can't tell you whether she's going to zig or zag next." Martin Kingfisher sighed happily as he turned on the hot water. "Life is grand because of it."

The thing about washing and drying dishes by hand in the Kingfisher kitchen was that there was something satisfying about occupying a space in the old-fashioned cramped space with two men who barely moved from their appointed spots, much less talked. He could get used to it.

Until they'd put away everything and Ash moved to block the exit from the kitchen—he was an immovable, solid object.

"I appreciate you helping Winter, but I can't shake the feeling that there's more here than meets the eye." Ash crossed his arms over his chest and Caleb noticed Winter's easygoing father had the same implacable expression. "Callaways aren't known for their charity or their honesty. What are you doing?"

Caleb talked himself out of the flash of anger. Ash was a big brother, watching out for his sister.

"I'm here to make my family proud." Caleb shrugged. It was true, but there was more, if he was honest. "And every day I'm here, the more time I spend with Winter, the more I realize how dumb my brother is. If I'd managed to convince her to agree to marry me, nothing would have shaken me. The minute she'd said 'stop' on the lodge, I would have moved the mountain to save The Aerie if I had to. Right now, my job is clear. Get the lodge built. Make all this worth it."

"And what about Winter?" her father asked. "How do we restore Winter?"

That was the harder question.

"Tell me what you want. Her old job at the reserve back? I can manage that." He could, probably. She'd set up these media days, the campaign would be back on track and the other Callaways would be too busy to bother with reserve business. The Kingfishers were focused on the reserve. It was the perfect solution.

"A job is easy enough to find. Winter can do anything she wants. You think she needs the Callaways?" Her father shook his head. "Not nearly as bad as they needed her. The reserve? She did more for that place than just about anyone else." He clapped a hand on his son's shoulder. "Winter doesn't need you or your family, but most of all, she doesn't need any more trouble from men who have their priorities messed up." His serious expression was so different from his amusement at the table.

All along, Caleb had kept his eyes on Winter's mother, ready to run for his life.

Her father was no joke.

Donna Kingfisher was fiery explosions. People knew where they stood with her.

Martin Kingfisher was patient, waiting for his opening. No man would see him coming if he messed up big enough to make him an enemy.

Then there was Ash, who actually had a gun and wore it every day.

Caleb's brother was lucky the Kingfishers had such high moral and ethical standards.

"What do you want from me? Name it. I'll do what I can to see that Winter gets it." Unless it was a reunion with Whit.

"Ask her. Then give it to her." Ash offered Caleb his hand. "And good luck digesting my mother's leftover tortillas. They stay with you a long time. Good news is, she's a great cook. Bad news is, she never gives up, either. One bad recipe and it hangs around until she perfects it."

Caleb gripped Ash's hand. This was the kind of conversation he could appreciate. Honest, tough, loving. This was family as he imagined it.

Now that it was time to go home again, what could he do or say to make the Callaway experience go differently?

If he was learning anything from his time

in Sweetwater, it was that everything could be changed for the better. Sometimes it was slow progress, like with the lodge. Other times, it went from fearing for your life to being sent home with leftovers over the course of a dinner. Change could happen. He wanted that for his own family, too.

As he was walking down the driveway, with a container filled with leftover tacos and Winter trailing behind him, he couldn't remember a better day. Not in a long time. "Thanks for this, Winter. Without you, I'm not sure I ever would have loved a day in Sweetwater the way I have this one."

She stopped suddenly. "A hike. A family dinner. That's all it took to win you over? No more scowling like you've hit the end of the road?"

Testing the waters, he stepped closer to her, the cold night fading as he stared into her dark eyes and wished for more than starlight. "Pretty sure all that had a touch of Kingfisher magic about it. That was the winning combination."

Her mouth dropped and the urge to kiss her was strong. So strong. "You're drunk on weird tortillas and the offer of a press conference."

He laughed. He couldn't help it. She was right but there was so much more.

"Your family is awesome. I'll wake up with cold chills when I remember your mother's eyes ten years from now. She's fierce. Like you." Caleb took her fingers between his, giving her hand a small shake. When she squeezed and then tangled their fingers together, he wanted to whoop in victory.

"Yeah, we're usually fiercely arguing by the time dinner is over. Ash and Dad go quiet and Macy watches like it's a drama on the big screen. I always wonder how my parents have made it this long when she's so intense and he's so easygoing, but it works." Winter sighed. "They took everything better than I thought they would. You had something to do with that."

Caleb decided not to mention the deadly, unspoken warning her father had issued. "I like knowing where you come from. Understanding Winter Kingfisher is one of those long-term goals a man might never accomplish but he'd also never regret the effort."

Maybe he shouldn't have been so honest. Winter blinked in surprise before looking away from him.

"You wouldn't be saying that to improve

Callaway-Kingfisher relations, would you? I'm already on board to assist with the lodge." She licked her lips, a nervous gesture that only made it more difficult to put any space between them.

"The only Kingfisher I'm concerned with is you." Caleb leaned in closer. "And the only Callaway I want you to relate to is me." Something clicked as soon as he admitted that. It was true, so true, but his emotions didn't matter until Winter felt the same.

"I don't suppose you'd like to support the arts in Sweetwater." Winter took a step closer and tugged on his jacket. "The gallery could use a wealthy benefactor like you to attend the grand opening next Saturday. Bring your checkbook, of course."

"I'll be there." He needed to go. She should walk back inside, where it was warm, but she wasn't moving away. Not even after he gave her the answer she wanted.

"Don't buy the bunny painting. That one's mine." She smiled up at him and it was impossible to stop. Caleb tilted his head slowly, carefully, and pressed his lips against hers. Warm breaths mingled in the night and she blinked slowly when he stepped back. "Why, Caleb?"

"I had to. I've wanted to, so I had to." He waited for her to get mad. Instead, she pressed her hand over her lips. "Should I apologize? I don't want to, but I will. I won't do it again."

She didn't agree, but he waited patiently as she studied his face. Instead of answering, she ran a hand down his arm to squeeze his fingers.

Winter glanced over her shoulder as she turned to go back inside. "See you Saturday."

Caleb ran a hand through his hair, frustrated and more alive than he could remember. Confused, too. She was the kind of woman who'd keep him spinning forever and love every minute of it.

But only if the whole world faded, leaving the two of them alone, without a single remaining Callaway to be found. Neither Senior nor Whit would appreciate that kiss.

Caleb had some hard thinking to do. If Winter did appreciate a sweet kiss that made him instantly want more, how much did Senior or Whit even matter?

CHAPTER ELEVEN

WORKING FOR JANET Abernathy had been an eye-opening experience for Winter. In a short time, she'd made a few discoveries. First, no matter how many decades Janet had on both her and Leanne, she could work circles around them both. She never hesitated in her decisions. Basically, Janet Abernathy had no time for the world to give her trouble. She was onto bigger and better things.

Second, arranging art had only a little in common with any home decorating Winter had ever managed in her own apartments. In the gallery that was taking shape beside Sweetwater Souvenir, she, Janet and Leanne had arranged and rearranged pieces until Winter was afraid they'd come full circle, right back to how they'd started.

But together, they'd done it. The gallery was complete with a striking window display certain to draw in the few tourists wandering Sweetwater's streets. When summer came?

The gallery would become one of Sweetwater's main attractions. Bold colors framed the delicate beauty of Leanne's painting of The Aerie from one direction on the sidewalk. Pedestrians who came from the south would get to enjoy the same bold stained glass pieces, but also see a featured display of her father's baskets.

And all the hours of arranging the pieces, moving them to try another layout, figuring out the fancy hanging system and the tools for framing and the inventory system... All of that had been a challenge Winter enjoyed. She and Leanne had worked well as a team, with Janet buzzing in and out.

She'd needed a busy week. Sweetwater Souvenir and Art had provided it.

Thoughts of Caleb and his kiss had filtered through all the noise too often, and if she'd had less to distract her, she might have done something silly. Sweetwater was small enough that she could find Caleb easily enough. She missed him, which made no sense. It had been too easy for him to slip past her guard. If he was a different kind of man, one who would use every one of her weaknesses to his advantage, she would be in serious trouble.

"Shelves are done. Table's set," Leanne mumbled as she paced back and forth in front of the old wooden desk Janet had insisted on painting. Gone was the scratched dark wood. Instead, distressed white paint helped the desk fade into the background.

Janet crowed when she marched in from Sweetwater Souvenir. "Even better than I imagined, ladies." She clapped her hands. "This place is perfect. Absolutely perfect." She studied them both. "How are we feeling?"

The question was directed broadly at the room, but Winter was certain that Leanne was the intended target. She hadn't stopped moving since Friday afternoon. Nervous energy radiated from her. "Fine. Fine. Fine. Everything's fine. I've been down the list. Checked everything off." She tapped the clipboard. "Macy uses a clipboard when she's running events. I borrowed her lucky clipboard. This is all going to be fine." She wrapped an arm across her stomach. "How would you feel if I called in sick? I'm going to vomit in the wastebasket so it won't even be a lie."

Watching Janet's jaw slowly drop convinced Winter that it was time to put Leanne in a quiet timeout. In less than half an hour, all the hard work would pay off. Neither Winter nor Janet had as much invested as Leanne. It had to be difficult to stand in front of something she'd created, and prepare to hear whatever anyone might say. Would it be harder to handle praise or criticism?

For Leanne, neither would be easy. She was accustomed to Sweetwater's criticism. How would the change to praise feel?

"Why don't you go arrange the storage room instead? We've got a mess to clean up before we can replace anything that sells tonight." When Leanne frowned at her, she nodded slowly. "Take your time. Move things around in there. Put everything in order."

Leanne's shaky nod wasn't convincing, but she disappeared into the storage room and closed the door firmly behind her.

"Good thing the place ain't got a back door. She'd be running into the night." Janet pursed her lips. "Did you tell her about the reporter you have coming to cover the opening?"

Winter frowned as she considered the question. She was never certain whether Janet was innocently tangling things or operating from a plan. She was devious with an innocent face. Learning to read her would take time. Had it been her suggestion? Yes, but Winter wasn't sure it was a good one or that she would have gone through with it except for Janet's urging.

"The reporter you insisted I contact and insinuate there would be an interview, here, in the gallery, in hope of some extra positive press will arrive in…" Winter studied her phone. "Ten minutes or less." Bailey Garcia had been calling every other hour for the last two days. Why? Winter wasn't sure, and she'd decided the only way to maintain the fragile truce with the Callaways was to stop speaking publicly.

When Janet had finally managed to get the details on who was calling, she'd demanded they capitalize on it. "When I refuse to talk about the Callaways, this will be the last chance we get."

She wasn't sure she was ready for the microphone to be thrust in her face again. For years, as the public outreach officer for the reserve, she'd smoothly handled all questions and small crises without much of a hiccup.

Then her brother had landed on the front page of every newspaper in the state, blamed and praised as the man responsible for stopping the Callaways in their tracks, and she'd had to fight to save his job. Considering that the Callaways had been the largest benefactors of universities, hospitals and charity events in east Tennessee, Ash's press during the fight over the lodge had not been positive.

Not that it would bother her stoic brother much.

Janet waved her hands. "We make good use of the chance we have, then. Make sure she hangs around long enough to get a shot of all the movers and shakers here in Sweetwater." Janet was fussing with items on the small table set up to serve wine and hors d'oeuvres, all provided by the kid out at the campground who'd shown a flair for appetizers. "You did make sure that cute Callaway boy got a special invitation, didn't you?" Before Winter could ignore Janet's nosiness and ask for a list of who Sweetwater's VIPs might be, the Kingfisher clan arrived en masse.

Her father was first through the door. "My baskets! They *are* pieces of art. I never believed it could be true, but here they are." He hugged Winter first and then Janet. "You will let me tell people how they're made, won't you? That would be a boost to the classes I'm teaching. Working with the seniors' center is fun, but I'm not sure it's doing much to pass the craft on to the next generation, if you understand what I'm saying." Winter watched her tall father bend his head attentively to Janet Abernathy and knew how powerful his enthusiasm could be. His charm was contagious.

"Dad, if we have a chance, would you be willing to talk on camera?" Winter asked. Could she pull that off? She wasn't sure. Bailey Garcia was coming for a political story, not small-town feel-good, but Martin Kingfisher could win her over, too. The way her father's eyes lit up made her laugh. If she didn't know better, she'd swear Enthusiasm was his middle name. "Our goal here is to make it clear that this is art with a history, a connection to this area. You can do that by talking about Einisi and how she passed this on to you." Winter nodded along to get his agreement. This was what she wanted to do with the gallery—tell the history of the people who'd lived here. As long as it made money, Janet was fully on board.

"Yes." Her father snapped to attention. "Your mother won't let me do that—tell long stories to everyone who asks—not anymore, but I'm ready."

Winter met her mother's stare and then wrapped her hand around her father's arm. "Do me another favor, too, can you?"

Some of the teasing faded, and she knew, no matter what she asked, her father would move mountains to make it happen. This was the kind of family she had. How lucky she was.

"Leanne is in the storage room. She's nervous about the crowd and answering questions about how she works. Could you distract her?" Winter knew there was no one in the room more qualified to put Leanne Hendrix at ease. Her father had done it more than once when Winter was a girl obsessively worried over grades and perfection and so much. He could do this.

Winter eased back as he knocked on the door. When it opened, her father said, "I heard you needed a big strong man to help with moving things. I couldn't find one of those so here I am instead. Point me to my doom."

Dad jokes. That's how he'd always managed to ease the tension in the room at home. He had a million of them, all usually exclaimed loudly.

Winter loved him for it.

She hurried back to hug her mother, who whispered, "This is going to be amazing." She'd corralled her long blond hair into four braids and then arranged those braids into… something. A ring of tiny roses dotted her crown. The original flower child had come out in full force to support her daughter. "I'll go hang out over there by the baskets to make sure your father stays on task." She marched away, the hem of her long skirt drifting as she moved. Her mother might appear to be the laid-back one of the Kingfisher couple, but she made the rules and they all marched to them. Thus, the homemade shampoo, the baskets that needed a new home and a hundred other strong recommendations a day.

"You sure it was a good idea to have us all here?" her brother asked from behind her. "I mean, the two of them are risky enough. Add me into the mix and…" He raised his eyebrows. Anytime her brother could go wordless, he would. He'd always been the strong, silent type, and when his job was in jeopardy, Winter had been frustrated to the point of anger with his inability to defend himself.

So she'd had to do it. Her guilt at putting him in that spot had helped keep her irritation under control. Otherwise, he'd be job-less and holed up in a literal cave somewhere.

Instead, he was here. At a social event. Wearing... "Is that a suit coat?" Winter drawled. The ranger uniform was his only fashion choice, usually. He looked so strange in civilian clothes that casual acquaintances might not even recognize him.

"It is." Macy Gentry stepped up beside him, lifted his arm and draped it over her shoulder. "I won a bet. Your brother doesn't like my shopping list. I like to shop the specials, you see? He said no one could eat a whole jar of dill pickles, but he never gave a time frame." Macy shrugged. "Or what I won when I proved him wrong. So I did it. It took a week, but it's worth it because look how handsome he is. The ranger uniform is nice and all, but I stare at that all the time." She tapped his chest—he was wearing a plain button-down. "This is date-night material."

Since the two of them had become a couple, Winter had seen changes in her brother that she welcomed. The way he wrapped his arm tighter to pull Macy closer was one of those sweet changes. The chaos brought on by the lodge report and the governor's attack on Whit had brought about at least one good thing. Ash and Macy were meant to be together.

"Wish we were spending date night alone, on a hike down to Otter Lake to find some constellations, but no. We're here. With people." He didn't sigh, but the minute change to his expression made Winter grin.

"Because you love me, big brother." She rushed forward to hug them both, shocking all three of them.

Ash squeezed her tightly for a second before stepping back. "Go. Mingle."

Winter noticed a group of reserve firefighters loitering near the door and tugged on her suit coat, prepared to move them farther into the gallery. This party was for the people of Sweetwater. Janet wanted to make sure everyone knew the focus of the gallery was their art, their stories, so this grand opening was taking place before the tourists hit. For Sweetwater.

She was arranging the proper words in her head to set everyone at ease when she remembered Bailey Garcia's imminent arrival. She leaned closer to her brother. "Bailey Garcia will be here. If you guys want to duck out when she arrives, I get it."

Ash considered that. "No. Bailey was a

big help during the lodge mess. No reason to avoid her now."

"What if she asks questions about the progress?" She would totally ask questions about the progress. Winter knew exactly why Bailey was headed to Sweetwater. The only interesting thing about the Kingfishers and even Sweetwater was the connection to that reserve, the bone of contention between Whit Callaway and the governor he intended to defeat in the next election.

"I'll answer them. Had a good talk with Caleb today when I drove out to check the road condition and materials. He's working a miracle so far. Got two different crews running." Ash tilted his head to the side. "Money talks loud enough to bring in crews from Knoxville, apparently."

Caleb Callaway again. He was either the subject of conversation or in her thoughts all the time. Would he attend the gallery opening? It wasn't his kind of thing. Neither was it Ash's, but her brother had put on a suit coat and changed his date-night plans. For her.

Caleb would be there. He'd done more for her with less to gain. Showing his face here would be a step in the right direction to change Sweetwater's opinion of him and he was smart enough to figure that out on his own. Why was she so sure she knew how he thought? That was a question that needed an answer.

All day long she'd come out of a daydream to realize she'd been staring into space as she remembered the way Caleb had looked at her while they'd shared a sunny spot on Otter Lake, and how he'd thoroughly enjoyed his mother's cooking. Bright sunshine, easy laughter—that's where the romance had come from, not Caleb and his handsome face.

But that kiss.

That had been romance and straight from Caleb Callaway.

Winter waved a hand in front of her face. The heat from her cheeks wouldn't go anywhere but it was the only solution she had at this point.

Half a second too late, Winter realized her brother and Macy were observing her mini meltdown. "I better…" She pointed over her shoulder and turned away.

Winter took advantage of the bustle around the doorway to rest her forehead against the cool glass. Caleb was notorious for dating Nashville's most beautiful women. Wealthy daughters and ex-wives who were movers and shakers in the Callaway social circle, beauty-pageant winners and even country-music stars. He knew women. It made sense that his attention knocked her off balance.

The fact that it was working was so annoying.

"Are you all right?" Macy asked from over her shoulder, so Winter straightened. This kind of behavior is what provoked people to ask that kind of question, which she normally dreaded.

"Sure. You never had a doubt we'd make tonight happen, did you?" Winter asked with a bright smile. This was the Winter Kingfisher people expected, not one confused over feelings she should not have for a man.

"Never." Macy shook her head firmly. "So glad you aren't waiting tables, though. That, I had my doubts about." Laughing with Macy brought Winter back around. She was Winter Kingfisher. She wasn't great at everything, but this? This was her element.

The reminder came in due course.

Because the Knoxville Channel Six News van had pulled up in front of the window.

Bailey Garcia had arrived.

It was showtime.

CHAPTER TWELVE

STANDING OUTSIDE ON the sidewalk and staring in the window of Sweetwater Souvenir was a new experience, but the dread in the pit of his stomach was familiar. He'd experienced it in December, when he'd followed Ash and Winter Kingfisher all the way back to the Otter Lake ranger-station open house. He'd wanted to be there to watch Winter win the battle over the location for the lodge in front of the town of Sweetwater.

At the time, he hadn't noticed any of the changes he now spotted in the town.

Probably because his mind was locked in on Winter Kingfisher.

She'd convinced him to take the brunt of the report being made public, ended her engagement and her employment at the reserve in one day, and done it with power and passion, with one fierce shove.

For the first time he wondered what might

have happened if she'd taken her win less publicly.

Would she and Whit have worked out their issues for the good of…whatever it was between them? Whether the answer was yes or no, there was the possibility she'd still have her job. No one could represent the reserve better than Winter Kingfisher.

That public showdown with the Callaways had accomplished one big thing: Winter had become a hero in her hometown.

He could see the admiration on the faces of everyone inside the new gallery.

Even kindly small-town people who depended on the reserve for their jobs took it personally when the rich jerk had pushed his way through, hurt one of their own. And the cold shoulders they could give to outsiders were the coldest. He should know. He could count on one hand the number of neighbors he'd managed to win over in his time in Sweetwater. Odella. Janet Abernathy. It was a short list.

But here he was, about to wade into the waters.

Because Winter had asked him to.

Caleb shoved his hands in his jeans and

wondered if he should have changed clothes. Again.

He had dropped the jeans he'd worn to the construction site in the dirty clothes hamper Janet had disguised inside the upscale bathroom on his way to the shower. These jeans were black.

"Dress jeans," Caleb muttered. He should walk back to his SUV and pull out the trusty silk tie. Then, through the window, he caught sight of Ash Kingfisher. He was bent low to hear whatever it was Odella was saying. That was a conversation he could walk up to and expect a reasonable, lukewarm welcome, anyway.

Odella didn't do anything she didn't want to. If he had nothing clever to contribute, she'd leave him standing alone in the center of a crowd.

But if anyone should greet him warmly, it would be the guy whose job he'd saved.

Except he was half a second from kissing the guy's sister.

Again.

No, you aren't. Seriously bad idea. Forget the hike and the dinner and the way she shines when she's talking about anything she loves.

"And stop staring in the window like the kid who didn't get an invitation to the party. You got invited." Caleb put his hand on the door and shoved it open. The familiar bells rang and a petite blonde he hadn't been introduced to popped her head above the counter. She disappeared again before he could figure out whether to acknowledge her hiding place.

"Callaway, haven't seen you in some time." Ash Kingfisher held out his hand, since Odella had moved on. Ash passed a cup of something punch-like, Caleb took it and lifted it to his dry mouth gratefully.

The grimace must have given his feelings away. "Yeah, it's been what? Three hours?"

"Be careful, that stuff is sweet. That's how you know Winter was in charge of the punch." Ash shook his head. "Can't explain it, but she'll put in twice the sugar and half the salt of any recipe she attempts. What I'm saying is, don't eat dinner at Winter's house."

Since it was easy to imagine laughing over a takeout pizza, Caleb nodded and gave a strangled laugh. Between his brother and hers, he'd be better off hiding behind the counter with the blonde.

"I promised Winter I'd stop by and view some artwork. With my checkbook. Here I am." Caleb closed his eyes and wondered if he sounded as out of it as he felt. It was a reasonable explanation.

If only Ash had *asked* for an explanation.

Ash Kingfisher's confused frown made perfect sense. "Uh-huh. I'm not sure I remember that."

Right. Caleb cleared his throat. "Glad you could stop by the site this morning. I'm pleased with the progress."

Ash nodded. "Me, too, and that you cleaned up the trash that was building last week."

"Sure." Caleb gritted his teeth. The suggestion that he'd let something go he shouldn't have rankled him. "I like sites to be neat."

"Sure." Ash stared over the crowd. Caleb wondered if they were done with the conversation. Since Ash Kingfisher was the quiet type, he wouldn't do much heavy lifting with small talk. Still, it was better to stand next to him to look like he had a friend. How sad.

"But in a place like this, we can't have that trash blowing away." Ash turned to him. "We've got conservation efforts going on down at the lake, up at The Aerie. That plastic blows into the water, and the otters get ahold of it, and we have a problem." Ash nodded. "See?"

He did. And he appreciated the clarification. "Got it. We're here to protect the land. Better, more consistent refuse cleanup will be in effect, Ranger Kingfisher."

The muscle in Ash's jaw clenched. "Might as well call me Ash, Callaway. I have a gut feeling this isn't going to be short-term relationship."

"Fine. Then I'm Caleb." What did Ash mean? Was he brave enough to ask?

"Want to know how many people, man or woman, my sister has invited over to be subjected to dinner at my parents'? Just two. Whit, which was never a success. Not with my mother, anyway." Ash held up one finger. "And you. Don't know what that means yet, but I know what it meant when I did it." Their eyes met for a split second before Ash returned to staring into the gallery and Caleb glanced back at the cash register, where the blonde was pacing.

His experience at the Kingfisher house had been fun, but apparently it was rare. The Kingfishers were hard to impress, but Winter had invited him in. Ash's one invitation had to be Macy, since she was glued to his side now.

But Winter had done it as an efficient way to get their plan for a media day underway, nothing more. Right? Caleb wasn't convinced, but the pleasure he felt at being one of the few in the Kingfisher inner circle made him smile.

"You see who Winter's talking to?" Ash pointed with his cup. "Bailey Garcia. Your brother would have elbowed his way up to the front of the room to make sure he got in some camera time." Ash's eyes were assessing when he turned back to Caleb. "What are *you* going to do?"

Good question. What was he going to do? From where he stood, he couldn't hear anything of what Winter was saying, but she'd given him her promise. The way she was motioning at a truly spectacular painting behind them convinced him that she was doing her best to sell the artist, the work and the gallery.

Had she taken her notoriety and intended to use it for the gallery's publicity?

Of course she had. She was that clever.

That didn't mean she was also using her time to trash the Callaway family.

"If Winter asks me for something, I'll do my best to make it happen. Simple as that." He wasn't sure what else he could say. He was ready to be rescued. Caleb checked on the blonde again. She'd rounded the counter, but both hands were tightly clasped under her chin. Was she praying? "Winter and I know where we stand."

"And where is that?" Ash drawled. "You don't act like a man who is passing through town, not around my sister. A normal guy, presented with the potential to show up at the family dinner or attend a new business opening in a place he's only visiting, would probably make some excuses. But here you are."

"We're..." Caleb sighed. Wouldn't he like to know the answer to that himself? Telling her brother that she was the first woman in a long time to make him stutter and sweat seemed like a bad idea. He refused to even think about the kiss, just in case Ash Kingfisher had any psychic ability. He and the Kingfishers were getting along. He had a feeling that might change if they knew, rather than suspected, that he and Winter had turned a weird corner into...something. "Business colleagues."

"Business. Colleagues." Ash didn't believe

him. It wasn't a great answer. There was no hint of satisfaction or relaxation in the man's face, but Caleb figured Ash wasn't willing to escalate the conversation in the middle of the party. When Macy stepped away and crooked her finger at Ash Kingfisher, he didn't even hesitate but sliced through the crowd. Whatever her question was, Ash pointed with his thumb over his shoulder.

"That's about me," the blonde said and vibrated with nervous energy. "This is when I miss alcohol the most. When I needed to be brave, it never let me down."

"Want me to get you out of here?" Caleb wasn't sure who she was or what her story might be, but terror was easy to read on her face. "I'm Caleb Callaway. We weren't introduced the first time we met."

"I wasn't sure you even saw me. Your eyes were locked on Winter. Your *business colleague*." Her dry tone was impossible to ignore. She managed to look up in his face. "I know who you are. We all know who you are." She offered him her hand and watched closely to see what he would do. "Leanne Hendrix, one of the few people in town who knows how rough it can be when people can identify you but aren't sure whether they like you or not."

Caleb shook her hand carefully, afraid too much pressure might shatter her in a million pieces, and said, "The artist. Right?"

Her eyebrows shot up and her expression transformed from terror to confusion and stayed stuck there. What had he said?

Then she nodded slowly. "The artist. That's my painting."

She moved forward one step. "I'm proud of it, and I haven't had a lot of things to say that about. My kids. That's it. But I do love that painting."

"You should. It's amazing. You're talented." He watched her straighten. Caleb realized everyone in the crowd had craned their necks to check out the back of the room. Where he was standing. Talking to the artist. "You're on. I heard you're going to be interviewed. Are you ready?"

She gulped. "No." Then she straightened her shoulders and marched to join Winter in front of the camera.

From his spot on the edge of the crowd, he watched as Winter seamlessly transitioned whatever she had been saying to an introduction of Leanne Hendrix and wondered how she'd developed that skill. It was part of what made her so good at her job—the ability to roll with new developments. He admired it.

"So, Winter tells me you're about to make us an offer we can't refuse. Got your painting picked out yet? The big one, the one she's standing in front of, sure would be pretty over your fireplace," Janet Abernathy whispered from her spot next to him. When she'd landed there, he had no idea. "That Winter, she's magnetic. Can't take your eyes off her, can you?"

Was she asking in a general way or him specifically?

"You ever meet her parents? Dad's an artist. You're going to want some of his baskets, too. Let me introduce you."

Before Caleb could confess he knew Winter's parents, Janet was towing him across the room by one sleeve pinched between bright red fingernails.

But at least he wasn't standing alone anymore.

And no one in the crowd was glaring at him.

This would be fine, after all.

"LEANNE IS A lifelong Sweetwater resident, but she's only recently discovered her natural talent for capturing the beauty of the mountains here." Winter gave her favorite polished smile. "Anyone who spends the day on Otter Lake or the trails of the Smoky Valley Nature Reserve will need to stop by Sweetwater Souvenir and Art to find the perfect keepsake to remind them of the day."

Bailey Garcia's expression had transitioned quickly from confusion to irritation to…cold displeasure. At some point, she'd realized that Winter had agreed to the interview she'd been requesting for weeks for her own reasons, but Winter had never promised to answer the questions Bailey wanted to ask. That was a PR tactic she'd picked up in the early days at her first job out of college. Working for an electric company had never been a dream, but in terms of controlling bad press, it had been a graduate course in public relations.

"On that note, I'll send it back to you in the studio, Harry." Bailey paused for a long moment while Winter braced herself. As soon as she could, Bailey thrust the microphone she was holding to her producer and turned on Winter. "What was that, Winter?

We had a professional relationship here. Pulling a bait and switch like that? It's the easiest way to build a bad name for yourself." Bailey crossed her arms over her chest, as if she was prepared to wait for an answer.

Leanne's arm brushed Winter's and she was reminded that the world around them hadn't stopped. She patted Leanne's back. "You did so well. Enjoy the party. That has to be easier than having a camera pointed at you." Since she hadn't seen Leanne speaking to any single person all night long, she had her doubts that it was, but she didn't need to be involved in this argument, either. When she saw Caleb's head over the crowd, she relaxed. He would help. A second before she waved to get his attention, he turned toward her.

As if he knew exactly where she was in the room and even that she needed him. Why did that send a warm shot of emotion through her?

It was nice not to be standing alone in front of the crowd, even if Caleb was halfway across the gallery. If she called him, he'd be there for her.

His dark eyes were assessing and then he nodded. When he was halfway through the crowd, Leanne surprised her. "I'll go talk to Caleb. I'll be fine."

She watched until Leanne met him in the crowd.

Then she realized who he'd been talking to: her parents.

Oh, boy.

"Is that Caleb Callaway over there with Ash?" Bailey Garcia asked, her voice a slow drawl that did not match the new alertness in her expression. It reminded Winter of how a napping bear might perk up and sound about half a second before it ate your face for having disturbed its winter hibernation. "And Macy Gentry, I see. Are those your parents?"

What did that matter? It was a small town. He had to run into all of them in a crowd this size. *Deflect the attention. Change the story.*

"He's staying in Sweetwater while he oversees construction on the lodge." Winter moved both hands behind her back. She was about to start gesturing. Almost everyone who addressed the media had a tell—something that betrayed nerves. Her hands were her weakness. She would start pointing and motioning dramatically in order to convince Bailey that everything was exactly as she said. "But you already knew that."

Of course she did. She'd interrupted work at the site. "How about this? I'll give you a recorded interview. We can talk about the lodge project. It's moving quickly." And she would sing Callaway praises.

"Are you also prepared to tell me why Caleb Callaway is doing your bidding? You were asking for his help, right? Across the room?" Bailey stared over the crowd at Caleb. "And he responded almost like a boyfriend might. Are you two dating?" Breathless excitement was the worst setting on a news reporter.

"Of course not. My history with the Callaway family is…rocky enough." This was where it got tricky. Caleb had asked her to speak well of Whit. What he didn't understand was that Bailey would keep coming until she discovered something else to dramatize.

"Caleb and I have discussed the lodge several times. He is here tonight because I suggested a visit to see more of what Sweetwater has to offer. This town owes a lot to the Callaways, so it's good to have a strong relationship with everyone in the family. This gallery is a huge new opportunity for this town and the area. I believe that he, in particular, and the other Callaways in general are recommitted to the protection of the land and history of the reserve. I'll be happy to say that again on camera. That's a great sound bite."

"Sure, because everyone loves it when a juicy feud ends with adult behavior and calm consideration." Bailey sniffed. They both knew that wouldn't entice viewers to tune in.

A story about Winter Kingfisher switching Callaway brothers? Ratings bonanza.

"Well, that's the story we have." Winter tangled her fingers together into a tight knot. When Bailey's eyes dropped to her hands, Winter had the sinking feeling that this reporter had done a close enough study to know her weaknesses.

Meeting Bailey's suspicious stare wasn't easy, but this was the part where training paid off. Any second, she'd get frustrated and leave.

"You don't mind if I hang around. We'll get a few crowd shots to show in the package that we put online." Bailey smiled slowly.

Almost as if she knew Winter was counting the seconds until she left.

"Please do. Have some punch. I made it myself." Winter did her best spokesmodel hand wave toward the refreshment table.

"And when you're ready to buy some of Sweetwater's finest art, let me know. I'm working on commission here." Her hearty laugh was fake, fake, fake. And everyone had to know it, but she needed a few minutes to catch her breath.

Then she'd have to rescue Caleb from her father's enthusiasm and warn him to be careful around the reporter. The Callaways wanted to squash the news. A hint of something between the two of them would pour gas on the flames and build a fire it would take years to put out.

Determined to pretend that everything was fine, Winter worked the room on her way over to the display she and Leanne had built of her father's baskets. While she wouldn't call the firefighting group of park rangers close friends, it was nice to see several of them and their significant others, as well as the law-enforcement rangers scattered throughout the room. Christina and Brett Hendrix were bundled together in one of the quieter corners of the room. Were they talking? Winter studied them more closely. It seemed they were only staring at each other and happy to do so.

Reminded of Christina's teasing at their

first girls' night out, Winter considered barging in between them. Getting even would be fun.

Sadly, she decided to do her duty and went to join her parents.

"If you're of a mind to offer classes, you know, fun activities at the lodge, birdwatching or nature photography, I'd be happy to throw my name into the ring for consideration. I know my way around the park." Martin Kingfisher shoved his hands nonchalantly in the pockets of his dress slacks. "Or there's always my basket-weaving class. It's calming. Therapeutic. I could include history, tell stories about my mother and hers. My grandmother made her own dyes, but I haven't gotten the hang of it. The trick seems to be—"

"What's the completion date for the lodge?" her mother interjected as she wrapped her hand around her husband's arm. Her teasing look and his chastened-but-amused one were so familiar, but it was sweet to be reminded that, in a world where things fell apart easily and often, her parents had been solid for forty years. One short sweet wedding in front of Yanu Falls was all it had taken. Her dad talked too much. Her mother loved him for it but did her best to be sure others loved him, too. "Why didn't we talk about this over tacos? We must have been preoccupied with other matters."

Winter quickly checked to see who might be close enough to hear, but the news crew was close to the door.

"No later than July first. The Callaways are planning a big Independence Day picnic to celebrate the grand opening." Caleb met Winter's stare. He didn't smile, but something about his expression reminded her of the way her father looked at her mother.

Like they might be able to guess what the other was thinking if they spent forty years exchanging similar glances.

"No fireworks." Ash shook his head slowly, his lips a tight line. "Fire hazard."

That wouldn't go over well with the Callaways, who always went with bigger, better and louder for their party aesthetic.

Whatever his first answer was, Caleb changed his mind and held up both hands in surrender. "Nothing goes forward without the okay of the head ranger. Speeches and tours, food of some kind. My mother is in charge of the party. I'll tell my father to cross off anything requiring lit matches."

"Indeed, and since construction is notorious for overruns of money and time, you might tell 'em to be considering a Labor Day celebration. Thanksgiving." The twinkle in her mother's eyes convinced Winter to stand down. She'd been prepared to argue on Caleb's behalf. He was working hard to meet the schedule. The evidence was there in the fatigue around his eyes.

Callaways never had been ones to dodge difficult jobs, even if her mother didn't quite approve of the rest of the family's ideals.

"I have my orders, Mrs. Kingfisher. Whit Callaway, Sr., will have my butt if I allow this project to run long." Caleb shifted back. "It got off to a slow start. That's why I'm here. My stepfather wanted someone committed to meeting the timeline and goals of the project here in town."

Her mother softened. "I get that. Some things are so important we only trust the people we really care about to handle them. The stuff that matters requires the best of the best. Your stepfather must have a lot of faith in you. We know this lodge matters. At least enough to go to political war over."

Caleb frowned as he listened. It was too bad they hadn't spent more time with nonverbal communication. Winter wanted to know what that frown meant.

"Caleb's been busy sourcing local, sustainable, green products, Mama. That's what he did with his company. This is going to be a lodge that Sweetwater can be proud of." Winter wasn't sure why she said it, except that she remembered other occasions when she was the only Kingfisher in a crowd of Callaways. Caleb, when he'd managed to show up, had been an ally.

He'd also sat shoulder-to-shoulder with her at her mother's picnic table, ready to defend her if the heat got to be too much. Winter battled the desire to slip her hand into his. In this crowd, such a gesture would send a whispered report around in an instant, alerting everyone, even her family, to the... whatever it was between them. Instead, Winter knotted her hands together tightly at her waist.

"Funny how sons in the same family can be so different." Her mother pursed her lips. "Man who wears those boots to an art gallery is showing people who he is, I guess. I appreciate that, almost as much as you clearing out my leftovers, Caleb."

Caleb squared off face-to-face with her

mother. "Thank you. Whit has made some mistakes. I have, too. He's got a good heart. He'll do the right thing."

Her mother's eyes narrowed and she nodded. "Fine. I accept that. Good people make bad decisions. Handling the consequences, though, that's where the real story lies."

Caleb's eyes met Winter's. He'd saved her from some consequences. Was he reminding her of that?

"Well, now that the serious portion of our evening is over, Martin, why don't you tell us how you create these baskets? Everybody, hit up the refreshments table. This is supposed to be a party. If the cops don't roll up with noise complaints soon, I'll know it's a pure failure." Janet Abernathy clapped her hands, and the frozen crowd resumed mingling.

Winter saw the news crew gathered around the door and realized they'd had more of an audience than she expected. Getting Bailey Garcia's agreement not to run any footage of that conversation would be next to impossible, but she should give it a try. Nothing terrible had been said about either Kingfishers or Callaways, but all the heat would come down on Caleb.

And the whole night had been a reminder

that he was dealing with fallout that he shouldn't have to.

He was doing it for her.

Winter tugged his sleeve, gratified when he instantly turned toward her. "Come help me with something in the storage room." She motioned with her head before turning, certain he'd follow.

Before they cleared the crowd, Bailey Garcia cupped her hands over her mouth. "Caleb, have you got a second? I'd love to get a quote." The crowd silently parted and the red light on the camera glowed. Winter had the urge to stop this. Unplanned interviews always went terribly wrong, but Caleb was smart.

"Here you are again, Ms. Garcia, telling Sweetwater's stories." Caleb's grin was handsome and slow, and it would convince any woman it was special and only for her. "I don't see any purchases. Surely you can't leave without making at least one." He covered his heart with his hand. "There's real talent here."

Bailey Garcia held out a microphone. "Mr. Callaway, I'm surprised to find you out and about in the town of Sweetwater. I've heard from some of your cronies you weren't too happy about this assignment."

"If that's true, I'd guess you heard it from someone I haven't talked to in a while. All work and no play makes a man say dumb things. What's not to love about this place? All I needed was a minute to appreciate it. Every visitor to the new lodge will find the same peace I have. This is important work and I'm happy to do it."

Winter believed he meant every word. If he was lying, he was doing it very well.

The reporter raised her eyebrows. "So the Callaways and Kingfishers seem…close."

This was the whole thrust of her questioning. Before Winter could step in to deflect, Caleb drawled, "Well, we have some common ground. Both families are proud of the Smoky Valley Nature Reserve."

That was a good answer.

"What about Winter telling me Whit's new girlfriend, Candace Hawthorne, was nothing more than a political stunt?" Bailey asked. "That sound like bygones are bygones to you?"

The urge to protest was strong, but Caleb stepped up again. "Honestly, after the way she told my brother the engagement was off, complete with a big splash of water on a cold night, I'll call that progress." He held out both hands. "Please, tour the gallery. Find something you love. You'll be getting a press release about upcoming media days where we will make the lodge building site open to the media and we'll answer all your questions about the project there."

Caleb turned his back and Winter had to admit it was a strong message. There was no way the delicate reporter was going to budge him from his spot. Winter was relieved until Bailey Garcia asked, "One last question. Are all the Callaways comfortable with how close Winter is with the governor?" Bailey smiled brightly. "The footage of her leaving the capitol a little over a week ago impressed me. She almost looked like a woman with the inside track to Richard Duncan."

Before Caleb could answer, Winter stepped forward. "Call me tomorrow, Bailey. I'll be happy to explain why the governor and I were discussing his education platform. It's not right for Tennessee, and I have high hopes the conversation might have swayed his thinking."

For a split second, she and Bailey were frozen in the center of the crowd. Was the reporter going to accept that? The news crew left while Winter was wracking her brain to come up with a way to smooth things over. Nothing came to mind, so whatever story broke, Winter would find a way to spin it. That was what she did and she was good at it.

If it was about a relationship between her and Caleb Callaway...

Well, she wasn't sure what she'd do, except hold on for another wild ride.

When the conversation in the room resumed, thanks to her father's loud question about who wanted to hear a story, Winter towed Caleb into the storage room and closed the door.

"It was a job interview. I got the offer. I didn't take it because Richard Duncan is nothing but a cautionary tale of how politics have gone badly wrong because of some. Believe me or don't, that's what happened." Winter crossed her arms tightly in front of her. "That's not what I wanted to talk to you about, though."

Caleb studied her face. "It was before the truce, right? Water under the bridge. What did you want to say?" His eyes weren't the clear green she expected when he was happy, but he seemed to be giving her the benefit of the doubt.

"Thank you." She shrugged. "That's it. That's as far as I thought it through. Thank you for helping me when you didn't have to and for coming to Sweetwater to build this lodge that will mean so much and for being patient with my hurt and anger and for coming tonight to support this gallery and town and for answering Bailey Garcia with a grace she probably wasn't expecting and I didn't deserve and for…everything. Thank you. I've been carrying around this guilt for dragging you into this, and…" She stuttered to a stop and smiled. "I'm glad you're here. That's all."

Caleb's lips twitched as he straightened. "That's a lot."

Winter nodded. "Oh, and one more thing…" Before she lost her nerve, she stretched up to press a kiss against his lips. The feel of his shoulders under her hands and the grip of his fingers on her hips were more than she imagined, so sweet. Right. As if she'd found the place she belonged.

When she stepped back, his eyes opened slowly. "You're welcome."

Winter laughed.

"I don't know what else to say. My brain is stuck in a celebration loop." Caleb pulled her tight against his chest.

"Then it's a good time to go shopping. Buy some art. Make sure you tell Janet that any commission goes to me. I've got to prove my worth here or I'll be twice unemployed." Winter grinned up at him, completely unconcerned about what came next for her.

For tonight, there was Sweetwater and her family and her friends and this gallery.

All her problems could wait until the sun came up again.

CHAPTER THIRTEEN

AT SOME POINT, the half smile that had been appearing now and then, ever since the gallery opening, would stop surprising him. Enthusiasm for the day made it easy to jump out of bed Monday morning before the sun came up. He drove into town to make his now-usual stop to see Odella. The first warning he had that something had changed was her solemn expression.

"Mornin', Caleb," she said as she handed him his two-slice to-go bag. "Sure was surprised to hear the news last night. Hope your mama has some good doctors. Nowadays, medicine works wonders, I hear."

Caleb slowly took the cup of coffee and slid a twenty across the counter. Since he had no idea what Odella knew or didn't know, he murmured, "Thanks, Odella, keep the change." He turned to leave and noticed everyone in the coffee shop watching him. He'd adjusted to being the center of attention, but there was something different about these stares. Instead of curious or suspicious, the expressions were somber, concerned.

When he made it back to the truck, his phone rang. "Hello?"

"Guess you heard the news. Headlines in at least four different newspapers about your mother's illness." Senior's voice was gravelly, as if he'd been talking for too long already and was running out of energy. "She's not doing well today. You need to come home. Get someone out at the site up to speed and come to Knoxville. We need to make some plans."

Caleb had too many questions to ask and not enough time. "Fine. Let me talk to Carlos, make sure he's got the work orders straight, and I'll be there as soon as I can." Caleb coughed. "How bad is it?"

The tense pause had him worried, but Senior said, "It's nothing we can't handle, son. Come home."

Caleb ended the call and rested his head for a second. Both crews were going to be working on the lodge, completing the framing for interior walls and running wiring and plumbing as each section was completed. It was a terrible day to miss because all the moving pieces had to come together. That was Caleb's talent.

Senior never skipped work. To call Caleb home meant he considered the situation there to be critical.

And then Caleb realized how the story must have gotten out.

Winter and Bailey Garcia and all those phone calls.

The interview that Caleb missed while he was chatting up Ash and Leanne Hendrix.

He'd assumed he and Winter had reached an agreement, but obviously he'd been wrong.

Winter had been biding her time to use her knowledge for her own benefit.

He didn't have time to confront her, but her old station wagon was parked in front of Sweetwater Souvenir. Before he knew what he was doing, Caleb was out of the truck and stalking across the street. When he nearly flattened his nose on the glass because the locked door didn't swing open, he forced himself to stop.

"Take a minute. No one should be surprised here. She's been pushing all along." Caleb braced his hands on his hips and studied the cracks on the sidewalk in front of the large plate-glass window.

Then the bells inside the shop rang. The door opened and Winter Kingfisher was framed in the doorway, as pretty and everything as she had been every single time he'd faced off against her.

Except this time, she'd hurt him in the only way that remained.

"What did you do?" he asked.

Her eyebrows shot up, the surprise almost believable. "What do you mean?"

"How could you have leaked this story of my mother's illness to your friends in the media?" He squeezed his eyes shut as something clenched hard in his chest. "You and I understood each other."

Anger, he could have handled. If she'd come back at him, eyes blazing and anger on her lips, he would have been fine. Instead, she wrapped her hand around his arm and squeezed. "I didn't. I wouldn't. I couldn't hurt your mother. She's always been kind to me. Tell me what's going on, Caleb."

"You don't know?" He huffed out a breath. "How is it that connected Winter Kingfisher, the one who knows all the people there are to know to help the reserve, is out of the news loop?"

She held out both hands. "I've stopped

scouring the news sites all day long for any mention of Whit Callaway to get over this. That's how I don't know what's going on. It's also how I'm moving on with my life, and for a minute there, I was happy to be doing so in a place where my path crossed yours, but I'm starting to have my doubts." Winter propped her hands on her hips. "What is your problem this morning, Caleb Callaway? You went from kiss to kill awful quick."

Caleb stepped back, unprepared for her to turn and go on the offense.

"It was one phone call. That's all it took. This morning on the drive in, I had a stupid smile on my face thinking how I might set up some run-in with Winter Kingfisher." Caleb pointed at Smoky Joe's. "Then my father called me home. Because the news of my mother's illness is hitting the front pages. She's upset. And this lodge, the one I've been killing myself to get built at his direction, is suddenly less important. If you don't understand what that means by now…" Caleb stopped. He couldn't put it into words.

Winter ducked her head. "Okay. I get you're mad and upset, but this is not me, Caleb. I didn't. I wouldn't. Why would I hurt her that way? Besides, I made you a promise that I was done coming after Whit. I trusted you when you gave me your word. You can't do the same for me?"

He wanted to, but it was impossible to forget how fiery she'd been the first time she'd stormed his office or how she'd talked about how Whit had let her down. Then there was her meeting with Richard Duncan. "What if it was the only way to get your career on track?" Caleb braced himself. He didn't want to go there, but he needed the truth. "Did you trade my mother's secret to get that job offer from the governor, Winter?"

Her jaw dropped. "I met with him the day before you told me about Marjorie's diagnosis, not after. And are you saying there's no possible way I could get it otherwise? I mean, my education, graduating at the top of the class and my experience in handling all the communication needs for the reserve, or even my ability to move inside all kinds of crowds along with his number one challenger. None of that would work, but the ability to whisper about your mother's diagnosis will open those doors right up." Her lips were so tight that her smile was almost a threat.

"It wouldn't be the first time you let a whispered secret do your dirty work for you."

Her gasp almost cut him off at the knees. He was mad enough to fight dirty, so he should go. Leave before he did something he'd regret forever. "I've got to get to Knoxville." Why wasn't it easier to leave her?

Because this was all wrong between them, but he couldn't spend the time to make it right.

"Richard Duncan is every bit the kind of man you think he is. I have no doubt he'd love inside dirt, Caleb, but I'm not who you think I am." Winter had followed him to the curb. She wasn't yelling but her voice carried. The coffee-shop crowd was glued to the window. "The next time you see me, you're going to apologize."

The hurt over her betrayal was too much. Time. Distance. Room to cool off. That's what he needed.

Caleb hustled to his truck and sped out to the job site, while he evaluated his choices on who to leave in charge. Ken Lowell had proven ineffective against Bailey Garcia, but surely he could handle twenty-four hours in charge. Reporters would likely wait for the media day to descend on the work site.

The media day.

The one Winter Kingfisher and her brother were planning.

Was that going to be a disaster, too?

Caleb was exhausted by worry when he got out of his truck. Both crews were working on the lodge in an effort to complete all the framing so the electrical and plumbing guys could start. By the time he had reporters at his site, he wanted people to be shocked at what he'd accomplished.

He wanted both Whitney Callaways to be impressed.

Caleb called loud enough that both Carlos and Ken heard and trotted over. He studied them. "I've got to go to Knoxville. Personal reason. I hope to be back tomorrow. Which one of you can do the job better than I can?" He'd never believe the answer, but the confidence to tackle the job was all he had to go on.

Carlos kicked a rock as he considered the question. "Not sure anyone can do it better, boss, but I'll keep us going until you get back." He met Caleb's stare head-on. "Scratch that. *We* will. It'll take us both. He'll focus on the trades. I'll make sure framing stays on schedule."

Ken nodded. "We got it, boss."

It was better than any solution Caleb had devised so he held out his hand. When they each shook it, he turned to go. "Call me if a crisis comes up."

They both waved and he was soon bumping back down the gravel access road to the pavement. As soon as all four tires were on asphalt, he hit the gas. On a normal, sunny day, the trip into Knoxville was an easy thirty minutes. He'd cross his fingers and hope all the law-enforcement rangers and state police were otherwise engaged.

Twenty minutes was his goal, and the work truck shuddered to a stop three minutes over that.

In a second, Caleb was knocking on the front door, hoping his mother might open it, her normal smile on her face. Instead, a maid he didn't recognize answered. "Yes, sir? How may I help you?"

The urge to move her out of the way with a firm arm was strong, but Caleb gripped his manners tightly. "I'm Caleb Callaway, here to see my parents."

Instead of hurrying him on his way, she dipped her head. Her lack of urgency... Was it a sign that things were not as grim as he'd feared? "Of course, sir. I'm Patrice, your mother's new nurse. They're in the library. Would you like me to show you the way?"

Caleb paused midstep to study her face. Was she joking? "Uh, no, I know the way." Her serene acknowledgment had him shaking his head as he trotted down the hall. Half a second before he shoved the door open, he noticed the clumps of dirt falling off his boots with every step. His mother would not like that.

Then the door was open. Senior and his mother were sitting on the couch, which had been moved to take full advantage of the sunshine pouring through one of the windows.

And Whit was nowhere in sight.

"Cal, come in." Senior didn't get up from his spot on the couch but pointed at the seat next to it. His mother straightened from leaning against his shoulder and patted the arm of the chair. From Caleb's spot in the doorway, he couldn't see any distress on her face. Instead, she seemed…happy. Truly content.

"What's going on? I broke speed laws and good judgment to shave seven minutes off the drive because you had me scared." Caleb dropped down in the leather armchair and tried to be grateful none of the dire possibilities he'd imagined were playing out in real time. "I left your precious lodge in the hands of foremen I'm not sure should be allowed to handle power tools." Not true but it fit his black mood. He deserved some answers. "Instead of waiting on Whit to appear, tell me what's going on right now."

"I told you, you should have explained on the phone call," his mother drawled and narrowed her eyes at her husband. "What if he'd been hurt because of the rush?"

Senior cleared his throat. "He wasn't. You know he doesn't listen under normal circumstances."

Caleb fought the urge to slap his hand on the armchair. "Listen, I thought we had a crisis. Somebody start talking. For once, just once in this family, let's lay all the cards out. What's going on?"

"Watch your tone, young man. There's a... *situation*," his mother said sweetly, "but we have a plan in place to handle it."

"Either I've been working too long and my brain is fried or you're being deliberately impossible to follow," Caleb said. "Talk or I'm loading up and heading for Nashville. There I will sleep for a solid week before scrambling to put my own business back together. I put it on hold for this, remember?"

Would he be able to carry through on the threat now that he was falling for the lodge and Otter Lake more every day?

If he had to. He'd learned he could do anything if the incentive was strong enough.

"Fine. Good idea." Senior leaned forward. "Whit isn't coming, anyway. He's on his way to Sweetwater to deal with Winter Kingfisher."

Caleb mirrored him, and was half a second from running back to the truck. "Handling" Winter Kingfisher was no job for Whit. One or both of them would get hurt. "What does that mean? Handling? I talked to her before I left town. She swears she's not the person behind this story." Did he believe her? Why couldn't he decide how to answer that question? There'd been no lie in her eyes or her voice, but it made too much sense.

"She's not the person behind this story, but I took a page from her book," his mother said, looking relieved. "Your stepfather does not listen to logic or reason on some things. I am one of those things." She smiled over at Senior, who had crossed his arms over his chest. "We've done things his way for long enough. Now, we're going to try it my way. No more hiding or pretending. The Callaway family is going to be open and honest, with each other, and with the voters and neighbors of Tennessee. Life is too short for all this strategizing. My way will eliminate all that running in place."

Caleb leaned back, speechless. What was there to say? Everything she said was true, but what did "her way" look like?

"I want Whit to run the campaign he wants, not what he thinks will win. I want to get out of this house. I want to see the lodge you're building. The Callaway Foundation? I want to investigate the school projects we're funding. And if I'm going to die, I want to truly appreciate every moment until then." She gripped Caleb's hand. "So, when a news reporter called to ask about my absence at the latest Foundation meeting, as if maybe there was some juicy news there, I told the truth. No more hiding. No secret maneuvers, not anymore. Nothing has changed with my diagnosis. The treatments are easy so far and I feel like myself, and while I do, I'm going to live my life. Senior is going to retire and help me do that." She shook her head. "I wanted you here today because if I let him put this off, he'll never make good on his promises to me. He loves Callaway Construction and politics and pulling the strings too much."

"Not as much as I love you. Everything I do is for you. You know that," Senior said. His gruff voice had a different tone than normal. And Caleb believed every word he was saying. "She outflanked me, Cal. Your mother zigged while I was watching for a zag, told that reporter everything and basically changed everything." His disgruntled frown transformed into a goofy grin as his mother waggled her eyebrows.

"I've still got it. You retire. Let me take the lead for a bit." His mother patted Senior's hand cheerfully.

"Retire. So what does that mean?" *Why am I here?* That was what he wanted to understand.

"Callaway Construction. I'm stepping down." Senior met his stare. "All my life, I've intended to hand it off to my boys. Now's the time. Your mother saw to that."

Caleb studied the dark red pattern on the rug under his dirty boots. "What does *that* mean? And where is Whit?" A bolt hit him. "You pulled me out of Sweetwater because Whit's going to take over the lodge project?" Emotion hit before he could see it coming and he was up and out of the chair. "I've put in time. That's my project!"

Senior blinked and faced his mom. "You were right."

"Of course I was. All he needed was the open door." She crossed her leg slowly. "If any of you had listened to me six months ago, a year ago, we'd all be much happier at this point."

Caleb bit his lip to prevent an angry interruption, but he could feel the tension in his jaw.

"Whit has his political career. He'll continue to serve on the boards, but you will run Callaway Construction. It's all yours. We have contracts in place that will have to be completed, but after that, you determine the direction of the company." Senior's lip curled up. "Take your ideas for Summit and make them all bigger because Callaway Construction can handle it. We have crews ready to go."

The possibilities that immediately opened in front of him made his knees weak. Caleb collapsed in the armchair again while he considered what that would mean to his life.

"From Knoxville? That's where you want this to stay, right?"

Senior's eyes narrowed. "It's yours, Cal. Knoxville or Nashville." He shrugged. "You could run it out of Sweetwater if you wanted to. With the right crews in place, you could do that. Callaway has some experienced project managers, but how big or small, whether you oversee every project or only what you want to, that's all up to you." Senior wrapped his hand around his wife's. "There. I managed to say it. You thought I couldn't." The way they chuckled together made Caleb feel like an outsider looking in.

"The only thing I ask," his mother said softly, "is that you make a place for Whit if he ever wants it. Politics seems like a calling, but even men with missions get tired of the work. He could be an asset to the business, as well."

Of course he could. Whit could work a room of wealthy donors like a pro. Drumming up business contracts was only a small step from that.

"We're going to announce this and some other changes we want to make at the media day at the lodge. That's going to be the place where we do our celebrating from now on." Senior tipped up his chin. "That's where the Callaway family got its start. This lodge is going to be our future."

They were both watching him but he wasn't sure what to say.

"You don't want this, son?" his mother asked quietly.

Caleb wanted to pace. Sitting still with all the pride, worry and passion tumbling inside him was too hard. Finally, he said, "This is what I've wanted all along. I never thought I'd have it. I didn't measure up. As a Callaway."

The glare his mother gave Senior was impressive. The only other person he'd ever seen use her eyes like a weapon in the same way was Winter Kingfisher.

"It was always my plan. I should have made that clearer." Senior nodded. "I assumed you'd appreciate it more if you had to fight for it." He ran a hand over his forehead. "That's how my father did things. Obviously, we were both fools." He smiled at his wife's complacent nod.

And Caleb had to laugh. The chastised expression on Senior's face was cute. They were cute together. Seeing them like this, away from the formal dining room, reminded him of the Kingfishers' exchanged glances at the gallery. Someday, if he was lucky, there would be a woman who could see every one of his flaws, remind him of them with one cut of her eyes and make him better every day.

Then he realized what a mess he'd left in Sweetwater.

He should call Whit to warn him about his accusations that morning.

But every part of him rebelled at the idea of helping his brother win Winter back. She deserved more. They both did.

"You want to take a look at the projects we've got going, the proposals we have lined up?" Senior asked. "Sooner we start, the sooner your mother gets what she wants."

Caleb smiled as his mother exhaled loudly. "I have a doctor's appointment at three. Patrice will go with me." She held up a hand. "You two talk business, but don't let him convince you he's not ready for something new, Caleb. Last night he booked us hotel rooms in New Orleans. Apparently, we're going to start all this with the vacation he's been talking about for three years." His mother pressed kisses to both of their cheeks and left.

Senior covered his cheek with his hand. "Can't lie. She's right. I hope you'll…allow me to be involved, but this is what I've always wanted. Sooner than I expected, but what I wanted. We had to wait for you to be ready."

Caleb thought back to how he'd lived his life, dropping in and out of the Callaway unit whenever he pleased because he'd convinced himself no one minded. And they'd been waiting for him to settle.

"I don't want to quit the lodge, Senior." Caleb wasn't ready to let it go. Not yet. "How can I do what needs to be done from Sweetwater?"

Senior tilted his head back. "Grabbed a piece of your heart, has it? There's something in the air there." He didn't ask the question Caleb was most worried about. If Senior wanted to know if there was someone in Sweetwater, what would he say? How would the admission that Winter Kingfisher was the kind of woman he'd go to war over ruffle the new calm waters? And if Whit succeeded in winning her back, would he still pursue his own feelings for her?

No. Of course not. He'd admired her from afar. He could do that again.

"Got a list of all the projects and managers working them." Senior pointed at the computer on his desk. "Do so much remotely that you could be in Timbuktu as long as the internet worked. Sweetwater is easy enough."

Relieved at the open door Senior had left him, Caleb stood and moved behind the desk. "Let me see what you've got."

Working with Senior was easy enough when they were focused on the construction projects Callaway had scattered all over Tennessee. Small builds, like houses, and larger projects, including a school outside Chattanooga—each one of them was interesting. He needed to visit all of them as soon as possible.

"I'll be bringing my own crew in, promoting some of them to head up projects." Caleb waited for his stepfather's objections, but Senior nodded. "You'll need at least one more solid project lead to take over the lodge. Hope you've got someone in mind."

He did. As he paged through the spreadsheets outlining Callaway's work orders and timeline, the sensation of falling into the spot he'd been meant for was impossible to ignore.

Only one worry remained: what to do about Winter Kingfisher.

CHAPTER FOURTEEN

WINTER SPENT THE first hour after Caleb's surprise visit searching for news on her phone. Instead of helping Janet and Leanne with cleaning up the gallery or planning their next step, she hunkered down on a stool behind the cash register of Sweetwater Souvenir and hunted for details.

Every story she read and the single video she found, the one starring Bailey Garcia, of course, mentioned that Marjorie Callaway had sought treatment for a health issue. People were speculating that it was either cancer or dementia. Every source she read was the same until she hit the Sweetwater newspaper's online list of headlines. One of them was written by Marjorie Callaway herself.

"Brilliant. So smart." The bells rang over the door and Winter craned her neck to make sure someone else would help the retired couple who'd come in out of the cool March morning. Janet motioned over her shoulder with her thumb, a direct order for Winter to clear out, so Winter moved back to the gallery's storage room to read the short, heartfelt announcement that the Callaway family was facing a challenge that so many other Tennessee families were struggling with. There were facts about how Alzheimer's impacted communities, what treatments were available and what Marjorie was trying, and at the end, a piece of encouragement for anyone struggling with the same situation, those with the diagnosis and the ones who loved them, that they should live every single day.

"'Don't put off until tomorrow what you can do today. We don't have to hide in the shadows, no matter what the diagnosis is. We have to get busy living. Start your treatment, but don't wait for a cure to be happy.'" Winter read the first sentence of the last paragraph out loud. "'Forget chores or obligations or errands. Skip those. Dreams and the things you've put off to try when life is easier or better or whatever your reason, do those today.'" She put down her phone and covered her face with both hands. Marjorie was right. And instead of listening to Senior or whoever gave her advice, she'd taken Winter's words to heart and moved out front.

It was a brave maneuver. Smart. The Callaways had nothing to fear from their political or business rivals. The truth was out and they were going to go on living.

"What are you doing back here?" Janet asked. She and Leanne were blocking the doorway, concern wrinkling both of their brows. "This ain't like you, hon."

She was right. It was almost like Caleb had blown the old her into little pieces with his confrontation and then Marjorie had come along and squeezed those pieces to dust.

"Caleb was here and he was mad. He accused me of being behind this news story about his mother." She pointed at her phone. "Marjorie Callaway wrote her own story. No one could tell it better. That's expert-level public relations right there and she just..." Winter snapped her fingers. "I was the strategist running Whit's campaign and life, even though I had to work my way around Senior, but there was his mother, right there, waiting for a spotlight." Winter closed her eyes. "I want Caleb back here right now and I want to shove that story in his face and I want to demand an apology, and then I want to wrap my arms around his shoulders and squeeze him until he can't breathe because he needs someone to do that because his mother is awesome and this news is scary but there's still so much hope and..." Her shoulders slumped. "And I don't know what else."

When she managed to open her eyes again, both Leanne and Janet had moved closer, almost as if they wanted to hug her or comfort her but they weren't sure how.

"Since when does Caleb Callaway's opinion matter so much?" Leanne asked softly. The former baddest girl in town had taken a turn for the quiet and insightful and Winter wasn't sure how much she liked it. Her face must have been twisted into a disgruntled expression. "Sorry. My therapist is rubbing off on me. In a good way."

Janet chuckled at that and some of the overwhelming tension in the room evaporated.

"Caleb Callaway started to matter..." Winter replayed so many different times when she'd been impressed with Caleb. Out at Buckeye Cove, when he'd shared with her and made her smile even after she'd tried to leave him in the dust on the hike down. Over dinner with his crazy enjoyment of her mother's home cooking. The way he'd known she needed his help at the gallery opening. The kiss.

"He mattered from the first time I barged into his office and demanded he care about Otter Lake." Winter shoved a hank of hair behind her ear and realized how true it was. "If he'd hesitated, I wouldn't have been surprised. If he'd said no, it would have confirmed my suspicions. Instead, he said yes and he told me to reach for more. Ash's job was one thing. The whole adding him to the board of directors? That was all Caleb. If he hadn't taken credit for slipping the report to Richard Duncan, how much harder would this life be right now. His opinion started to matter right then and there. He did something good for me and never once expected to profit from it. Instead, he's had to put his own plans on hold." And she still felt the guilt over that.

Her shoulders slumped. She hadn't done what he accused her of, but she was still plenty at fault. Then she realized what she'd admitted to Janet and Leanne.

"So he didn't leak the report and save The Aerie?" Janet pursed his lips. "All along I've been giving that boy the benefit of the doubt because he'd done a good deed, and he didn't even do it?"

Winter began pacing. "He did more. I did that, released the report to protect The Aerie, but he protected me. And Ash. And made it possible for Ash to correct the problem, strengthen the reserve. Caleb did that. I didn't ask for that. He did that on his own."

"He's kind of annoying, the way he always manages to do the right thing when you least expect it." All of them turned to see Whit Callaway standing in the doorway.

They must have shared an angry, surprised expression because he held up both hands. "Sorry. I used the door. There were bells. No one heard them."

Janet covered her heart with both hands. "My superpower is on the fritz! I didn't even know there was a rich person in the vicinity, much less about to walk into the store."

Leanne laughed and shook her head. "You're tired. You need to rest. Come have a seat."

"No way. Not with this Callaway. He broke our girl's heart." Janet crossed her arms over her chest and moved to stand next to Winter. "He won't get another chance."

Winter appreciated the effort, but all of her

confusion and just…lostness had come down to this point. She needed to talk with Whit. "Janet, it's okay. My heart is safe enough."

Janet narrowed her eyes. "Well, you be careful, young man. Her heart might not be in any danger, but your neck is. Do you hear me?"

Whit nodded solemnly and moved aside as Leanne led Janet out of the storage room. Whit leaned a shoulder against the open doorway. "Can we talk here?"

Her first instinct was to demand to know what he wanted to talk about.

If this was another confrontation about his mother's story, Winter would not be caught off guard this time. Whit would be sorry. Someone would be forced to call the cops for his protection.

All of that must have crossed her face. Whit held up his hands. "All of that? That's not what I want to talk about. I have two things to say, then I'll leave."

Winter marched over to the stepstool she'd been using as a chair and sat. "How did you find me?" He'd be twice as shocked as Caleb had been when he saw what she was driving, so he hadn't spotted her car and dropped in.

"I went to your house. I hoped your dad

was there. He was not." Whit stepped inside and leaned against the wall. "These paintings are amazing. Caleb's working up some kind of commission with the artist for the lodge, isn't he?"

Winter blinked slowly. Not yet he wasn't, but he would be as soon as she whispered the suggestion in Janet's ear. Because that was inspired.

"Local artists. That fits with the Tennessee heritage he's going for." Whit studied the stacked canvases against the wall, almost as if he had the urge to flip through them.

And that was the reminder that she didn't need that they'd always been more alike than they were different.

"What did you want to talk about?" Winter asked. There was only way to get through this. Face it all directly. She'd tried the easy way out. That never worked for Kingfishers and it wouldn't start now, especially if the Callaways were changing tactics to face the truth head-on. The whole idea was exciting.

"First, an apology. I'll do it in public, too, since I'm the one who dragged this on the stage for everyone to observe, but between you and me, I'm sorry." His solemn face made it hard not to trust his words. "I messed up. I messed up first by shoving this project through. Senior's had this dream for a long time. I swear, most of the trouble in my life and with my brother goes right back to wanting to win Senior's admiration." He rubbed his forehead. "Caleb and I had it, but getting ol' stone face to show any emotion is just… Doesn't matter. That's what I'm trying to wrap my head around. I had reasons for what I did, but they still hurt you and I owe you more than an apology for that. You were my best friend in the world. And I made the worst mistakes." His lips were a tight line.

Since she'd never once imagined Whit Callaway, Jr. could say he was sorry, she knew it had to be a struggle.

"The marriage idea was dumb, Whit. Why did we try that again?" Winter asked.

He rolled his eyes. "The consultant. The one Senior hired when we first started talking about the capital. He wasn't worth half of what Senior paid, although I appreciate the investment. Happily married candidates, or at least those who can pretend to be, poll better with voters. Who cares what they say? As long as they look the part…" He gave two thumbs up. "Dumb. Like my 'stunt' with Candace Hawthorne."

Winter grimaced. "I had nothing to do with this story about your mother, but I did say 'stunt' to Bailey Garcia." Should she apologize for that? The urge was strong. As long as they were getting things off their chests, she should clear the air. "I was having a bad day."

He laughed. "It's okay, we both had our reasons, but I never thought you had anything to do with Mom's story. She showed me her final draft before she sent it to the Sweetwater newspaper. Senior was the only one who didn't know."

"And Caleb." Winter rubbed her hand over the center of her chest, amazed all over again at how the memory of Caleb's angry face made her heart hurt.

Whit watched her until he said, "He's in Knoxville, taking over the reins of Callaway Construction. After this lodge, he'll be stepping into Senior's spot full-time."

Winter studied Whit's face. They'd been such good friends, sharing laughs over late-night pizza and standing side by side to win city-council elections. "You okay with that? It should leave more time for Senior to work with you on this campaign." She wasn't certain that was the best thing for Whit. If she

considered their history, everything had gotten out of whack the minute Senior had come
on board.

"Except Mom's got other plans. They'll be
traveling. She's decided someone who runs
the Callaway charity should see the projects
she's been funding. That means visiting all
four corners of Tennessee, although first
they're taking a vacation in Louisiana." He
shrugged as if he couldn't understand why
anyone would do such a thing.

Winter smiled. That was one thing she and
Whit would always be in sync about. Vacation time confused them both.

"That's the other topic I wanted to talk to
you about. My campaign. I need you, Winter. Please come back." Whit met her stare
without flinching. "No one can argue that
you were the magic behind our success. You
know what I want to accomplish. This thing
with the teachers and Richard Duncan? Education is the keystone I'm willing to live
and die by, and he's out there, shooting off
his mouth. I mean..." Whit shook his head.
"I need to win this election. You're the key
to that. Senior is out of the picture. Moving
forward, it's you and me."

Winter studied her nails, worrying the cuticle of one thumb. Did he mean as a couple? How was she going to do this? Now that she'd seen the possibilities, she would never marry for his career or hers. "I can't marry you."

Whit tilted his head to the side and then laughed out loud. "Sorry. I didn't do a good job of explaining. I want to *hire* you. Pay you to advise me. Like professionals. We'll be smart. We're going to do this the right way, even if it is the hard way. No more stunts. Sound strategy and policy. That's it. I'll win or I'll lose, but the voters of Tennessee will know who Whit Callaway is." He held both arms out. "Sometimes dumb, but always trying to do the right thing."

For the first time since she'd walked out of the capitol after leaving the report on Richard Duncan's desk, Winter knew what she wanted to do with her life. This was it. She was never meant to be the unofficial power behind the man. Her place was behind the podium, running meetings, setting goals for the Callaway team. This was the career she wanted: helping a good man who had some bad ideas but a solid heart lead the state they both loved.

"It's not going to be easy, not with our

history." Winter stood and walked over to stand in front of Whit. "You've been out there, stunting. I've been over here trying to cause trouble and mostly failing. We've got our work cut out for us."

Whit raised his eyebrows. "You are not wrong, but we're Callaways and Kingfishers. Hard work doesn't scare us." He held out his hand, and Winter slipped hers inside before wrapping her arms around him. The hug reminded her of all the times they'd celebrated together. There was no more or less between them than shared purpose. Never had been, but that had seemed like enough.

Until Caleb Callaway had met her toe to toe.

"I have a couple conditions," Winter said and Whit blew out a gusty sigh.

"Sure you do." He thumped his head against the wall. "Hit me."

She waved her balled-up fist in front of his nose. "Don't you do anything to threaten the reserve or my brother ever again." Whit nodded firmly. "And I'm going to live here in Sweetwater. I can't go back to Knoxville, not now that I remember how much peace Otter Lake brings me. I'll drive down there to work with you. I'll hit the road with you, but I'm going to find a place here that is mine. All mine. Win or lose this campaign, I'm going to have a home to return to."

Whit smiled. "Easy enough."

Relief washed over her. The uncertainty about her job had been a weight. She loved the gallery and she'd continue to work there, but this was her calling.

"How soon do we start?" Winter asked. "I've got the media day at the lodge to complete and then..." She held up both hands. "I want to work."

Whit nodded. "About that. The plan is to announce Senior's retirement, ramping up the charitable foundation, Caleb's promotion and hiring you all in the same spot. Think you can get a larger group of reporters there with the promise of more than one story?"

It was easy to imagine eyes lighting up when she suggested it to her contacts. "I can definitely do that." That meant Caleb would return to the lodge at least one more time. What was she going to do about it?

"How are we going to handle this relationship moving forward, Whit?" Winter asked. His frown was easy to read. "I'm going to be dating. Someday, you will, too."

He sighed. "Right, about that..." He smiled.

"If your question means what I think it does, I want you to be happy. That's all. Reporters will try to stir something up and we'll… What did you used to say?"

"Hit them with the story we want them to tell." He'd been listening to her. This was going to work.

"Yeah. I can be taught." He slung his arm over her shoulder. "If I'm going to be spending more time in town, I should do some damage control. Should I start with the ladies out front? The older one was ready to gut me with a ballpoint pen."

"She's a good start, but lesson number whatever we're on is never, never say the 'older' one about women who can vote. Her name is Janet. She's awesome, but she could hurt you if I let her. Buy a painting. That's one sure way to her heart." Winter laughed and was amazed at how easy it was to let go of all her anger and hurt. With one apology, Whit had convinced her that what came next was going to be better.

"Did you ever tell me how you found me this afternoon?" Winter asked, curious again. No one in Sweetwater would have given him directions.

"I mentioned I'd stopped by your house.

Had to talk to your mother." Whit shivered. "Where was your dad?"

"He's been teaching classes at the seniors' center." Winter chuckled at how grim Whit was. "You okay?"

Whit sighed. "Your mother is scary. I hope that's the last time I have to meet with her alone again for a long time."

"I know what you mean." She grinned at him. "How soon am I going to get a paycheck? Until I move out of my parents' house, you run the risk of meeting her."

Whit pretended to consider. "I'll leave a check before I go. Payment for this media day. That's what we'll call it. Know any good Realtors? If this is headquarters, we may both need new places."

Winter laughed. "Let me introduce you to Janet Abernathy. She's going to be your number one fan. Fast."

Eventually, she was going to have to figure out what to do about Caleb, but it was nice to know what came after her media day for the lodge. She'd needed that purpose. Having it made it easier to focus on what she wanted next. As soon as Caleb returned to Sweetwater, she'd get started on it.

CHAPTER FIFTEEN

WHEN CALEB ROLLED up to the lodge's job site early on Friday morning, he hoped he was prepared for an onslaught of both Callaways and reporters. Leading them through the lodge would be easy enough. Instead of falling behind schedule while Caleb had been stuck in Knoxville for the past four days, it seemed that Carlos had worked some kind of magic. The walls were fully framed. In his quick tour, when he'd made it back to Sweetwater late the night before, he'd found electrical and plumbing and the first rounds of drywall were up in some of the guest rooms on the second floor.

Had he actually been holding his crew back all this time?

Caleb shook his head as he climbed out of the truck, hard hat in hand. Carlos waved to him and trotted over. "Boss, good to have you back." He motioned toward the lodge. "I hope you don't mind, but I made a few changes. The progress on the cabins has slowed, but the lodge itself is ahead. I wanted to take advantage of the weather and the trades on hand. Next week, they'll move to the cabins while we focus on interior walls. After that I plan…" Carlos slowed to a stop in front of him. "I plan to follow your direction. You're back, right?"

This confirmation that Carlos was ready to lead was all Caleb had needed. He held out his hand. "This is outstanding, man. You're promoted to lead project manager. We'll talk to personnel at Callaway Construction to get everything official next week. The lodge is your first project. Make it a good one." When Carlos gripped his hand hard, it was impossible to ignore the emotion on his face. "You do good work. Keep it up."

Caleb slipped on the hard hat. "Show me what happens next." This was the role he was going to have to get comfortable with. Supervising. Guiding. Less climbing joists and swinging hammers and more developing his people skills. He wasn't sure how that would work out, but Senior had faith. Caleb would, too.

They were standing over the architect's modified drawings, discussing the new finishes Caleb had requested to fit with his all-Tennessee plan, when the first news van squeaked to a stop. "Wave them in. Park them off to the side. When my family gets here, send them up to the front." Caleb didn't want his mother having to walk on the rocky, uneven ground any more than necessary.

Carlos nodded and trotted toward the van as he hollered for assistance. Caleb stared hard at the lodge plans and wondered if taking over Callaway Construction would mean losing the best parts of the job. Then he realized he'd always loved setting the parameters, establishing the rules for each build, the most.

This could work.

When the black sedan that had to be carrying his family parked in front of the lodge, Caleb wondered if he should have gone for the silk tie.

"Nope. No matter what, I'm not a tie kind of guy." He hadn't worn one in Nashville or Knoxville. When he moved operations to Sweetwater, they'd be polo and logo kinds of people. Goodbye, formal Callaway tradition.

His stepfather slid out of the sedan's driver side and went around to open the door for his mother as Whit got out of the back seat.

Caleb tensely waited to see if Winter joined his brother. When Whit slammed the door shut, Caleb relaxed a bit. Did that mean the campaign to win Winter over had failed?

His day was sunshine and smiles at that point.

"Mama, I can't wait to show you what we're doing." Caleb relaxed into his mother's hug and then braced himself against the hard clap of Senior's hand on his shoulder.

"You ahead of schedule now?" Senior asked.

Caleb nodded. "Yep. All I had to do was get out of the way." He pointed at Carlos, who was directing a small line of news cars over to the side of the site. "That's the guy who's going to finish this up. Carlos was part of Summit, but next week, he'll join Callaway Construction."

Senior raised his eyebrows. "Cannot argue with this progress."

He shoved his hands in his pockets and went to examine the building.

"Wow. Pretty over-the-top with his praise, isn't he?" Whit said from behind Caleb.

Their mother chuckled and went to join him.

Now that Winter was nowhere in sight, it

was easier to welcome Whit. Caleb offered his hand and then stumbled back when Whit threw his arm over his shoulders. "We're about to make all this work out, Cal. You see that, right? Mama's going to be happy. Senior will be busy making that happen. Now is when we do what we've been waiting for."

Caleb studied his brother's face. If he'd been rejected a second time by the woman who he'd planned to marry, wouldn't he be sadder?

"Where's Winter?" Caleb asked, determined to stop waiting and get his life going.

Whit grinned. "I wondered where you stood. I mean, with her, it was kind of easy to see. She was annoyed about your confrontation. I knew asking you to bring her on board was a big job. I didn't know it would get you into this much trouble. I hurt her feelings, but you... Man, you messed up large." Whit squeezed his shoulder. "She'll be here in a minute. If I were you and I were as desperate to fix things as you must be to come out and ask that," Whit said with a shake of his head, "I'd be rehearsing the grandest of all apologies."

The urge to knock the grin off his brother's face was strong. Then he realized what Whit was saying. "You don't care if I try to make something between us work?"

Whit stepped back. "I care because she's the best friend I've ever had. Neither one of us was in love, but that doesn't mean I don't love her. You get that, right?"

Was he telling the truth? Caleb studied his face and couldn't find a lie. "I do get it."

The chug of an ancient station wagon interrupted them and the slide of horror across Whit's face was enough to make Caleb laugh.

"That's what she's driving? Does it run on vegetable oil?" Whit muttered. "Has to be her mother's car."

Caleb crossed his arms over his chest as he watched Winter step out of the car, a black pantsuit her armor and a stack of bright yellow hard hats in hand. She marched up to them. Caleb tensed, ready to defend himself against whatever attack she might launch. Instead, she thrust a hard hat at Whit. "Put this on. Better optics." Then she was off in pursuit of Senior.

Whit whistled. "Oh, man, you got a long road ahead of you, but I believe in you." He thumped the hard hat on his head. "She's worth it, too."

Then he was moving toward the group

of reporters gathering at the base of where the steps leading up to the completed lodge would be. Someday. Caleb could see it in his head.

"You ready to start the tour?" Winter yelled, her hands cupped over her mouth. Since she was staring at him, Caleb got the picture. It was time to make this happen.

"Yes, ma'am. Let's start in what will be the grand lobby." He pointed toward the end of the building that would have the most spectacular view down the valley toward Otter Lake.

Caleb did his best to charm the reporters while giving them information on the completion, the materials used and the Tennessee companies providing them, and the plans for the smaller cabins dotting the mountainside. This was his shot to convince everyone watching that the Callaways were building something meant to last beyond the reserve itself.

At the end of the tour, after he'd exhausted all of his facts and figures, Winter gathered the group right back where they started, at the base of the lot facing up to the lodge. "Before you all go, the Callaways have some information on upcoming events."

Caleb watched all the reporters brace themselves, notebooks and recorders and cameras at the ready.

Then Senior stepped forward. "First thing, I'm announcing my retirement. That's nothing important, but most of you have heard of Marjorie's Alzheimer's diagnosis. Something like that can change some priorities, so we're going to focus on the Callaway Foundation for a bit. That's her first love and she's mine, so we're pretty excited about that."

Caleb crossed his arms over his chest, the blip of warmth at Senior's words hitting him hard. He and his stepfather had been at odds, but the way he loved his wife was an inspiration.

Senior held up a hand to still the flurry of shifting and paper turning as the reporters absorbed his statement.

"There's been some speculation about whether Whit would withdraw from the campaign. Dumb idea." Senior shook his head in disgust.

Caleb turned to catch Winter's reaction. Her wrinkled nose suggested she might have gone a different route, but no one directed Senior.

"Callaways are Tennessee. Have been

since my great-great grandfather made it here and staked his claim with a few head of cattle and hard work." Senior tilted his head up. "We've made mistakes, for sure. Top of the list is damaging our alliance with the Kingfishers, the family who loves the Smoky Valley Nature Reserve like home because it is home. We'll be working to repair that, but first and foremost, I want to tell you about Winter Kingfisher. This lodge right here? It's better than we ever imagined it could be, thanks to Winter Kingfisher." He pointed at her and the crowd of news media followed. "She's taking over as Whit's campaign manager. And she'll run it to win it. Richard Duncan ought to be shaking in his loafers right now."

Caleb was grinning at Winter's discomfort at unexpectedly being the focus of the media's attention, when Senior added, "And all my life, I've been building Callaway Construction for my son Caleb. It's his time to take the company where he wants. You will see big things, new things, beautiful projects like this lodge. Bet on it."

Caleb gulped hard and did his best to remain expressionless because now the cameras were on him.

"That's it." Senior clapped his hands. "Total Callaway-Kingfisher domination headed your way straight from east Tennessee, as it should be." He laughed, pleased with himself and how things were turning out. Somehow, he'd taken the whole mess and pretended it has been his plan all along.

That was a handy talent to have.

"Y'all have a nice drive back home and don't forget the lodge's grand opening in July." Senior frowned. "Hey, before y'all go, what about running a contest to come up with a name for the new lodge?"

Caleb swiveled fast to see Winter's reaction. She'd frozen in her tracks and was scribbling on her notepad. When she gave him a thumbs-up, Senior laughed like a kid. He was practically gleeful, pulling strings and making trouble.

Bailey Garcia ignored Winter's shepherding hand and turned back. "Mr. Callaway, I have one quick question for you if you have the time." She motioned the cameraman closer. Whatever it was, she expected it to be the best part of the news story. "When I was at the gallery opening last weekend, I noticed a connection between Winter Kingfisher and Caleb. Is there a new romance in the works? And if so, how is that going to rock the new version of the Callaway-Kingfisher alliance?"

The hush that had fallen over the crowd of reporters and the construction crews gathered to watch would have been funny if it had happened to anyone else but Caleb.

Since the question was one of those worrying thoughts that had floated through his brain now and then while Senior was drilling him on earnings and upcoming board meetings, Caleb might be the most interested person in the crowd at his answer.

But he wasn't going to look at either Whit or Senior. If they lost it at this point, thinking he'd been flirting instead of doing what they'd asked of him to manage her, their fragile agreement could unravel in a mess of knots.

When the silence was too much, he chanced a look at Senior. His stepfather had rocked back on his heels and was considering the question carefully. His mother stepped in front of Senior. "Never ask this man *feeling* questions." She smiled beautifully. "Every mother knows this, but we hope for the best for our sons. We want them to find smart, caring women. Winter Kingfisher is definitely that. We'd be happy to add her to the Callaway Sunday dinners again."

"But on Caleb's arm instead of Whit's?" Bailey asked, following up. "How does Whit feel about that?"

Whit's charming grin was easy, but Caleb didn't envy him being put on the spot. "I didn't expect to have to remind you of this, but the only opinions that matter are Caleb's and Winter's." He wrinkled his nose. "Let's be honest. In this spot, it's really Winter's. Caleb would be lucky to have her and he's already dug a deep hole. If he can get out of that, I wish them happiness. She's my best friend. Always will be. He's my big brother. I admire him. Always have." Whit shrugged. "We'll have to see how this goes, but if we can't all get along, I'm voting to keep Winter this time. The woman is smart, you know?" The arm he wrapped around Caleb's shoulder had the right mix of teasing and affection. And if Caleb had to guess, the reporters were eating it up.

Winter's expression was harder to read. She seemed…irritated. If he had to name it.

But she slipped on a professional smile. "Thank you all for coming. If you need to get in touch with follow-up questions about the lodge, please contact the ranger station. I'll be sending out a press release about the contest to name the lodge. The winning suggestion will have a week's stay at the lodge, a prize that should get people interested."

Caleb couldn't hear the rest of what she said, but it was impossible to take his eyes off her.

"Be smarter than me. Don't mess this up." Whit squeezed his shoulder.

"That's it. You really don't care if we…" Caleb wasn't sure what to say. Fall in love? He might have already done that.

Whit was serious. "She deserves the best. I've always believed you were the best." He shrugged. "Not sure where that leaves the rest of us, but we'll figure it out. If you have the guts to go for it. She's the one."

Caleb chuckled. Winter was fielding questions and jotting notes as she went. None of the Callaways were worried about her control of the situation because she was the best.

What was he going to do to convince her that his stupid inability to trust her at her word was a momentary lapse?

CHAPTER SIXTEEN

"NEVER WOULD HAVE guessed that there was something one of the mighty Kingfishers couldn't do as natural as breathing, but climbing is not a talent of yours," Leanne said from her spot next to the ladder. "Get down. Let me give it a shot."

Winter stepped down slowly, grateful to take a deep breath as soon as she had both feet planted on the floor. Leanne made a good point. The fact that Winter hadn't known how much she hated ladders until she started working at Sweetwater Souvenir was something to consider. There had been other frames to hang. Had someone else always done the climbing for her?

"I don't do cameras. You're afraid of heights." Leanne shrugged as she trotted to stand on the top step, the one that left no gripping room on the side of the ladder. Every muscle in Winter's body tensed, as if she was prepared to catch Leanne when the ladder tilted. "That imperfection makes me like you more."

Winter rolled her eyes. "Everyone I know seems to have a running tab of things I don't do well. Someone with a shaky opinion of themselves would have a difficult time around this town." She clutched the sides of the ladder, determined to save Leanne from a fall.

Although, now that she looked, the ladder's legs were much more solidly planted than they had been when she'd been frozen in fear.

Life was that much more solid when she was on firm ground, apparently.

"I have the reverse problem. Town seems to be shocked I can do anything right." Leanne paused, then she straightened her shoulders. "But we're changing that. I'm making a difference in my own life." She gripped the painting and carefully eased it off the hook. No white knuckles required.

Winter tried not to take that personally.

When she caught movement outside on the sidewalk from the corner of her eye, Winter turned, hoping Caleb Callaway had come to his senses and was ready to grovel. She would hesitate for a split second and then she would kiss him. More than once.

Missing him for a week had been difficult.

Seeing him standing up in front of all those reporters, flannel and denim and charming Callaway smile and his stepfather's affection and his brother's admiration… Well, they weren't done. She knew Caleb Callaway all the way down to his soul. Did she know his favorite color? No, but she knew the kind of man he was and she wasn't done with him yet. He had some making up to do, but she'd show him the way.

"That's the fourth or fifth time I've caught you studying the street." Leanne stepped down one rung and leaned back against the ladder, the bunny painting Winter had claimed but forgotten to buy clutched in her hands. Was she comfortable up there? Impossible. "Who are you watching for?" Leanne blinked innocently, as if she was prepared for Winter to lie so that she might pretend she believed her.

"I'm just curious about the crowd on the street," Winter grumbled and stepped away from the ladder. The problem with having actual friends instead of acquaintances was that they knew too much.

And the friends she had couldn't let a single thing go.

"Oh, I expected you were hoping to catch sight of Caleb Callaway." Leanne waggled her eyebrows. "Anything exciting about to happen?"

"After the way he accused me of leaking a story to hurt his family?" Winter shrugged. "I'd be a fool to give him another chance, wouldn't I?" She didn't want to be obvious but she valued Leanne's opinion.

"I heard of a man who fell in love with his ex-wife's best friend, a woman close enough to be called a sister. And since he was one of those paragons of virtue, it was completely out of character, but somehow, the man, his ex and her best friend had formed a family for the two kids they all loved." Leanne hopped down the steps and leaned the painting against the wall next to the large piece she'd named *Disappearing Sweetwater.*

Leanne was always ready to talk about Parker and Riley, her kids, but she didn't mention Brett and Christina's relationship often. "Situation like that would be hard to get through, I'd guess."

Instead of staring holes in the drywall or watching her hammer trick, Leanne met

Winter's gaze. "It has its moments, I can't lie about that, especially when I wonder what life might be like if I hadn't made the choices I did." Then she smiled. "But those days, thankfully, they fade. Now my time is filled with happy kids and friends and the knowledge that life falls apart sometimes, but it also goes on." She rested an elbow on the ladder. "If you were to ask any one of those people if a woman could fall for her ex-fiancé's brother and expect the world to go on spinning, they'd all say yes."

Winter took the hammer Leanne offered her, questions tumbling around in her head.

Leanne moved the ladder. "And that's all that's between you, right? History and your broken engagement?"

Winter wanted to trust Leanne with everything. She wanted advice.

And she wanted a friend she could tell the not-so-great things she'd done and know that person wouldn't leave. "I was the one who leaked the report and stopped the lodge. Caleb took the heat to help save Ash's job." Winter ran a hand through her hair. "And he kissed me. Twice." She grimaced. "One and half times." Technically, she'd kissed him the second time, but he'd responded so well, he deserved part of the credit.

Leanne frowned as she studied the ladder. "What is a half kiss? Never mind." She patted Winter's shoulder. "Explain that at girls' night out. I'm certain I'm not the only one who needs the answer to that." Then she held Winter's hands. "So, what are you doing here? The Winter Kingfisher I knew and sort of resented wouldn't be waiting on a man to make up his mind. Forget what people will say. What do you want?"

Easy. She wanted Caleb to come through for them without having to tell him a single thing.

Was she being silly? What man could read minds?

"You'll be okay if I take the rest of the afternoon off?" Winter asked, determined to pretend to be her old self even if she was still wobbly. Wasting time like this made no sense. She and Caleb could be making progress, but not if she waited until he realized the next step. She was the one with the plans. It had always been that way.

Leanne pointed at the window. "Almost done for the day, anyway." The sun was setting behind the mountains, so a gray shadow had fallen over the street. "I'm going to make a few phone calls, notify our buyers that next week they can pick up the paintings they purchased. Janet has the new software system installation finished, so all the commissions and…stuff will be easy to track." She sighed. "It's hard to believe something I made actually sold."

"Almost every piece we put out sold," Winter said drily. "Pretty soon you're going to have to get over the 'unassuming artist' persona."

Leanne frowned. "So now we're going for plain talk, are we? Playing hardball." She nodded. "Fine. You have an excellent excuse to find Caleb. He bought those paintings. The one you loved from the beginning and the one you wanted to own. It's almost like you have the same taste." She winked. "Or he was buying the things you love because you love them. Maybe you could negotiate some kind of resell on the rabbit painting." She waggled her eyebrows. "Otherwise, you'll have to go to his house to visit it whenever you want to see it." She made a sad face. "The hardship, right?"

Winter laughed. She recalled Caleb standing in the middle of the room, staring as if lost at all the artwork.

Until she'd mentioned how much she loved the two paintings that he then quickly bought. What did that mean?

"I don't know where he lives." She sniffed. How hard would it be to find out?

"I heard an interesting tidbit about Caleb Callaway the other day while Janet was talking to Regina on the phone." Leanne pursed her lips and shoved a shoulder under the ladder to move it away from the wall.

Her curiosity was impossible to tamp down. The jingling bells next door put the conversation on hold. "Be right back," Leanne said.

"Mrs. Kingfisher, what brings you in today?" Leanne said loudly enough to carry into the gallery.

And possibly out on the sidewalk. Did she mean it as a warning?

Curious, Winter walked over to investigate.

"Janet and I have a business meeting—" her mother pulled up the voluminous knit thing she always wore as a winter coat and looked at her watch "—in ten minutes. I'm early." Her happy shimmy sent fringe dancing.

"You didn't tell me you were doing business, Mom." Winter stepped closer to study the large cardboard box her mother had placed on the cluttered counter. "What's inside?" She tried to lift one of the flaps but her mother smacked her hand.

"Kingfisher Apothecary. That's what's inside. And we aren't doing business yet, but we will." Her mother smoothed wisps of curls that had escaped her blond topknot. Seeing her mom that way, with the tamed hair and the flashing watch that she'd actually checked, reminded Winter of kissing her mother's cheek before she marched out the door to go to work. "Some people prefer all-natural products, shampoos and lotions that don't destroy the environment." She smiled benignly at Winter. "I've included my new shampoo, the one I made for you. Even you can't argue with the results. I'm going to call you my spokesmodel."

Her mother was right. Once she'd started tinkering with her formula, the gray goop had worked better and smelled nicer, and fighting over shampoo had become a thing of the past. Being the spokesmodel for Kingfisher Apothecary would be easy enough.

The bottle she pulled out was beautiful. There was no other way to describe it. Amber glass with a silver cap and a large tag tied around the neck with twine. Winter studied the logo on the tag, a finely drawn bird with hand lettering. The back listed ingredients.

"Glass bottles seemed my best bet, but I've concentrated the formula so a drop is all you need and this bottle could last months. I got the labels printed at the old-time print shop in Pigeon Forge. They use plant dies and recycled materials. This is something I'm proud to put the Kingfisher name on."

Her mother straightened her shoulders and faced off against Winter as if she was prepared for Winter to do her worst.

"I wasn't listening," Winter said slowly. "I'm sorry. I thought this was a hobby, like Dad's baskets—not a…passion or a calling." She blinked slowly. "Why wasn't I paying attention?"

Her mother shrugged a shoulder as if it wasn't important. "I don't give up easily."

She didn't. She never had.

"Based on the spokesmodel," Janet said as she entered, "I bet we can work a deal. I do love meetings that start on time, and the results are impossible to argue with." She checked the tag and saw the price. "Whoa."

"It's that good." Her mother's shrewd stare transitioned into a smile. "First bottle is free, then we discuss the pricing. How does that work?" She waited for Janet to dig through the box and sniff some lotion.

When Janet nodded and offered her hand for a shake, static popped between them.

"I have something that can help with that." Donna Kingfisher reached into her box of apothecary items, snagged a bottle and waved it like a television spokesperson. "Antistatic spray. Works for your clothes and hair, and it will leave you smelling like sunshine."

She squirted her own clothes to demonstrate, spreading spring sweetness through the shop. Janet inhaled deeply. "Got any potpourri like that? That could do a big business…" Winter's mother reached into her box again and pulled out several jars. "Ladies, we're busy. We've got some negotiating to do."

Winter and Leanne were chuckling when they returned to the large storage room.

"Your mom is a character, too. I should have guessed every single Kingfisher had talent," Leanne said with a shake of her head as she waved a hand at the stack of her father's baskets. Had it grown since the last time Winter was in here? Her mother had claimed they multiplied when no one was watching. "Artists, inventors... Dinnertime around your table must be epic." Leanne turned away before Winter could figure out what she meant. Epic good or epic bad?

"You might not know this with one look, but Donna Kingfisher has high expectations of all Kingfishers. Nothing we do is epic. It's expected." That's what made struggling to figure out her next step so frustrating. Now that she was employed and preparing to run Whit's campaign again, she could face her mother.

And do it without coming across as a brat.

"Guess she's as careful to encourage you when you need it, then." Leanne paused. "Being a mother is hard, no matter how good you are at it."

Since she and her mother had always been the ones to argue loud and long, Winter knew every one of her mother's failings.

Just like her mother could list her own.

"She ran away from home before her last semester of college, escaped New England for a summer spent at the reserve waiting tables in the campground diner. She and my father met and got married at Yanu Falls. Kingfishers have been here for generations, but my mother is the one who taught us to work for what we loved." She owed her a lot.

"And you're a lot alike. Riley and I can argue for ten minutes before realizing we actually agree." Leanne tangled her fingers in front of her and nodded her head knowingly until Winter took the hint. "That's how family goes, or so I've been told. Kingfishers wouldn't be immune."

"We work for what we love, and fight when we have to, don't we, Winter?" Her mother was standing in the doorway. "Do you need help loading the paintings?"

"I don't have a delivery address." Feeble. Weak. So weak. Every woman in the room was speaking volumes without saying a word. "But I could."

"I was going to tell you where he lived, offer to do the dumb drive-by that Christina and I used to do in high school. Every cute boy with a bad attitude was on our Friday-night tour." Her teasing grin faded. "But you're past that."

Janet tapped her chin. "It's a delivery.

There's no conflict in giving you the address to the house he offered to purchase at a nice price. Full price." Her smile was smug. "Why did I wait so long to try this real-estate thing? I'm a natural." She scribbled the address on a piece of paper. "You and your mama load up. Me and Leanne are going to go choose our next batch of paintings." She wrapped her arm around Leanne's shoulder, but paused. "Winter, you are coming in next week, aren't you? Or is Knoxville calling? Big-time politics gonna fit in small-town Sweetwater?"

Leanne met her mother's stare. "Sweetwater's home. I'm not sure I'm ready to buy yet, but if you have other places in mind, make a list."

Janet pursed her lips. "Hmm, rentals are hard to come by." She raised an eyebrow. "Regina and I'll put our heads together."

"Rent shouldn't be an issue. I have my fingers crossed for a solid commission check." She blinked innocently at Janet. "I have one coming, right?"

Janet nodded. "You are gonna be one happy salesperson, my girl." Then she turned to Leanne. "Think Christina would be interested in renting her cabin? I mean, it's down the hill from the ranger station, but it's real close to Caleb's new house. The one he's buying here, in Sweetwater, instead of renting. It's almost like the kid is content here and planning to make this home. I did not see that one coming." She winked at Winter over her shoulder before she and Leanne disappeared into the storage room. Their giggles drifted out on the air.

Winter and her mother exchanged a glance. "I'll grab the big one, you get the other one and the door." Her mother marched across the room and handed Winter the beautiful rabbit painting. "That Leanne has real talent."

Winter agreed as she pushed on the door. "I wanted to buy this one."

"Maybe it's a gift. For you. Caleb had to stare at every painting to decide whether this was the rabbit he wanted." Her mother shrugged as she waited for Winter to open the back of the station wagon. "Doesn't seem like his style." She motioned with her chin at the large painting of mist. "This one is more like it, that view of the valley."

Winter considered that as they carefully arranged the paintings. Her mother was right, but how did she know that? She hadn't seen his face while they'd gazed out at Buckeye Cove.

Her mother stared down the quiet street. "You know, most everyone forgets that I didn't grow up here, surrounded by Otter Lake and all this." She crossed her arms over her chest. "I found it, too. Sort of like Caleb has. Like Whit should have if he could have gotten his act together." Her disapproval was easy to hear.

"How did you find it?" Winter asked. East Tennessee seemed a strange place to take a summer vacation as a college student. Beaches. Those were the places to go.

"Had a boyfriend. He wanted to hike and fish and camp." She covered her heart with both hands. "And I was in love." She batted her eyelashes. "Or I thought I was."

Since she'd met Winter's father here that summer, things had changed. And quickly.

They'd changed so much that after graduation, Donna Kingfisher had come back to Tennessee and gotten married at the top of Yanu Falls.

"Twists and turns, Winter. Life is all about them. When you settle in, it's an adventure instead of a detour." She patted Winter's shoulder. "And it can take you some exciting places."

Since her mother had been Whit Callaway's number one critic, Winter had been afraid to ask her opinion of taking the job.

"Whit's a man you vote for and trust that you won't regret it. That, I'm sure of." Winter would guarantee it.

Her mother nodded. "I guess I see that. Now that you aren't engaged, I like him better. When he showed up at the house, I didn't even want to yell at him to get off my lawn. It was always you that I was worried about, not the job. I didn't want you to give up the best for...Whit." She smiled. "Working for him? Much easier."

"No skeeves, then?" Winter asked.

"Nope." Her mother held her arms out at her sides. "Skeeve-free and happy."

"Even if another Callaway shows up at the dinner table unexpected."

"As long as he eats like my boy Caleb, I'm in." Her mother frowned. "That's who we're talking about, right? There's not another brother hidden away somewhere."

Winter laughed. "Not that I know of."

"Wouldn't put it past them, although Senior Callaway is a man in love. I like that." Her mother pointed at the driver's side. "You gonna keep stalling until it's full dark? We should get moving." The door creaked as she pulled it open. "Set him straight, then get on with life. That's the only way to do this, Winter. Men? Even the best ones need help sometimes. They will talk themselves out of every good thing if you let them go too long. When your father gets like that, I hit him with a kiss. Works like magic. Key to happy marriages, I'm certain."

Winter was grinning as she started the station wagon. "All right. Tell him how this is going to work out and if he starts losing his way, hit him with a kiss. Good advice, Mom."

She sniffed. "Your grandmother passed it along to me and I've never regretted following it." She leaned in and wrapped her arm around Winter's neck. "I'm proud of you, baby. You made it through something hard and you're better for it. You deserve the best. It's for you to say if that's Caleb Callaway or not, but he's got something."

Winter hugged her mother and nodded. Her mom was right.

Her mother stepped back. "And from now on, you're going to listen to your mother." She was waving slowly as Winter pulled out of the parking spot. The older she got, the smarter her mother was. How did that happen?

Winter tightened her grip on the steering wheel. The sun had disappeared behind the ridge of mountains, so there was no doubt where Caleb would be. Construction would be done for the day. She was about to make her case on Caleb's home turf, the place he was actually buying and planning to call home.

That seemed right. She was ready.

CHAPTER SEVENTEEN

WORKING CONSTRUCTION SITES was a challenge that Caleb would never get tired of. At the end of his second full day back in Sweetwater, he was pleased with the lodge's progress. Carlos was smart and constantly thinking of ways to improve the process. When the lodge was finished, he'd be ready to take on something bigger. The other Callaway Construction projects were waiting. Soon, Caleb would have to travel to check on each of the seven largest projects to evaluate their progress.

Senior had meant what he'd said. By the end of next week, Senior and Caleb's mother would be in New Orleans, eating beignets and not worrying about the lodge or the campaign or the business.

Or at least they'd be giving it their best effort.

Caleb had carefully plotted a trip that would take him away for a full week.

Seven days away from this spot that had filled him with such peace.

The work was exciting. Spending so much time away from here was less so.

The house Janet Abernathy had talked him into was going to be his base. The peace had settled into his bones. Leaving would be tough, but knowing he'd found his place in the world was satisfying. It was also going to be the blueprint for his business going forward. Tennessee's history and materials and future, that was going to be Callaway Construction, whether it was a house or a high rise they built.

Falling in love with a place had been a shock.

Realizing that he couldn't leave this town and get on with the business without clearing the air with Winter Kingfisher was, too. Nothing made sense without her somewhere in the picture.

But the way to fix his immense failure escaped him. Words were all he had and they were not enough. So he returned to his thinking spot.

This cozy corner, next to the warmed rocks and protected by the second floor's balcony, was the perfect hideaway. When summer arrived, he might never go inside.

Until he'd plopped himself down there the first night, Caleb had been certain living in Sweetwater for any amount of time would make him miserable. The urge to go and see and do and not be alone with his thoughts had been strong. That had been the story of his life—living fast to ignore that weird feeling he was missing something. What could that be? He had money, a job he loved and was a regular in enough Nashville hot spots that he never had to be alone.

But in Sweetwater? Alone. Plenty of time to worry about his mother, the jobs he was missing, what he should be doing and whether he'd ever fit in with the Callaway family.

When his phone rang, Caleb snatched it off the cushion, hoping somehow Winter needed him for something. That was the opening he was waiting for. Instead, the display showed his brother's name.

"What's going on, little brother?"

"Need some advice, but I wasn't sure you'd answer." Whit cleared his throat.

Since his little brother was addressing his earlier, unspoken attitude, hitting the nail on his uncooperative head, Caleb said, "New policy. When you call, I'll answer, Whit. I promise."

"Fair enough, Cal. Me, too." Whit's tone was serious.

"What's the question? I live to advise." Caleb stretched out his legs. Was he about to ask about policy or even what to do to help their mother? Caleb knew almost nothing about the first one, but he'd considered asking Whit his opinion on the second. He'd almost decided to step back and give his parents some time together. A vacation could work miracles.

Or so he'd heard.

"Winter is determined to make Sweetwater home, even though Knoxville is much easier for us to work from. Got any ideas on how to convince her otherwise?" Whit asked. The silence on the call seemed expectant, like Whit was messing with his mind.

"Nope. I'll be moving Callaway Construction headquarters to Sweetwater as soon as I can find the space. She's on the right track." Caleb left it there, even though he was certain he knew what Whit wanted. Junior was poking at Caleb's wound, trying to make him do something about Winter. He would. As soon as he found a solution he liked.

"Have you talked to her? Planted the idea in her head that we all need to be near Sweetwater for some reason?" Did Whit know that some kind of sly tone had crept into his voice? He was a good politician, but the little brother would never outsmart the older brother. "What about staff, Cal? How will we find enough people willing to work all the way out there?"

"They can live in Knoxville. So can you. The commute's easy." Caleb pressed his head back. "But I'm going to live here."

Whit's disgruntled sigh was loud and clear. "Fine. You won't play along. Why haven't you made up with Winter yet?"

"It's only been a day. And how do you know I haven't?" Caleb asked. Did the guy have cameras up or something?

"It's been almost a week since everything blew up. You'd sound much happier if you had resolved things."

His brother was right. That was annoying.

"It's on the agenda for tomorrow. I needed to plan." A few more hours... Was that enough time?

"Good."

"Was that the reason you called? To prod me into connecting with Winter?" Caleb shook his head. How did he feel about that, his little brother checking up on him? It was a brand-new experience and it would take some time and effort to adjust.

"That and I was hoping you might have an idea about a rental property. For me. If this is where the home base is, I need my own place. You don't want me crashing with you."

His brother was correct about that, too. They'd end up squabbling with each other in minutes.

"Janet Abernathy. Sweetwater Souvenir. I don't know if she has other properties for sale or rent, but if there's a place for you around here, she'll find it for you. You'll be proud of it, too." Caleb tried to imagine what a meeting between Janet and Whit might be like.

"I've met her. When I went to talk to Winter about the job." Whit cleared his throat. "She's kind of scary."

Caleb frowned as he considered that. "If you're Winter's friend instead of her enemy, you'll be all right. I wasn't either, was more in the middle, but Janet helped me. She will help you make the best of whatever you want in Sweetwater."

"It's too bad there's no new construction there. Something out of town where you can have bigger lots. I could see some demand for that, since, as you mentioned, Knoxville is an easy drive." Whit paused. "If only there was a construction company with a connection in the area that could put up some upscale homes. Best of the best. That could turn a profit."

While Caleb was still formulating his answer to that idea, which was good—almost as good as setting up a consignment agreement with Leanne Hendrix for artwork to fill the lodge—his brother said, "Good luck with Winter." And hung up before Caleb could answer.

"Little punk." Caleb would have asked for advice. He honestly needed direction.

He pulled his coat tightly against his chest and closed his eyes. He was so comfortable. He could rest here on the porch for a minute.

Before the cold got him, Caleb realized he wasn't alone. When it was harder to open his eyes than he expected, he wondered if he'd actually fallen asleep.

Maybe the cold was freezing his eyelids. He should get up.

Then he saw Winter Kingfisher sitting on

the lounger opposite him, her legs pulled to her chest, arms wrapped tightly around them. She was watching him, the corners of her mouth curled as if a smile lurked below the surface.

"When did you get here?" he asked, his voice was unexpectedly gravel-like, which was another clue that he might have had an unscheduled nap.

"Interesting way to start the conversation." Winter shook her head. "I guess I expected some surprise. I also expected you to be inside with the heat. I got here about four grumbly snuffles ago, when I decided to investigate the light after my knock went unanswered. I left the two paintings you bought at the gallery next to your front door. Snoring is cute, but sleeping outside? That's weird."

She had a point. "Cute, huh?" *She* was cute, bundled up against the cold in a thermal fleece and heavy jacket he remembered and a fuzzy knit hat with bear ears that he didn't. Caleb blinked slowly. "Sleeping inside lacks creative flair, even if it is smarter or safer. Obviously, you give me more credit than you should. Want some coffee?" He did.

"And then nothing else to say? I sneak up on a sleeping man, but his calm reaction is to invite me inside for a cup of coffee." Winter raised both eyebrows. "I don't know if Sweetwater has any criminal activity, but there are bears. What if one mistook you for a tasty snack? How is it you were sleeping out here, anyway?"

Good question. "Early mornings catch up with me before I know it. I'll be glad when summer gets here. I love this spot at the end of the day, so I stay right here as long as I can. I missed it while I was in Knoxville, so I'm glad to be home. Dozing off is new." Caleb scrubbed a hand through his hair. "I've always worked hard, but this project and then stepping up to lead Callaway Construction…" He shook his head. "I've been burning the candle at both ends all week. Hasn't left me time for what I really wanted to do." Caleb reached over to take her hand, her fingers chilled against his.

"I'd find it hard to give up, too." She stared over her shoulder. "I'm guessing that's a tiny view of Otter Lake. These trees. The size of the lot is right. Janet has a good eye. I didn't know it existed." Winter shivered. "I thought I knew everything about the reserve and these mountains. In the summer, these two chairs could be the nicest spot in the whole area."

There, in the cozy corner of the long, comfortable porch, the silence between them was easy. There was no tension, just the low-level hum of…something. Instead of wasting his time, trying to get poetic to give the buzz a name, Caleb said, "I'm sorry. I messed up. It's even harder to get over since I managed to exceed expectations the first time you asked me for anything and this time I just…" He shook his head. "I blew it. You care for my mother. You aren't the kind of person to hurt someone you care about, certainly not to get revenge."

She wrinkled her nose. "Well, to be fair, you've saved the day several times already." She tangled her fingers through his. "That showed me who you were. I have an unfair advantage. You don't know me, as well."

That shocked him. "But I do. I knew you from family dinners and all the praise Whit and my mother rained down on you and the intelligence that radiates from you. I knew you from your family. Your brother is the best at what he does and determined to protect this place. I do know you, Winter."

She nodded. "Okay. Then we both agree

that my determination can get me in trouble. This story might have been one of those times."

"Are you letting me off the hook?" Caleb asked. In her place, he would have struggled.

"Of course. You didn't want the lodge build, but you stepped up to make it the best it could be. I did the same thing with this media day. We're pretty well matched, I'd say." Winter's lips curled up at the edges.

Was she saying what he thought she was? They were a match. Like, a *match*?

"What do you think we'll end up calling the lodge? The contest was inspired, wasn't it?" Caleb said.

"We?" she drawled in response. "What will *we* call it? The Callaways will be making the final determination. I figure it'll be something like Callaway's Pride or Callaway's Folly or Callaway's Don't You Think We're Awesome Because We'll Tell You Why We're Awesome If You'll Stand Still For Five Minutes And That's The Short Version."

Caleb pretended to consider that. "I'm not sure that will fit on a sign." He tipped his head to the side. "Maybe it will but it'll take longer to put up a sign that big than it does to build the lodge."

"The Callaways are pretty amazing. Some of them more than others. Lots of raw talent for me to work with." Her pursed lips relaxed and Caleb realized he needed to either get closer or move the whole thing inside. From here he couldn't see her face.

And he wanted to see her face.

Looking into Winter's eyes across his desk had tilted his world on its axis.

Caleb lifted the edge of the quilt. "We can go inside or we can share this. I don't want either of us to freeze to death. I have a company to run, and you have all kinds of havoc left to wreak."

Winter huffed out a breath before tugging hard on the old quilt and motioning to him to shove over. "Chivalry is dead, obviously. Instead of giving me, a visitor to your home, the quilt, you just…don't."

"Chivalry was me inviting you inside. I have heat in there. I have a fireplace, a gas starter, hot coffee—all ready for company. This is just common sense, and maybe a little strategy to get you into my arms." Caleb smiled as she plopped down next to him.

If he'd had to make a long list of things

that he was certain would never happen, this wouldn't have made the list, because who could have imagined it? Winter Kingfisher was snuggled up next to him under a simple old quilt in the dark night. And they weren't fighting.

If he'd had to guess, this was the way any life they built together would go. Immovable object meeting irresistible force over and over again. The only question would be which would win? Every day. Every moment. Maybe they both would.

His arm tucked under her head, they stared out at the clear sky through the canopy of trees. He'd thought the spot was perfect before. With her here, it was. Nothing could make it better.

Unless it was about twenty extra degrees.

"You let me know when you're ready to start talking. It's Winter's...weird outdoor sleepover and I'm living in it."

"Out here, you have stars." She sighed happily and then pointed. "The Pleiades. Can you see them?" She moved closer to him, almost touching, and pointed at the cluster of bright stars. "They're easiest to find as night first falls. For Cherokee, they're known as The Boys. There were seven boys who refused to come when their mothers called. They were too busy playing games, so their mothers gave them rocks for dinner instead of corn and sent them away. Those boys were mad at their mothers and they started to dance. They danced and danced, rising higher. All but one of them was too far to reach, and six of the boys landed in the night sky. The seventh, you ask?" She tilted her head toward him, a teasing grin on her lips. "His mother pulled him down but he fell so hard and far that he went into the ground. She watered the spot with her tears until one day, a green sapling grew in its spot, a tall slender pine that would one day reach the night sky."

Caleb watched her face, content to listen to her talk for as long as she wanted.

"The moral to the story? Always listen to your mother." She grinned at him. "That's how my grandmother told it to me, anyway."

"Smart lady. It runs in your family." Caleb returned her smile, because there was no way he could help himself, but his curiosity about her visit was strong.

If she hadn't walked right out of the night to surprise him, he'd say Winter wasn't sure what she was doing there, either. He had the urge to help her.

"I heard you're looking for a place in Sweetwater." A lock of hair fell over her forehead, covering her eyes, so he brushed it back.

Instead of answering, she leaned back to look right at him. Before he could tease her or ask what was going to happen next, she pressed a kiss against his lips. Warm, sweet and all too brief, this kiss was about making things clear between them.

"My mother, who is so wise and gets wiser every day, taught me that men will get themselves into trouble if we let them talk too much. The best way to prevent that is to stop them with a kiss." She brushed a hand over his chest, stealing Caleb's breath away. "What do you think of her advice?"

"I like it. Donna Kingfisher, outstanding cook and wise woman. I'll have to thank her the next time I see her." He liked her family. He hoped this advice was proof that they liked him, too. It was as charming as Winter Kingfisher's sharp mind and pretty smile. The one she wore as she stared out at the sky—that one he'd seen before. He was happy to see it again.

"You know, you barged into my office and demanded action. Tonight, you barged onto my porch and demanded—" Caleb motioned between them "—this. It's almost like you take what you want, Ms. Kingfisher, without considering the consequences. But there are consequences."

She nodded. "I'm ready for them. Whatever happens next, I know I'm on the right track. With my career. With you. Even if you messed up. Big-time." She raised an eyebrow.

"This is where I apologize." Delighted with her and the night and the possibility right before him, Caleb held one hand over his heart. "I'm sorry, Winter. I won't make that mistake again. I promise. The Callaways are turning over a new leaf—it's called honesty."

"You were always pretty honest, Caleb." Her soft smile was all he needed. They were going to be okay.

"Come inside. We'll hang my artwork." Caleb pushed back the blanket, stood and swept Winter up into his arms, her gasp transforming to giggles. "I have a few surprises up my sleeves, too, Winter Kingfisher."

She seemed to be struggling for breath

herself when she wrapped her arm around his shoulders. "Coffee. Food. Art. In that order. And we need to talk about the rabbit painting. I told you about that one. It was supposed to be mine."

Caleb toed the door open with his boot. "I got it for you. Before I knew I would need an apology gift. It's a thank-you, for helping me out with the reporters and for making the lodge better than it could have been if Callaways had been left to their own devices." Once they were inside where the fire was going, Caleb set her down gently.

She was breathless when she gazed at him through her thick eyelashes, the cute bear hat slipping to let her dark hair swing into her face. "And now?"

"If you'll forgive me for doubting you and your heart and your word, you can have that painting." He traced a finger over her eyebrows. "And whatever else you want. If I can give it to you, I will."

Her slow smile was as bright as the break of sunshine over the mountains after sunrise. He loved it. He wanted more, at least one more for every day.

"What about your heart, Caleb? I gave mine away to this guy who does not know how to hike or how to come inside from the cold. I'm looking for a replacement." Winter raised her arms to his shoulders, each inch slow and sweet.

"The painting. My heart. It's all yours." This close, her lips were impossible to ignore. He lost track of time until she stepped back, the loud growl of her stomach comic relief. "Sorry. Dinner and then we hang art."

She nodded. "I cook better than I hammer. We should divide the work evenly."

Caleb leaned back. "There's something Winter Kingfisher doesn't do well?"

She raised an eyebrow. "I also don't climb ladders. Deal with it."

Caleb pretended to consider it and wondered what she'd do if the told her how much she resembled her mother in that moment. Since that was a good thing in his eyes, he decided to keep it quiet. "The cook doesn't clean. Or hammer. Or climb ladders. No problem."

Before he stepped back, she squeezed his arm. "Are we going to make this work? With all the family drama and the politics and the traveling you'll be doing and I'll be doing and Sweetwater watching and all of it?"

Caleb laughed. "How can you even ask that?"

She frowned. "It was a silly question, wasn't it? I'm a Kingfisher."

"And I'm a Callaway," Caleb answered, proud of how easily it rolled off his lips.

"We do whatever it takes." She winked. "But now we do it together…" Then she twirled out of his arms and into his pristine kitchen.

"Together. I like how that sounds." Caleb smiled at her. "Think it'll be easy, the 'together' part?"

Winter slipped a hand over his shoulder to pull him closer. "Maybe. Maybe not, but it's definitely going to be worth it. Isn't it?"

Winter's energy and intelligence added up to a challenge.

And Caleb loved it. It would take time to come up with the proper answer to that, but he'd do it. He had a lifetime to work it out.

EPILOGUE

November

WINTER REALIZED THE pace she'd set to reach the bottom of the trail to Buckeye Cove was closer to a jog than a sedate walk and paused just before the last curve. If she'd tried that pace down the aisle in a church, the whole congregation would be scandalized. Reminded that all eyes would be on her in a minute, Winter straightened the long ivory skirt she'd chosen to hide her sturdy shoes.

"Well, thank goodness," her mother gasped from behind her. "Are you wearing your running shoes, Winter Rose Kingfisher?" Her mom braced a hand on her dad's shoulder for balance and bent to inhale slowly.

Since the answer was hiking boots, Winter kept her mouth closed. Her mother wasn't traditional but that might be too much for her. There would be time for truly fabulous shoes at the reception.

"She's in a hurry," Winter's father said. "Guess that's the opposite of cold feet. I like it." He draped an arm over Winter's shoulders and tugged her closer. "It is excitement, isn't it? Not nerves?"

Winter shifted the woven basket her father had proudly presented to her that morning to press a hand over her anxious stomach. The basket, her bouquet, was filled with flowers from her mother's greenhouse and plenty of dried lavender. Because this was going to be a family affair. Whereas the big splashy party, the one they were throwing for family and friends, as well as business associates of Callaway Construction, and supporters of Whit Callaway, would strain the capacity of the Callaway Aerie Lodge at the seams that evening.

Here, along Otter Lake, the spot where she'd always done her best thinking, Winter was going to marry Caleb Callaway. Nothing in her life had felt more right. Since the election was over, her job was a question mark again. Caleb was traveling to meet Callaway Construction crews all over the state and loving every minute. The two of them were busy, but it was easy to come home to Sweetwater.

It was so easy to come home to Caleb.

"Nerves. Excitement. It's hard to say right now. I've got a lot to do today to pull everything off," Winter said and then waved off her mom as she started to protest. "Number one on that list? Enjoy every minute of my wedding."

Her mother nodded firmly. "That's right."

Her father laughed. "Donna, Winter negotiated a wedding for the Kingfishers and a party for the Callaways. She's got all of this under control. Our daughter is smart."

"You've always been my biggest fan, Dad. Thank you." She squeezed his waist, grateful to have his steady presence there at her side. Only one other man in the world would be more welcome.

"And you and I have always been too much alike." Her mother blinked slowly. "We are. We are desperate to move, even if it's in the wrong direction because we can't stand to wait. Remember how panicked you were to figure out what came next after your engagement was over and the reserve job was gone?" Her mother wrinkled her nose. "Could you have ever imagined this was where you'd end up?"

Was she really going to agree with her

mother? She was. "No, I couldn't. Thank you for keeping me from shooting off the wrong way."

"Luckily, Ash and I, we've learned a few things." Her father's eyes were warm. "Sometimes you have to give life a minute to catch up. Great things are coming but you're outrunning them."

Her mother tipped her head to the side as she considered that. "I think it all happens when it's supposed to. Look at us. I'd just been dumped by the boy I'd followed from New England and clung to even though I knew he was a mistake from the minute I crossed the state line, and boom! In walked your father." She tapped his chest. "It's about being open and ready."

He sighed. "I'd already lost count of how many meat loaf sandwiches I'd eaten, Donna, just waiting for you to be done with that guy." He nodded as she shook her head. "And I'm thankful to him every day because he got you here, but I wished him gone for at least five days before you noticed me at all."

Winter was stifling laughter at her mother's dumbfounded expression. Her father straightened.

"Ready to go get your groom?" he asked as he squeezed her mother closer.

"Yes. Ready. I hope in forty years Caleb and I are telling each other different stories about the same event." Winter hugged her mother and led them down the rest of the trail.

"How many other stories am I telling the wrong way?" her mother asked just before they reached the bottom of the path.

Her father winked over his shoulder. "That's the only one, dear."

"When your parents appeared but you didn't, I thought you might need help." Caleb had paused below her on the trail. He was wearing the same jacket he'd been wearing when they'd met again in Sweetwater Souvenir. It matched his nicest jeans, the white button-down shirt and the sprig of lavender pinned to his lapel. Winter was sorry she'd missed the first time Senior had gotten a good look at their dress code for today, perfect for a wedding in the Smoky Valley Nature Reserve, not the Knoxville church Senior had pushed for.

"Does everyone expect me to get cold feet?" Winter asked.

Caleb's shock was reassuring. "Uh, no, I thought you were handling a media circus. I can't believe we've made this informal gathering with half the town of Sweetwater, the Callaways and the next governor of the state of Tennessee, and not one camera crew has shown up. I imagined you chasing the reporters out of the parking lot. That's all." He stepped closer. "Let's go get married."

When he held out his hand, it was the easiest decision she'd ever made to slip her hand inside his. They finished the short path down to Buckeye Cove, where their guests waited on blankets beneath the sunshine on the banks of Otter Lake.

The golden ripples of the lake.

The smiling faces waiting for the two of them to arrive.

The connection between her history and her future.

This was exactly what Winter had wanted.

As they stopped in front of the minister her mother had recommended, Ash and Whit stepped up to join Caleb.

Macy dropped her lucky clipboard, the one required to monitor the schedule for the evening's gala/reception/election-win celebration at the Callaway Aerie Lodge—the full name the Callaways had finally chosen—and tugged Leanne up to stand next to Winter. Beyond where they stood, Christina waved the camera; she'd been drafted as the photographer for the ceremony. The constant clicking that carried over the light breeze suggested she was taking her job seriously.

Emotions welled up at the sight of the women who'd become real friends, the kind of friends she needed, thanks to returning home to Sweetwater. Desperate for a distraction, she turned back to Caleb.

He was frowning.

"What?" Winter frowned back at him. Was Caleb Callaway about to ruin everything with his own cold feet? Panic blazed through her mind until she got a grip. No way. He was as solid as the mountains surrounding them.

"That day you brought me here, you told me this place would make things clear, but it's you." He shook his head. "You're the key, Winter Kingfisher, not this beautiful place. You make things so clear for me. Everything, all the distractions fall away, when I see you. The same thing happened when you barged into my office. You made everything make sense. That's why I love you."

Winter gulped and then blinked her eyes quickly. She felt the same, but had no hope of being able to say it.

Words were her life. How had he scooped her?

"I had to say it." Caleb took her hands. "Now I'm ready." He planted his boots firmly and stared intently at her. In that second, she could remember the way he watched her across his desk as she'd stormed his office. She'd have said then he was dependable, bright and the kind of guy she was ready to trust.

The hard lump in her throat made it hard to swallow. Winter pressed one hand to her throat and cleared it.

"What's going on," Caleb asked softly.

Winter just smiled.

"Winter doesn't do emotions like this." Whit grinned and thumped Caleb on the back. "Except when it comes to you."

Whit's words helped her gain control. "I…" She coughed and tried again. "I love you, Caleb Callaway. You were the hero I needed when I didn't think I wanted one.

You'll always be that guy, the one who steps up for what's important to me. To us." She squeezed his hands. "Whatever comes next, I'm ready for it, as long as we're together."

His slow smile settled everything for her. The emotions were okay. With Caleb, she was okay.

"Reverend, I'm going to kiss the bride before the ceremony. Could you look away for a minute?" Caleb asked just before he pressed his lips to hers. Right there, beside Otter Lake, with her family and friends and neighbors watching, Winter understood that, no matter what her plans were, absolutely nothing mattered except standing right beside Caleb Callaway.

And that was a nice thing to hold on to.

The minister cleared his throat. "Maybe I better take control of this ceremony."

Everyone laughed, including Caleb, who was beaming as if she was the only person in his world.

He got her. For better or worse, Caleb Callaway understood her and what she needed to get herself together. How lucky she was.

Winter narrowed her eyes at Caleb as her

lips curved into a grin that matched her husband-to-be's and said, "Hit it, Minister."

The minister nodded. "Friends, we are gathered here today to witness this celebration…"

* * * * *

For more great romances from
Cheryl Harper and her
Otter Lake Ranger Station miniseries,
please visit www.Harlequin.com!

Get 4 FREE REWARDS!

We'll send you 2 FREE Books plus 2 FREE Mystery Gifts.

Love Inspired® books feature contemporary inspirational romances with Christian characters facing the challenges of life and love.

FREE Value Over $20

YES! Please send me 2 FREE Love Inspired® Romance novels and my 2 FREE mystery gifts (gifts are worth about $10 retail). After receiving them, if I don't wish to receive any more books, I can return the shipping statement marked "cancel." If I don't cancel, I will receive 6 brand-new novels every month and be billed just $5.24 for the regular-print edition or $5.74 each for the larger-print edition in the U.S., or $5.74 each for the regular-print edition or $6.24 each for the larger-print edition in Canada. That's a savings of at least 13% off the cover price. It's quite a bargain! Shipping and handling is just 50¢ per book in the U.S. and 75¢ per book in Canada.* I understand that accepting the 2 free books and gifts places me under no obligation to buy anything. I can always return a shipment and cancel at any time. The free books and gifts are mine to keep no matter what I decide.

Choose one: ☐ **Love Inspired® Romance Regular-Print**
(105/305 IDN GMY4)

☐ **Love Inspired® Romance Larger-Print**
(122/322 IDN GMY4)

Name (please print)

Address   Apt. #

City   State/Province   Zip/Postal Code

Mail to the **Reader Service:**
IN U.S.A.: P.O. Box 1341, Buffalo, NY 14240-8531
IN CANADA: P.O. Box 603, Fort Erie, Ontario L2A 5X3

Want to try 2 free books from another series! Call 1-800-873-8635 or visit www.ReaderService.com.

---

*Terms and prices subject to change without notice. Prices do not include sales taxes, which will be charged (if applicable) based on your state or country of residence. Canadian residents will be charged applicable taxes. Offer not valid in Quebec. This offer is limited to one order per household. Books received may not be as shown. Not valid for current subscribers to Love Inspired Romance books. All orders subject to approval. Credit or debit balances in a customer's account(s) may be offset by any other outstanding balance owed by or to the customer. Please allow 4 to 6 weeks for delivery. Offer available while quantities last.

Your Privacy—The Reader Service is committed to protecting your privacy. Our Privacy Policy is available online at www.ReaderService.com or upon request from the Reader Service. We make a portion of our mailing list available to reputable third parties that offer products we believe may interest you. If you prefer that we not exchange your name with third parties, or if you wish to clarify or modify your communication preferences, please visit us at www.ReaderService.com/consumerschoice or write to us at Reader Service Preference Service, P.O. Box 9062, Buffalo, NY 14240-9062. Include your complete name and address.

LI19R

THE FORTUNES OF TEXAS COLLECTION!

18 FREE BOOKS in all!

Treat yourself to the rich legacy of the Fortune and Mendoza clans in this remarkable 50-book collection. This collection is packed with cowboys, tycoons and Texas-sized romances!

Get 4 FREE REWARDS!

We'll send you 2 FREE Books plus 2 FREE Mystery Gifts.

Harlequin® Special Edition books feature heroines finding the balance between their work life and personal life on the way to finding true love.

FREE
Value Over
$20

Get 4 FREE REWARDS!

We'll send you 2 FREE Books plus 2 FREE Mystery Gifts.

Harlequin® Romance Larger-Print books feature uplifting escapes that will warm your heart with the ultimate feel-good tales.

FREE
Value Over
$20